GIRLS,
CRIMES,
and the
RULING
BODY

BARRY R. ZIMAN

Archway Publishing books may be ordered through booksellers or by contacting:

Archway Publishing
1663 Liberty Drive
Bloomington, IN 47403
www.archwaypublishing.com
844-669-3957

Cover Illustration: Mark Levine

ISBN: 978-1-6657-0863-0 (sc)
ISBN: 978-1-6657-0704-6 (hc)
ISBN: 978-1-6657-0862-3 (e)

Library of Congress Control Number: 2021912696

Print information available on the last page.

Archway Publishing rev. date: 08/17/2021

For Arthur Ziman, Eileen Ziman Ravin
and Josie Moralidad Ziman

CHAPTER 1

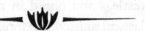

Her beautiful, young life was now almost over. All that remained for her to complete was a final semester class, coupled with an internship. Even with no particular plans for the future, she was eager for college graduation in the months ahead. She had opted for an internship at the legislature not out of ambition but instead to put an early end to academic drudgery. There was no pressing financial worry that demanded part-time work, for she had been granted most of what she wanted by the privilege of diligent parents and middle-class money. Occasionally, she was accused of snobbery by virtue of her striking good looks and aloof attitude. In reality, it was a projection of youthful confidence. It was an audacious confidence fed by the lofty and beguiling belief that she would be famous someday. This stubborn conviction of personal destiny was only natural. To this moment, she had been lucky in the insouciant way that youth allows. Self-doubt, drugs, suppressed demons, and sudden disaster had taken a toll on many of her friends, but not her. She felt comfortable and carefree entering the limousine on a naive whim of romantic adventure. Now those impetuous feelings faded with the duration of the ride and the rapidly decreasing light of the day.

With an exit from the highway miles before, the black limousine left behind the traffic of suburbs and shopping malls. With every mile advanced, modern life receded in the distance.

She could see a slice of the driver's face in his rearview mirror. He seemed dark and sullen.

Seeing her restless and bored in the back, the driver asked, "Perhaps some classical music?" His foreign-sounding accent seemed to her strange, even contrived.

"Sure."

He turned on the car stereo. A soothing but sad lullaby of piano, violin, and cello filled the car.

"Schubert," she observed. The driver glanced at her again through the mirror, quizzically.

"I took four years of piano under parental coercion. 'Andante Con Moto,'" she sighed. "You're lulling me to sleep," she added while watching the moving view, silently wondering upon her destination. Daydreaming in the back seat, she was oblivious when the car exited the highway. The luxury limousine cautiously weaved down narrow country roads, twisting through a rustic landscape of bare trees, dilapidated houses, and dormant, modest farms not yet recovered from the harsh winter of upstate New York. For her, the passing rural scenery seemed forlorn and impoverished. From the plush, expansive comfort of the back seat, she silently wondered about the nature of their unseen lives that passed in a blur. There was only sparse traffic on the road. This could not be a direct route, she thought. Perhaps the driver was lost.

"Are you really a chauffeur? Do you know where you're going?"

"I drive you, yes" was his fragmented response.

The car then turned off the well-paved, narrow road they had traveled on for miles. It then crept deeper into a forest along a rough unpaved gravel road, spitting small stones from the rear tires. The sleek car moved through the elongating shadows of tall pine, maple, and oak. The irregular road parted the premature darkness of the divided forest while spring twilight clung in purple hues to the treetops. She found a switch for a car light and checked her watch: it was 8:20. After an hour of driving, the destination now seemed absurdly remote to her. The driver had kept his eyes on the road, oblivious to her. He was entirely taciturn, having only spoken to extend her lover's invitation to enter the vehicle for her ride and to ask if she wanted to listen to music. Clearly, to her, this trip was at the direction of her boyfriend, as he had hinted at a surprise event for her upcoming birthday. As far as she knew, she was on a ride to a romantic destination where he awaited her.

"How much longer?"

The chauffeur did not answer.

Several more minutes passed.

"How much farther?"

The chauffeur did not answer.

Impatiently, she crossed her long legs and jiggled her sneakered foot in the air. She removed her cell phone from her purse and began to fiddle with it, and to her dismay, there was no cellular service.

"I don't have cell service," she whined to the driver, who ignored her complaint.

"Can you hear me?" She rang out loudly this time, with agitated concern.

The driver mumbled his response. "Sorry, lady. My hearing not good. Not far go now."

Some minutes later, she could see the dashboard illuminated and the car's headlights were now visible ahead, scattering light against the tree line. The twenty-one-year-old with blonde hair and a pert nose sat upright in the rear seat, alert with curiosity. After turning another sharp corner, a house unexpectedly appeared, submerged in a pool of blackness now only illuminated by the dual beams from the limo.

Without a word from the driver, the car came to a stop in front of the structure. The young woman frowned in both bewilderment and disappointment. The two-level home appeared architecturally modern. Secluded behind a five-foot-high stone wall, the location was clearly not the exotic or luxurious location she had envisioned during the ride.

Impatiently, and almost as impulsively as when she had entered the car, she pushed the rear door open and was ready to bolt toward the house, nearly forgetting her purse in the process. Realizing her error, she darted back to retrieve it from the back seat and then slammed the rear door shut. She expected the driver to exit from his side to attend to her and make sure she was at the right location. He did not. Suddenly, and to her amazement, the car moved away and then the driver abruptly did a U-turn to depart. She watched as the rear red lights of the limousine, like an angry red face, dissolved in the distance.

An outside light, perhaps automatically triggered by her approach to the home, flicked on and illuminated the facade, but the front door had not opened. She called out her boyfriend's name, irritated at the driver leaving her alone. She opened a gate and then gingerly moved down along a jagged path of stone steps. She knocked on the front door and then pushed and turned the handle, expecting it to open, but the door was locked. A window glowed dimly with internal light, but the house was silent.

There was a sharp screech from the depth of the woods, from an unseen crow. The bird cry startled her, making her look over her shoulder and setting her heart pounding. The young woman scanned the surrounding woods. All was still. Annoyed, she turned back and, with greater insistence this time, banged on the door with her tiny feminine fist.

Dressed in shorts, her bare legs were now chilled down to her socks and sneakers. Locked outside, she was alone, with the envelopment of night around her. She was about to consider her plight, and her options, when uncertainty lifted with the audible turn of a cylinder lock, and then the door opened. Her young lover appeared, dressed in jeans and a freshly pressed shirt. She adored his physical presence and felt a rush of reassurance. Cathy Wilet sighed, and her momentary fears quickly evaporated.

"Sorry, baby, I didn't hear the car. The limo is gone?" he asked and then emerged from the cabin with a beckoning smile.

"Where the hell are we? What are you thinking?" she demanded.

"I thought you deserved a chauffeured ride."

"A limousine for me? I can't believe you. What is going on? All that wasted money on me." Now, suddenly, she effused childish excitement for his benefit, and in a swift transition of emotion, she lifted her chin and pursed her lips, ready to accept his mouth from above.

It was an unusually protracted and tender kiss, followed by a constraining embrace that placed her head against his chest. His powerful, muscular body wrapped around her like a protective blanket, engulfing her in a wash of freshly splashed cologne.

"Spending on you is never a waste. You're worth it," he exclaimed as he hugged her close and furtively eyed the dark and desolate road beyond the stone wall.

She looked up into his face as he held her. "Why didn't you just pick me up? What is this place?"

"I wanted to apologize for my bad behavior and surprise you. We've got some privacy now."

He led her into the cabin. Inside revealed a spacious floor-to-ceiling panoramic glass wall that opened to the now dark tapestry of the woods and a skylight to the violet sky. She was pleasantly surprised. He took her gently by the hand and gave her a brief tour. In the open space was a contemporary kitchen containing stainless-steel appliances, cherry wood cabinets, and granite countertops. There was a plush living room with a huge tan couch that encircled a stone fireplace and a newly remodeled bathroom with travertine tiles and bright fixtures. She presumed the place was a rustic retreat furnished for some urban professional, perhaps a state legislator given the proximity to the capital, who was obviously interested in remote privacy or discreet passion. She was oblivious to the fact that the house was stripped of personal identity, by design. There were no photographs or books or details of ownership. She did not know the owner of the cabin, nor did she think to inquire; this was an irrelevancy to her, for in a childlike, trusting way she did not care.

Because of the current phase of their relationship, being alone with him in this remote location was curious and unexpected. For the last several weeks, he had treated her with brusque indifference, and several times with even outright hostility, for which he was always routinely apologetic afterward. Now he was a romantic gentleman with some inscrutable motive that was beyond sex. She had always been a compliant and willing participant in their sexual antics. The passion between them was frequent and usually confined to her cramped room in an off-campus apartment, with her shrill screams of orgasm echoing off the thin walls and to her neighbor's irritation. Now she could scream as if some horrific crimes were being committed and no concerned person could hear her.

Several hours after she arrived, the remnants of a fire smoldered in the living room fireplace. A bouquet of twenty-four fresh pink roses adorned with a white frill of baby's breath lay cradled in a chair. They had consumed a dinner of shrimp, mussels, and pasta, and the pots and plates were left in place. Two ashtrays were filled to the rim with their expired cigarettes. Several empty bottles of beer and a bottle of wine were propped on the bare wood floor, and the fire glinted off these objects. The cabin was dark and aromatic with cedar, smoke, and pine. The smoke was a pungent mixture of hastily smoked cigarettes and slowly burned-up wood.

Inside the bedroom, he smothered her in kisses and uncharacteristic affection. His sweat in the cabin's chill smeared over her as it rolled from his bare, muscled body. She was impressed at all this affection after they had climaxed in near perfect unity. Sometimes, he could be a clumsy, selfish brute of a lover who turned contentedly in bed after he had discharged. But tonight he seemed especially attentive.

He caressed her softly with each physical move elaborately rehearsed in his mind. He needed to play the romantic lead now, for everything he ever wanted was at stake.

"I love you, Cathy," he whispered in her ear. He had practiced the articulation of the line so that it rung with sincerity.

Suddenly, incredulously, she pushed his hulking body back and off her.

"What did you say?" She was utterly taken aback. The room now seemed to undulate from the wine she had been drinking or from her pulse that, like a fired piston, now sent tremors through her body. The unexpected emotion emanating from her young lover seemed to create a dangerous entrapment.

He enjoyed Cathy in a purely physical way, as it was a sex-driven relationship. He suspected the feeling was mutual, as she had not sought to encumber him with the greater obligations of a more complex relationship. However, their relationship, now in its fourth month, had become a complex web lately spun with mutual suspicion. The fact that he was able to convince her to stay the night, secluded with him, was a major achievement. He had expected her to resist, maybe even physically. They had a contingency plan for that event, but it had not been necessary.

"I said I love you, Cathy. What's wrong?" he asked, trying to sound as gentle and sweet as possible. His face was close to hers.

"I just need to think for a second," she said. She was trying to breathe and think calmly, but her world seemed to be spinning. She could not decipher why he had her brought to this remote location. She turned on her side, away from him. The curtains were open, and only pale moonlight painted the room. They were alone here, isolated for miles. Outside was a dark forest that led into the still icy

7

mountains of the Adirondacks. In the night, the wind, when it stirred the woods, loudly snapped the winter-brittle branches.

"What can I do to convince you I love you?" he said softly in her ear, trying to regain her attention. Being a twenty-three-year-old, the role of avid, attentive lover tightened his throat and tensed his jaw muscles. Each word required a stupendous effort of feigned sincerity.

She turned to face him, and then she stretched her smooth leg seductively across him. He was not insensate to the erotic length of her leg across him, for he felt himself harden again. He liked pounding into the soft smallness of her body while her legs were over his shoulders and twisted around him. She stroked the sinewy bulk of his right arm, adorned with an eagle tattoo, wings upright.

Her voice rose softly. "I just don't understand you. First we have an understanding that there should be no commitment in this relationship. Now you're acting like a lovesick puppy." Her own inapt comparison made her stop and self-mockingly laugh, for even she could not reasonably correlate him with the image of a puppy. He was definitely not a puppy in any metaphorical way.

"I don't understand any of this. You should check on the fire," she said.

He glanced out the doorway to the next room. "It's almost dead," he said, suppressing a thought. "But wait." He rose naked from the bed, his muscular frame evident in the weight of his movement on the mattress and across the floor. He went to the next room. She heard him moving some objects, perhaps a drawer being opened. He climbed back into bed and as he came up close, she could see a smirk of evident pleasure.

She turned toward him and placed her hand on the broad barrel of his bare chest.

"Look, I'm sorry for all I put you through," he said, with every appearance of earnestness. Then his hand came up to her face, and she could see he was holding a small velvet box. She opened the box and removed a ring from inside. The room was dark, but she could feel the ring being pressed into her hand, and she could see the glitter of a gem.

"This is for you," he said simply.

She wanted to assess the ring under the light, but instead she just placed it on the appropriate finger. Her throat palpitated and words were impossible. She drew in a deep breath and then looked at his grinning face. He seemed elated, almost giddy, with this act of romantic audacity.

She looked at the ring on her hand, and unconsciously her head bobbed in amazement.

"There is something I have to tell you," she said hoarsely.

The corners of his smile straightened, and his eyes squinted critically.

"What? What?" he asked, annoyed. He was not accustomed to surprises from her; she was usually very predictable.

"The prosecutor's office asked me about the files."

He frowned and brought his hand up to her tiny chin. She almost flinched, thinking he was going to hit her.

"Did they ask about me?" he asked casually. His mouth was dry, and perspiration rolled under his arms.

"No. I never mentioned you. You told me I didn't have any reason to worry," she said with sudden concern. She pushed him back and sat in bed with her arms crossed over her bare breasts, with a feeling of exposed emotion and vulnerable nakedness.

"Of course. I was only kidding," he said with a strained laugh. He sat up and put his arms around the bare smoothness of her back.

"Why did you even bother talking to them?" he asked.

She felt emotions welling up to the point of tears. His arm slipped around her slim body in muscled, firm control of her. He began to feel her convulse on the verge of tears.

"It's fine. You need to trust me," he said cajolingly with a smile. She stifled the surge of emotion. For a few moments they were still, and then he felt he could proceed.

He had rehearsed the question, but even as the words flowed, he knew that it sounded artificial and unnatural.

"So will you marry me?"

Her blue eyes fluttered down to the ring and then turned toward him and up to his face.

"I'll think about it." She could not envision marrying him, but she had no experience in these matters or the protocol for these situations. She wanted to confer with her friends, with her mother, father, and others, before rendering any hasty judgment.

"OK. Sure. Take your time. I know I hit you with this out of the blue. Cathy, we need to trust each other; if this is to be a relationship of love and marriage, we have to trust each other."

She looked directly at him and nodded her head in thoughtful assent to avoid a direct conflict while her heart beat a steady drum of displeasure at any thought of marriage.

"I need to know what you did with the files. Are they at the office?"

Her mouth gaped open in consternation. "I thought you were going to ask me about the engagement?"

She wanted to crack his hard face with her soft hand. He had skipped over the serious real-world subjects of marriage and love, jettisoned the weight of these things, and was back to his lofty, artificial world of political intrigue.

"You keep asking about those damn files," she said, annoyed. She knew now that coming here to be with him was a mistake.

"The governor—" he said before she cut him off sharply.

"The governor and the district attorney and the Speaker, I am so sick of politics. I hate it all," she said bitterly.

"These are important matters, Cathy," he said solemnly. "People's futures are on the line. Powerful people."

"So you've told me a dozen times," she said, unimpressed by his solemnity.

He nudged her and pulled her into a supine position, close to him. She placed her head on his chest and listened to the strong thumping of his heart. He put his arm around her, ensuring her intimacy. Each of their movements embodied the tumult of their relationship.

"Look. I know the DA talked to you. Did you mention me or not?" His voice became tinged with impatient hardness.

"Will you stop it? I feel like you're interrogating me. You are throwing so much at me at once. I need to sort through it all."

"Look, sweetheart, I just need to know about the files so that we can start our life together with a clean slate." His voice softened again, and the word "sweetheart" struck her like a tuning fork and reverberated. He had never used that word. It seemed unnatural, she thought.

He wanted her focused on his question, so he reached over and took her thin wrist.

She glared at him. "I did not give the governor's precious ombudsman files to the DA. The files are still at the office, and no, I told you already. I did not give them your name. I was waiting."

"Waiting for what?" he asked harshly. "I've proposed."

"Do you think there is a connection? I wasn't waiting on a proposal," she defiantly exclaimed as she tried to pull herself up, but he held her tight and pinned her down with his weight.

"You're hurting me. You're such a brute," she whined in a way he interpreted as playful but in reality expressed pain. Unconsciously, he had tightened the grip on her wrist. The pressure he exerted was a function of barely suppressed rage and the fact that he could never gauge the force of his strength. He released her and she turned on her side, away from him. He leaned back up against the headboard, sighed deeply, and realized a desire for a cigarette. He rose naked from the bed in the semidarkness and scanned the cabin room for the pack he had put down. The sound of the fire hissed and snapped in the living room, but the light from the hearth had considerably died down in the adjacent room. He moved toward the dresser and stumbled over their commingled clothes scattered on the floor.

"Switch the table lamp on," he said.

"No," she said sharply, looking up at the ceiling and feeling strangely bruised and confused with her own emotions. She wholly regretted having stayed here with him and now felt trapped.

He shook his head in frustration and silently mouthed the word "bitch." His dark hair, normally slicked back, fell down over his forehead, obscuring his bright blue eyes. He groped across a chair and found a mangled pack with a plastic lighter inside. He withdrew a cigarette and lit it up, drawing the smoke deep into his powerful lungs, and then released the smoke in a jet aimed at the wooden ceiling beams.

"Want one?" he asked, with the cigarette dangling from his lip.

"It's a bad habit. I need to quit," she said bitterly. He couldn't see her expression, but her words had a sudden hostile edge. She seemed in a bad mood. This was customary between them. After sex released the passions, the void between them always filled with equivocal emotions, including for her a sense of trepidation that ebbed and flowed like a tide. He had occasionally frightened her, but never enough to run crying or screaming from a bed, or now from the cabin. She found in the course of their relationship that he could act like a careless brute, but the sex between them was fulfilling and he had never struck her or done real violence. Now he was utterly and completely out of character, oscillating between attentive lover and his usual core gruff self, and she debated in her mind his inscrutable motives.

"It's a legal vice, smoking, and life is too short anyway," he remarked.

"Maybe it shouldn't be legal and maybe you're shortening it." She sat up in bed with the cover up to her waist. Her tiny breasts were provocatively erect.

"You know, Cathy, one minute you're hot and the next minute you're cold."

"I think you're describing yourself," she said. "You better not have lied to me. You know I could care less about the governor, his files, and all the rest of them. Politics isn't life. It isn't love. It's nothing to us," she stated in shrill disdain. "It's just the crap that goes on around us."

She glared at him and then fell back in the bed, again staring up at the ceiling.

He strode over to the window, looking down into a moonlit gully of trees. He eyed the woods to confirm their isolation while he puffed on his smoke. Outside, only invisible nocturnal creatures were moving in the darkness.

"You're so damn difficult. Beautiful, but difficult." He crushed the cigarette against the pane of glass. He sat on the edge of the bed and drank the now warm remnants of a beer. In the dim light, she then noticed another tattoo on his back. "Did you get another tattoo?"

"Yeah. It's an eye to keep watch over you when my back is turned."

She sat up and brought her face close and studied the inked eye on his smooth skin that looked back at her.

"What were you thinking?" she asked, wondering why he had opted for another tattoo. She did not like it.

"I didn't think you would come here."

"I didn't know I was being driven to see you," she said flippantly, for in reality the driver told her the destination was to see her boyfriend.

"How are we getting back without the car?" She had not seen his car parked outside.

"I guess we're trapped here," he said as he climbed back in the bed and lowered his face over hers. He brought his mouth toward hers, and she receptively opened her mouth to receive his tongue. She ended the kiss abruptly and again pushed him back. Wild thoughts, fears, and desires were dancing in her mind, pulling her in a dozen different directions.

"You know, before I got in the car there was a cute guy that tried to pick me up," she remarked in a not very subtle attempt to evoke jealousy. He leaned on his elbow and listened to her with limited curiosity.

"Maybe I should have gone with him," she openly mused. "Maybe we would have fallen in love; had kids together. Sometimes those moments just materialize and you are left wondering: What if? Maybe I would be rid of you," she teased with a smile, caressing his face with her hand.

He laughed heartily.

"That is some way for my future wife to talk. Who was the guy?" he inquired casually.

"I never saw him before." For a moment, he seemed dejected to her, almost hurt by her taunt. "You know I'm just kidding. He was slim. I like my men big and strong."

Their eyes met in a long, silent look at each other, neither knowing what the other was truly thinking.

She rose from the bed and knocked over a near empty bottle of red wine. The residual wine splashed crimson upon the pine floor planks. She set the bottle upright and went to a mirror that hung on the wall. She switched on a nearby light that sat on the dresser and reached over to her red purse. She pulled from the purse a brush and began to untangle the knots and curls in her blonde hair.

In the mirror, she saw him rise from the bed too. She thought he was heading toward the bathroom. Then she saw him move around the room, but she paid no special heed. When he was out of view, she scrutinized the ring under the light. The glimmer of light from the ring was dull and possessed a yellowish, hazy tinge: a spurious stone, perhaps a cheap piece of refined glass. The diamond was a grossly apparent fake. His reflection appeared again in the mirror, with his broad back toward her and the tattooed eye watching her. Then she saw him move, and this time she saw him with what looked to be a golf club. In the reflection, he looked like he was playfully practicing a golf swing. She turned from the mirror. And then she could see the metallic blur of the golf club slice through the air.

There was a second of recognition of impending violence that she could not fully comprehend. At the moment of impact, she could actually and distinctly hear the club shattering the skull bone protecting her fragile brain. She was rattled by an explosive jolt of pain that violently knocked her to the floor. Inside her head, an exploding, blooming hemorrhage fire grew like a fierce inferno almost ready to consumer her. Consciousness fluttered but was maintained. Clutching her head, she could feel the horrific wetness of blood as it gushed from her wound.

"What did you do?" she screamed. "Why? Why?" she shrieked in terror.

Looking up with blurred vision, she could see him assessing the effect of his action in an expressionless and methodical manner. Then, in horror, she saw the club coming again, and she went into a fetal position with her hands over her head. This defense was futile against the impending blows. She took a last gasp of air, and then her full-throated, piercing scream filled the cabin, echoing eerily in the nearby woods, utterly unheard. The lethal action of the club was followed by another and another and another until the screams expired. Her pretty features were disfigured and her eyes transfixed, blue and blank, as the last breath eased from her lungs with a bubble of blood. Even then, the strong thump of Cathy Wilet's young heart resisted against the dying of a ruptured body while he watched, calmly.

CHAPTER 2

Three days had passed and her body had not been discovered. There was no criminal trail and no ransom note. Her life was now a matter of public speculation and a subject of police investigation. Her face was reduced to a blurred black-and-white photo, reproduced and disseminated with frantic effort and fearful effect. The certainty of her physical being, once encompassed by a lively circle of family, friends, lovers, roommates, teachers, and students, was now nothing more than a mysterious void from which authorities were working to discern a direction, a clue, a trace of forensic evidence. This was a netherworld, thought Ryan, a tenuous existence that hung like a question mark in a moment of time, preserved now only in the mortal memory of loved ones afraid to relinquish their faith.

It was the critical importance that attached itself to any sighting, no matter how fleeting or unlikely, that kept Ryan McNeil agonizing over what he may have seen. He had tried to put the whole matter out of his mind, to bury it like some bad dream. But the news reports were a constant, nagging reminder. Seeing her was the equivalent of seeing a phantom. There definitely would be skepticism, for his story did not fit with the facts that were known. The whole business was a depressing distraction, and Ryan did not feel in the mood for a distraction. Life was simply too good and full of promise.

It was morning. For months, Albany was locked in a brace of snow and ice. Through the stark whiteness of winter, Ryan rode the bus to and from work. Now it was April, and those conditions were a melted memory so that he could stroll comfortably in shirt, tie, and khakis under an electric-blue sky and in bright, breezy sunshine. He walked briskly past Washington park on his right, under emerging green branches and deciduous pink, yellow, and white blossoms. Across the street for several blocks, indistinguishable, three-story row houses quietly concealed their inhabitants.

Aside from the flutter of birds and the occasional passing car, the street was serene. Soon the days would be warmer, and the weekend crowds, including Ryan, would rush to the park for its abundant shade, a small lake, and open ball fields. But for now, only a few pedestrians quickly passed him, fellow commuters on their way to work, intent on business. Ryan knew he was different from them. Spring always certified his relative youth and imbued him with a kind of natural high—spring fever. The sensation was so strong that it pulsed almost palpably in his blood. The season signaled his sex drive overload since his days in high school. In those not so distant days, Ryan would easily succumb to the simplicity of desire. He just felt like he was one step ahead of death itself, and he wanted to taste all he could of life itself before its ephemeral sweetness was pulled from his lips.

Ryan paused. He had walked to the vague spot where he had last seen what he thought to be Cathy Wilet. Her disappearance had intruded on his otherwise carefree and relatively uncomplicated life. He had become entangled, even if it was only superficially, as a possible witness in a criminal act.

While the intrusion of sudden tragedy into the world of youth was usually met with the immaturity of exaggerated response, Ryan was largely unperturbed by Cathy's fate. Unlike his peers, Ryan, through personal experience, had been tempered and learned to accept these occurrences without trauma or trepidation. Cathy Wilet was gone; she was probably dead. Bad things happen. Parents die in auto accidents—as his did. Kids are kidnapped, murdered, or die young. Young girls vanish into oblivion. Evil and misfortune exists; this was no surprise for him. The disturbing and intrusive aspect to Ryan was that he was remotely involved, albeit as a bystander, in a criminal act. The desire to rid himself of any connection with this unpleasantness was overwhelming and imperative.

He resumed his walk and moved closer to downtown, but Albany still moved at a slow pace with light traffic and sparsely traveled sidewalks. However, on these streets there were visible reminders of Cathy Wilet floating in the air. For affixed with tape to the many streetlamps and traffic signs were the black-and-white posters he had come to dread. She had become a visible ghost in daylight. The image of her and the details of her disappearance confronted him at every turn. He picked up his pace.

Two more blocks up, amid the sleek splendor of modern office buildings, incongruously stood the six-story state capitol building. Built more than a century ago, it was lavishly constructed in a lazy era of patronage, a castle-like structure, gothic and gray, with ornamental turrets, gargoyles, and dark cornices. Proclaiming the importance of the structure was a block-long lawn, vivid now with fresh plantings of long-stem roses and bright yellow tulips.

Ryan walked the pavement that traversed the lawn, passing by a flowering spray of water from a solitary fountain. On this morning, the scene had a picture postcard quality. The modern concrete-and-granite Legislative Office Building was across the street from the stone-gray gothic capitol. Ryan quickly crossed the street and bolted up the steps with customary exhilaration for his twenty-four years. He pulled open the ponderous brass door entrance. Only a few people loitered in the marble-encased atrium. Unrecognized by the small crowd, he swiftly headed for an elevator.

The elevator brought him down to the underground mall of the Empire State Plaza. He walked through the mall. Like the streets, it was mostly empty. There was no legislative session that day, so most of the staff, lobbyists, bureaucrats, and protesters were conducting business elsewhere or residing peacefully in New York City. Because of the relative absence of people, the sound of his shoes striking the floor audibly reverberated.

The inconspicuous capitol police station was next to the capitol cafeteria. Self-consciously, he looked around to see if anyone was watching. Assured of his anonymity, he pulled open the glass door emblazoned with the seal of New York. Inside, the police station appeared deserted. There was an unmanned reception area and an empty waiting room, and behind the gated area were three empty desks. He called out, and a burly uniformed policeman with arms the size of hardcover dictionaries emerged. He held coffee in one hand. He looked at Ryan rather aggressively and asked, "Can I help you, sir?"

"I'm here to talk with someone about the Cathy Wilet disappearance," Ryan answered casually.

"Is Detective Brennan expecting you?"

Ryan nodded negatively.

"Your name is?"

"Michael Baker," responded Ryan as he averted direct eye contact and instead perused the safety brochures displayed on a mounted rack. He had chosen the name that morning.

Ryan sat on a hard plastic-and-metal chair in the waiting area. The fluorescent lighting was harsh and the station so silent that there was an audible electric hum emanating from the light above. The white walls were largely blank and the paint peeling in places. A framed photo of the governor, looking directly and sternly at Ryan, hung on the wall across from him. The last police station he had been in, more than seven years ago, was in the Bronx; it had looked and felt nothing like this. That station was controlled pandemonium, with cursing and fighting and phones ringing shrilly. This station appeared almost entirely deserted.

He began to have second thoughts about coming to the police. Suddenly, two uniformed policemen emerged. They were in jovial conversation, and one carried a clipboard. The officers were oblivious to his presence. The atmosphere took Ryan aback; he was expecting more activity in light of the girl's disappearance. Maybe he had nothing to add to this investigation, he thought. The two uniformed officers moved through the gate, politely nodded to Ryan, and exited. Ryan had no great affinity for the men in blue.

Ryan looked at his watch and then at a clock on the wall. He had been waiting twenty minutes. The soundless sweep of the clock was interrupted by the sudden shrill ring of a phone. The initial sound startled him. It took several rings before another officer slowly emerged and answered the phone. The officer spoke on the phone with his back turned as he leaned on a desk. It was a whispered conversation, perhaps a personal one. After a short time, the officer concluded the call, turned, and, with a look of surprise, noticed the young man darting out the front door.

CHAPTER 3

Three days earlier, Ryan was sitting in the nearly empty balcony of the ornate state assembly chamber, watching the legislators below debate the merits of the death penalty. The outcome of this debate was a foregone conclusion. Both the state senate and the assembly had for the last seven years routinely passed the death penalty bill. Unfortunately, for the supporters of the legislation, the margin of victory was never sufficient to override the perfunctory veto of the governor, who had been in office for two terms and was the nation's most eloquent and ardent foe of capital punishment. As a result, New York State had no death penalty sentence, and the punishment was not likely to be enacted as long as the governor remained in office.

An obvious complacency was evident. Assembly representatives sat at their historic desks, gossiping, reading the newspaper, even ostensibly dozing. The royal-red-carpeted assembly chamber was furnished with one hundred and fifty mahogany desks and black leather reclining chairs arranged in a semicircle before a four-foot-high elevated rostrum where clerks and presiding officers congregated. Anchored on either side of the rostrum were two flags and behind the rostrum an imposing brass replica of the great seal of the state.

Over the assemblage precariously hung a one-hundred-year-old chandelier that could obliterate most of the state's democracy in one monstrous plunge. To avoid such a catastrophe, four large pillars of polished granite framed the chamber, rising as formidable bulwarks to support the vaulted ceiling. Ryan was perched above the chandelier and positioned in the balcony over the Speaker rostrum from which the proceedings were directed. From this vantage point, he could see all the activity on the floor except for the presiding officer and clerks directly below.

Assemblyman Caluzzi, Republican of Staten Island, had the floor and was screaming, with great emotion, into his microphone.

"These people that kill at random are animals. Animals. They have no respect for life Why should we allow them to live out their years in the dignity of prison? My grandmother lives in Brooklyn. She is terrified to walk the streets. What kind of world is this where my ailing grandmother lives in fear of being killed and these murderous hoodlums have no such fear from the state," said Caluzzi with a flourish as he looked over his seemingly apathetic audience.

Assemblyman Caluzzi harangued the chamber of legislators for twenty minutes, concluding with, "We must kill these animals; inflict pain and death."

Spontaneously, when Caluzzi concluded, the audience came to life. There were howls of approval. The Republican side of the chamber was on its feet with thunderous applause, not for Caluzzi really but for the cause at issue: the death penalty. Ryan noted that some of the conservative Democrats were clapping, but party loyalty dictated that they restrain their enthusiasm. This was, however, a rare vote where the rigid rule of party loyalty was set aside and legislators were set free by the ranking leadership to vote their conscience or in conformity with their latest polling data.

The applause and Caluzzi's stirring speech were all conducted with an ironic wink and knowing nod among the legislators. The general opinion, among both Democrats and Republicans, was that Caluzzi was a clown—a clown who invariably wore flamboyant ties and spoke in fractured, nonsensical sentences. His understanding of issues was limited to the direction that the assembly Republican leadership gave him. Caluzzi was, to both parties and to the institution as a whole, a flagrant embarrassment. He was not the first, and as most seasoned legislators and staff knew, he would not be the last clown to be elected. However, the most distressing aspect of Caluzzi's presence in the legislature were rumors that now publicly swirled around him. For Ryan was aware, as was most of the assembly chamber, of hushed speculation that Caluzzi's brother was connected with organized crime in the city and might even be an enforcer or, to the point of absurdity, a contract killer. Caluzzi, it was also rumored and reported in the *New York Herald*, was the target of a Manhattan grand jury investigation.

Ryan leaned all the way back in his chair, propping his feet up on the vacant row of seats in front of him. The legislature presented as theater. It had a colorful cast of characters, but the story was retold to the point of ennui. He was fighting to stay awake, waiting for Somatos's speech. Assemblyman Green, conservative Democrat from Long Island, was speaking on the floor.

"Who are we to permit these killers to live? If we can save one innocent life by enacting this legislation, let us do it. Shakespeare wrote that violent delights should have violent ends. Let us deliver that violent end to those who terrify our citizenry, make our streets their predatory jungle and our children fearful. Let us restore the rule of law and order and put fear into the cold heart of every killer."

Assemblyman Green remained standing and accepted the applause of the chamber. About fifty years old, Green was elegant in style and manner. His gray hair swept back, his face tan, he was a photogenic presence who was rumored to be contemplating a primary challenge to the governor. Ryan knew Green's greatest weakness was his aristocratic demeanor that alienated the New York City population. For that reason, Ryan was sure Green could never succeed in a challenge to the governor.

By the time Assemblyman Somatos was on his feet, Ryan had grown weary of the monotony of the debate. The arguments flowed like a river that had already cut a deep, predictable path in the vast terrain of public discourse. Twenty minutes after Green spoke, Assemblyman Nickolas Somatos, Democrat of the Bronx, rose to his feet in his rumpled suit and adjusted his microphone. His dark hair was slicked back, and Somatos looked his audience over with the faint hint of a mischievous grin and then paused for supreme dramatic effect.

"Mr. Speaker, I rise in opposition to this measure. I stand here today mindful of the public's growing clamor for the death penalty. The death penalty is an easy remedy for desperate politicians trying to appease the fear and anger of our society. For the death penalty controversy is not about facts. The fact is that as long as humans are flawed in judgment, then our legal system is imperfect and innocent men and women will be executed.

"The debate is not about equal justice under law, because as long as the rich can afford better lawyers, with eloquent and elaborate legal defenses, then our system of justice is unequal. And the debate is not about deterrence, because we all know that the death penalty has never been proven to be a deterrent. Crime has a cause. Perhaps all crimes do not have the same cause, but they all have some cause. And we would be foolish to believe that we could stamp out murder by the fear of the death penalty."

Ryan noted that the usual background din of the chamber had quieted. The side conversations, whispering among aides, and chattering among the groups standing on the corners of the assembly floor had ceased.

Somatos's speech continued, and his voice, which had started low and crisp, was growing louder and more commanding. Somatos's face was sanguine and demonstratively serious. Ryan wondered if his demeanor was the manifestation of genuine emotion or from the exertion of this oratorical effort.

"Justice must be something more than the interest of the stronger. I stand here today to tell you that if this legislation is enacted, our society will be taking another step backward. And with strong conviction I state that this backward march is not into civil order. It is a retreat into something quite the opposite, something sinister and ugly. I oppose the death penalty not because I embrace the guilty, but because our society needs to walk toward the light and not return toward the darkness."

Somatos concluded. The Democratic side of the chamber erupted in a sustained, enthusiastic ovation. Ryan was awed as the legislators jumped to their feet and howled approval. The pro tem chair was gaveling the chamber to order but in a perfunctory way. Somatos wiped his brow and basked in the adulation bestowed by his party.

Somatos glanced up to the balcony and gave Ryan a look that conveyed satisfaction and appreciation. He had read Ryan's speech in its entirety, unedited. The absence of spectators and reporters allowed Somatos to test Ryan's words. And the chamber's clamor confirmed for Somatos that Ryan's words moved people.

Twenty minutes after Somatos spoke, the legislators dipped their magnetic voting cards into the voting machines beside their chamber desks, and as predicted, to the last man and woman, the bill passed 94 to 51 as scored on the lights of the huge electronic tally board. The result was anticlimactic, for the governor's veto would again be sustained and the death penalty measure would again fail. Ordinarily, Ryan would go down to the members lounge and speak with Somatos afterward, but he felt drained by the protracted oratory. He opted to go straight home. He walked the deserted underground passage from the capitol to the Legislative Office Building and took the elevator to street level. Opening the door, he felt a refreshing rush of spring air. It was late, about 7:25, Ryan noted from his watch, but the sky had retained light, and spring fragrantly embraced the city.

He was three blocks from the capitol, walking up Western Avenue, almost at the corner of the park, when he noticed the girl. She had abundant blonde hair and slim, tan legs, and she moved with an erect stride that was confident and, to Ryan, somehow sexy. She wore a jacket, unseasonably revealing shorts, and white sneakers. She was carrying a red purse. Ryan appreciated her legs and her hair from behind. He picked up his pace and stood side by side with her at the corner of North Capitol Street and the corner of Washington Park. While she looked ahead and waited for the light, Ryan assessed her ample bosom and placed her age at twenty-one. Undoubtedly, a college student, he thought.

She glanced over at him but offered only the hint of a smile.

"Work around here?" Ryan asked, trying to moderate his quickening pulse. Ahead, the signal light changed and allowed them to proceed.

"You're asking because you're interested?" she asked stiffly, walking forward.

She was answering his question with a question. Not a favorable sign.

"Just asking."

"You've caught me at a bad time; otherwise I'd say let's have a drink, but not tonight, OK? Besides, I have a boyfriend. And he is a big guy, a really big guy," she said with a mischievous wink. She was both flirtatious and defensive. Ryan debated whether to offer her his business card. However, as was his temperament, he backed off with a resigned "OK, good night."

Ryan picked up his pace to get ahead of her. He considered his options as he walked. Feeling rather audacious, he turned at the corner to look back and attempt a second pass at the girl. She was not there.

Ryan scanned the street and park and could see no girl. He turned back and began to retrace his steps. At the point where he had approached the girl, he spotted a luxury black sedan that appeared to be stopped with the rear door open. Before he walked any farther, the door shut. Then its front tires turned and the car aggressively pulled in front of the oncoming traffic, eliciting several irate motorist horns behind it as it sped past him. He knew she must be in the back seat.

He paused and considered the allure of money and power. Resuming his walk home, he reflected on his lack of financial resources. He hated the thought that he would lose a woman over money. Nevertheless, a quick accounting of his life showed promise: he had a beautiful girlfriend who adored him, a job of importance that fulfilled him, and the possibility of power and money to come. He felt on top of the world, and that feeling stayed with him as he made love to Caroline through the night and up until the next morning. It was an omnipotent feeling of contentment that did not leave him until he saw the first poster of the missing girl.

CHAPTER 4

$\mathcal{S}$he was born in Suffolk County on Long Island, twenty-three years before Ryan met her, the daughter of divorced parents and a deceased mother, prematurely dead from breast cancer. Unlike Ryan, who was an only child, she had three sisters: two older, one younger. The two older ones had married doctors; the younger one was dating a lawyer. Caroline Tierney was a beguiling blonde with extraordinary blue eyes, capable of captivating most men. She was quick thinking, hot-tempered, and, in Ryan's estimation, extremely proficient in bed.

Ryan was very pleased with their relationship, and despite the straying flirtation on the street, his physical and emotional loyalty to her was intact. For the past year she lived with Ryan in what appeared to be a state of mutually deepening romantic endearment. Ryan, in sum, liked where the relationship was going. He knew that he was capable of marrying this girl.

But there were elements in Caroline's nature that mystified him. He met her when she was doing an internship at the Albany legislature during her final year at the State University of New York.

She was not particularly interested in policy. She was bored by the art of legislation, the negotiation, and quid pro quo that created consensus and allowed idealistic ideas to transmute into legislation and then into law. She was, however, keenly interested in deciphering the confluence of power and money and sex.

Rumors about her life flowed profusely at the legislature. The nature of the rumors piqued Ryan's curiosity and inspired him to ask her out. The most provocative of the rumors to Ryan was that she had an abortion as the result of a pregnancy with Assemblyman Carnam of Long Island. Carnam purportedly paid for the abortion, which was noteworthy in light of the fact that he was a pro-life Republican with four kids, a wife, and an arm that was shattered in war.

He had asked Caroline about the rumor after they had been dating for a while. Caroline always offered some glib response that never effectively answered the issue. In true political mode, she would not confirm or deny the veracity of the allegation. Ryan figured that the truth was somewhere in the middle between the allegation and something innocuous.

They were in bed, and the 11:00 p.m. news had just led its broadcast with the police search for Cathy Wilet. There were no leads and no new developments, so the reporters had to focus on grim-faced police spokespersons and skyward shots of police helicopters combing the wooded area near the Colonie Center mall—her last confirmed sighting. Wilet's parents lived near Buffalo, but an affiliate station interviewed them before their flight to Albany. The parents, as expected, looked stricken. The news reporters noted that Wilet's father was chief financial officer for Amaterasu Corporation, a Far East conglomerate. With that fact, reporters speculated about the specter of a kidnapping.

"You'd better not get involved," Caroline said emphatically as she jumped from her side of the bed when Ryan told her he was considering going to the police. "Your career is on the line here. You think Somatos wants you mixed up in a murder investigation?"

"Who said anything about a murder," snapped Ryan.

"Don't be naive. A twenty-one-year-old girl who vanishes the way she did is probably dead. It makes me shudder." Caroline actually made a shuddering movement and crossed her bare pale arms. Twice she had gone over to a pack of cigarettes and laid them down on the dresser. She was trying to quit, and she rarely smoked this late in the evening and then only after she had been drinking. Instead, she sat down in front of the vanity and began to vigorously brush her hair, leaving slender golden souvenirs within the bristles. Ryan watched her intently and began to feel aroused.

"Look, Ryan, if she is dead there is nothing you can do to change that," she rebuked.

He considered that Caroline was ruthless in the extreme.

"Have you considered, Caroline, that maybe my sighting could help catch the murderer?" There was no immediate response.

"Should we now assume that she is dead?" Caroline asked. She was regaining her composure as she smeared moisturizing cream on her hands. Ryan contemplated that the result for the missing girl was the same, regardless if he came forward.

"If you go to the police, have you considered that they may regard you as a suspect? And how does that advance your political career?" Upon asking the question, she turned off the light and slid into bed. She snuggled up close to him. The pleasing contours of her body curved into a familiar position.

Ryan considered that statement. He could tolerate being a witness; felt it to be an obligation. The thought of being a suspect was a possibility he had not weighed.

"Perhaps I could not give my real name. Just give them the information," Ryan said as he turned slightly and focused on her pursed wet lips that seemed to speak silently to him.

"You're just asking for trouble."

She playfully began to stroke his arm and chest and spoke to him softly: "The news said she was last sighted on Colonie Avenue at seven p.m. Why would she be walking away from the capitol at seven thirty p.m.? It probably wasn't her you saw. You can't possibly be sure."

"I'm certain it was," he said softly as his hands fondled her breasts and his erection hardened beneath the covers.

Caroline stopped her movements and pondered the facts while Ryan kissed her neck. Suddenly, he was pushed aside and then felt a strong punch to his arm. "You were trying to pick this girl up."

Ryan was startled. He had subconsciously submerged that fact.

CHAPTER 5

Assemblyman Nickolas Somatos seemed internally pained as he sat in his leather swivel chair and listened attentively as Ryan described the situation. His eyes moved back and forth from Ryan to the statute bust of the god Zeus that sat prominently on his credenza as homage to his Greek heritage. Somatos was seeing his political future evaporate in his mind. He envisioned headlines screaming how his chief of staff was a suspect in a young girl's disappearance. With each word Ryan spoke, Somatos began to wince and his stomach acids churned. Almost immediately, he pulled open his desk draw and popped an antacid pill into his mouth. Somatos remained silent and mostly inscrutable as Ryan paced his office and narrated the sequence of events. Now that Ryan had finished, Somatos exploded in red-faced rebuke of his protégé.

"Don't tell me you're going to risk it all," he berated. "Just don't tell me you think you're going to save the world this way. Write them an anonymous letter, for Pete's sake." Somatos rose from his chair and began to pace his office while Ryan remained still.

"Ryan, you're the best and I mean the best political operative in the capitol. You could bring your credibility into question." Somatos pulled a cigarette pack out of his gray suit pocket. He looked down at the pack and seemed to lose his train of thought.

Ryan noted with amusement that Caroline also the night before had lunged for the cigarettes in response. Smoking was prohibited in the legislative building, but that didn't stop Somatos from occasionally closing his door and furtively huffing on one.

"Nick, I have to do something," Ryan stated assertively.

Somatos withdrew a cigarette, put the pack back into his pocket, and looked down at the frayed edges of his gray trousers and well-worn scuffed shoes.

"What does Caroline say?" he asked with eyes averted.

"She thinks I should not get involved."

"She's a bright woman, you know that." Somatos held the cigarette aloft between two fingers and licked his lips. Ryan frequently thought of Somatos as wolf like in both cunning and temperament. The image again came to mind as he watched him absorb this latest crisis. Somatos went to the window, put the cigarette in his mouth, and quickly pulled a gold lighter from his pocket to ignite it. The flame briefly lit his swarthy face with an orange glow.

Nickolas Somatos always had the appearance of needing a shave and despite his current age—fifty-one—he possessed a full head of dark hair, combed back and held in place by some slick substance. A self-made man who had gone through three wives, he was a former delicatessen owner, gregarious and gifted with the uncanny ability to reinvent himself. His education ceased at the high school level, when he entered his first entrepreneurial activity; nevertheless, the lawyer legislators with Ivy League educations never intimidated him. He felt eminently secure in relying on his street smarts.

"I'm not going to tell you what to do." Somatos was composed now and evaluating the legalities as he spoke. "But I will tell you this," he said as he turned to Ryan and held the cigarette again between two fingers. "I have no desire to blunt the arrow of my own ambition."

Somatos's metaphor lingered in the moment, and Ryan was expressionless.

He leaned closer into Ryan. His breath was hot in Ryan's face. "You better think every move out carefully, because there will be potential fallout from your actions. So be smart."

Somatos turned to face the tinted vertical strip of window again while he puffed furiously on his smoke. Outside the soundproof glass, his wolfish eyes looked down on the relative tranquility of the capitol lawn, being presently mowed, and the iridescent spray of the solitary fountain. Somatos considered his position; he was the ultimate city politician, and his sights were centered on either Congress or the mayoralty of New York. Sarcastic and caustic is how the *New York Herald* characterized him. Yet the city seemed enamored with his persona. He was the last wolf in the pack; the class of colleagues he rose with were either dead, indicted, or in jail. However, Somatos knew he lacked the tender sentimentality that needed to appeal to a broad audience.

Divorced for three years now, he had no kids, no wife, and no friendly family image to put on the cover of campaign literature. However, his oratory was on fire now. Ryan had breathed new life into his words and his legislative record. Somatos's ethics had never been called into question; until now he appeared beyond reproach. Now he wondered if his chief aide was going to entangle him with Cathy Wilet's disappearance.

CHAPTER 6

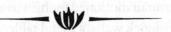

"Sir, I'm sorry. You are waiting for?"

"I'm here about the Cathy Wilet case," Ryan said shyly as he rose from his chair.

"I'll get Detective Brennan," the officer said as he disappeared out of sight.

Ryan did not sit back down but began to pace nervously, like a caged animal, in the bleak confines of the waiting room. He was almost ready to again pull open the station door and flee when a stout, red-faced, middle-aged man in mismatched tie and sport jacket emerged from the rear of the office. The detective's gut protruded above his belt, and his paunch seemed to cushion a black holster and the stubby revolver that hung there. He looked to Ryan like a man ready for retirement.

"Sorry for the delay. You're here about the Cathy Wilet case?" he asked as he swung open the gated partition. His aftershave, an astringent scent, struck Ryan.

"Yes, I have some information that may be helpful," responded Ryan casually.

"I'm Detective Patrick Brennan, and I'm assigned to the case. Let's talk in the back." The detective smiled and waved Ryan forward. Even in these back offices, the station was eerily silent. As they moved down the hall, he noticed that the detective in front of him walked with an authoritative swagger; a gait, no doubt, produced from many years of carrying a belt laden with weapons and other police paraphernalia.

Detective Brennan motioned for him to enter a small conference room with cinder-block walls, a metal table, and four austere chairs. Ryan assumed it was some kind of interrogation room. However, there was no specious two-way mirror as he had expected.

Detective Brennan was six months away from retirement after an uneventful twenty-five years of tenure on the capitol police force. In six months, he planned to be in Florida, fishing every day. The Cathy Wilet case was a sudden onus that he did not need. Fortunately for him, he was not the lead investigator. Unfortunately, he had been assigned the grueling task of interviewing whoever walked in the door with information on the case. It was a tedious role and, he believed, mostly a waste of time. Very little useful information had been proffered. He had taken so many statements from so many students and interns in the past week that their faces were now a commingled and largely irrelevant blur. Albany, New York, and the university were not used to this kind of crime.

Detective Brennan sat across from Ryan and set on the table before him a long yellow legal pad and a pencil. He looked at Ryan and pegged him as a legislative intern, maybe a little older; maybe one of those $15,000-a-session interns just out of college and who thinks he's got a load of power.

"I'm sorry, I didn't get your name," Brennan inquired.

Ryan had to pause to recollect the name he had given the previous officer.

"Michael Baker."

"All right, Mr. Baker, you've said you have some information on the disappearance of Cathy Wilet. Is that correct?" Brennan asked with a tinge of impatience. It was early in the morning, and a long day lay ahead for him.

Ryan was somewhat taken aback by the tone of his voice and the fact that his affable demeanor had melted. He seemed now, to Ryan, almost accusatory.

"That is correct, Detective. I believe that I saw her the night of her disappearance."

"Are you certain it was her?" he asked with incredulity.

"Yes, she was the girl in the photo that's been posted around town."

The detective scribbled some notes that Ryan could not read upside down.

"Where and when did you see her?"

"It was a little before seven thirty p.m. She was walking down Western Avenue away from the capitol. She was about to cross North Capitol Street."

"Seven thirty p.m.? In what direction?"

"West, I believe, away from the capitol and toward the direction of the SUNY campus."

Ryan watched Brennan scratch more notes with thick, calloused hands. The detective sighed.

"Mr. Baker, as you may know from reading the newspapers, our last sighting of Cathy Wilet was almost thirty minutes before your claim. That sighting was on Colonie Avenue, across from the mall, almost twelve miles away. How can you be sure it was Cathy Wilet you saw?"

Ryan paused and then calmly recited the details he had witnessed.

"She was wearing a white blouse, carrying a red purse, and she had on shorts and white sneakers."

Detective Brennan looked up from his pad with what Ryan assumed to be the intense, practiced stare of a veteran police investigator. While parts of Ryan's description were accurate, all that information had appeared in the press.

"You sound like you were very attentive to her, very close?" asked Brennan.

"Yes. Close enough."

"Where do you work?" inquired Detective Brennan as he casually leaned back in the chair.

"Hubbell Wright Investment Firm on North Central," Ryan answered nervously. There was a tightening in his throat, and the flow of words had become difficult. He now measured every word before he dared to utter it.

"You're not a student and you don't work at the legislature?"

"No," responded Ryan firmly.

"You're sure of the time you think you saw her?"

"Yes, it was seven thirty. I know that definitely because I looked at my watch after I passed her."

"Mr. Baker, what were you doing down by the capitol?"

"I got out of work early and was meeting up with some friends to go drinking down on Western."

"A little early in the week for a drink," observed Brennan with a wry smile.

"Not if you're Irish."

Detective Brennan chuckled and then considered the twenty something white male in front of him. He was a fine-looking young man with a full head of dark hair and expressive blue eyes. He wrote down the name Baker and circled 7:30 five or six times until the tip of his pencil split. The information that Michael Baker was now imparting did not fit. This kid, Brennan thought, must be mistaken.

"Well, thanks for coming in. We'll look into it." Brennan stood up.

Ryan, still seated, confusedly nodded his head in assent and then realized he was being graciously dismissed.

"Wait a second, this is important," stated Ryan sharply. "What kind of investigation is this? You've got dogs and helicopters up there by Colonie woods and I'm telling you I saw her by the capitol." Ryan became suddenly aware of the intensity in his voice and demeanor. Stay calm, he thought. *Don't be suspicious. You don't want to be a suspect.*

Ryan stood up and hovered on the precipice of leaving but then decided to take one more pass at the matter.

"It was a limousine that she got into."

Brennan, still standing, scowled incredulously. "What limousine?"

"I believe she got into a black limousine," said Ryan simply.

"Did you get a tag?" asked Brennan with increasing interest in the young man before him.

"No. No tag."

Brennan shook his head and visibly scoffed. He thought for a moment back to his training: abduction by limousine was absurd to him. He was not an expert on abduction, but he knew the FBI statistics on the ways young girls go missing. No girl had ever been documented to have been abducted by limousine.

"What are the facts here? Did you talk with this girl?"

"Well, we didn't exactly chat. She said she had a boyfriend."

"The girl you spoke with said she had a boyfriend? Anything else?"

"Well, did you talk with the boyfriend?" inquired Ryan.

"Did I talk with the boyfriend?" Brennan repeated, mocking Ryan. "Look, you don't tell me how to do my job," said Brennan, annoyed. "Some of your information matches up, but some doesn't with respect to the time of night. I have no information on any limousine. And yeah, she had a boyfriend, but that doesn't mean anything. What pretty young girl doesn't have one? We did talk to him, and he has an alibi. He has got the best alibi there is: he and his assemblyman were working down at the legislature until the eight fifteen adjournment."

Ryan corrected him: "Seven thirty adjournment."

"No, eight fifteen p.m.," Brennan rebuked. "Mr. Baker, I asked you earlier. Do you work at the legislature?" he asked emphatically.

"No."

"So why are you telling me precisely the time the legislature adjourned the night she disappeared?"

Ryan shut his mouth and ceased to breathe. There was protracted tension in the air between them. Silently, they eyed each other. Ryan intimidated; the officer assessing Ryan. Ryan did not look like a killer, a misfit, or any kind of a miscreant. In fact, to Detective Brennan he looked like the other fifty or so legislative interns and well-meaning students who had walked in his door over the last three days.

"Mr. Baker, we have received an outpouring of information from the community on this case. We are fairly confident that our leads placing Ms. Wilet near Colonie Center; our last confirmed sightings."

Brennan looked Ryan up and down. Many of the kids he had interviewed knew this girl and as a result were emotionally distraught.

"Did you know Cathy Wilet?"

"What?"

"Did you know her from the university or through her internship?" he asked firmly.

"No," answered Ryan defensively.

Brennan shifted his posture, leaning close to Ryan's face and lowering his voice.

"Then how could you be so sure it was her you had seen? I have a witness on a bus up near Colonie that knew the girl and saw her there. The witness knew her," repeated Brennan for emphasis. "You're probably mistaken either about the time or the sighting."

Brennan put a hand on Ryan's shoulder consolingly. "Look, when these kinds of things happen, people get upset," he said. "Our last abduction case in Albany was seven years ago. It's not something that happens here."

Brennan had already surmised that Wilet was abducted by force on the road up near the mall. It had to have occurred on one of the roads up there that had little traffic. An experienced detective knew abduction by force down the block from the capitol was not feasible: too many witnesses. The likely scenario for the police was that the abductor was probably some male pervert in his early forties, a habitual sex offender, driving a van and cruising through town when he saw an opportunity to grab her without attention. Maybe he asked her for directions while he grabbed her by the hair and pulled her into the van, envisioned Brennan.

The investigation was aimless and meandering in the absence of physical evidence or a credible witness to the crime. All of Wilet's friends had been interviewed. There was a long, consecutive series of boyfriends, and none could be considered a likely suspect. She didn't run away. Wilet was dead; Brennan knew it as a matter of professional judgment, and the only thing that the police could competently do at this point was find a body. A body with forensic evidence was all he could hope for: closure for the family and a smooth road to retirement.

"Anything else, Mr. Baker, that you need to tell me?"

"No."

"Nothing to confess?" the officer asked without any obvious jest and to Ryan's discomfort.

The last question punctured Ryan's confidence and pushed him into full retreat. He felt foolish and was ready to leave. "No. Nothing else."

"OK," said Brennan, affable once again, with a smile.

He led Ryan out of the room and down the hall and held the gated partition open for him. Before Ryan exited, Brennan called him back. "Wait. Here, take this," he said as he reached into his jacket pocket and pulled out a business card inscribed with the capitol police logo and his name and a phone number. Ryan slipped the card into his wallet. "We will be in touch if new information comes to light." said the detective. "Did you leave your name and number with the desk sergeant?"

Before exiting Ryan turned and said, "Yes I did." It was a lie. He felt both relieved and bewildered. However, he had faithfully discharged his civic obligation. He felt the relief of having a heavy burden lifted. Maybe he was mistaken in thinking he had seen her that night. There are many women who could have fit the description. At any rate, he wasn't a police investigator and he had too much to lose. Importantly, Assemblyman Somatos did not want him mixed up in the business of a missing girl.

CHAPTER 7

After he left the capitol police station, he thought of calling Caroline on the phone from Somatos's office. Then he thought better of the situation and instead opted to tell her over dinner that evening. He called her at work to coordinate their evening plans.

She was still in her business attire when Ryan returned home. To Ryan, she always looked sexiest in her work clothes. She was working in a law office and toying with the idea of taking the law school admissions test. However, in the past three weeks she had also considered becoming a paralegal, working in real estate, or taking up lobbying. Her life with Ryan was not confining, and they both enjoyed the relative liberty of youth not yet burdened by the awesome responsibilities of life. He suggested that they go out for Chinese food.

Caroline and Ryan leisurely walked the six blocks to the restaurant along tree-lined streets that stirred in lingering sunlight. They walked past the downtown SUNY campus, where students were sitting on window ledges, drinking beer, and tossing Frisbees around a green lawn amid the dancing shadows of spring.

Caroline had graduated two years ago and Ryan was out for three years. They both now watched the festival of college life with a detached appreciation and almost nostalgic feeling. Both of them were primed to make their mark on the world. Ryan wondered if their mutually soaring ambitions would drive them together or apart. Caroline, for her part, was consumed with the pursuit of money. Ryan could see that riches fascinated her, making her envious eyes sparkle like reflective gems. Her obvious obsession with money worried him, for Ryan was fascinated with exercise of political power and had no immediate financial aspirations. Nevertheless, he wanted that glimmer of excitement in her eyes to not be distracted by things that he could not immediately attain nor even promise at this point in his life.

The restaurant was cheap Chinese, for both Ryan and Caroline had limited budgets and they could reasonably satiate themselves with this indulgence.

"When do you think Somatos is going to give you a raise?" inquired Caroline while she held a dumpling aloft with two chopsticks.

"His budget is expended for the year; I told you that."

"My point, dear Ryan, is that Somatos is now using your material unedited. You showed me those clippings from the newspapers. They're constantly quoting Somatos now. He needs you. If you press him he will cave." Caroline was leaning in and pressing her point with eager blue eyes.

"You're always so sure of yourself," said Ryan with a wide grin.

It was between the appetizers of dumplings and the arrival of the entrées when Ryan told her.

Caroline dropped her fork and pursed her lips, and then the words flew forth in summary condemnation. "You went to the police; tell me you didn't go to the police. You are so damn stupid."

"Yeah, I did. I had to."

Caroline looked down at her plate, put her hands at her sides, and petulantly stopped eating.

He felt the need to say something to allay her feelings.

"Look, it was just routine. They didn't even seem that interested. Most importantly, I gave them an alias. They don't know where I work or who I am."

Caroline tentatively picked up her fork. "Sometimes you're not only stubborn, you're stupid as well, and it's a bad combination." Caroline was clearly incensed, but he felt confident that after a few drinks and some lovemaking, her vexation with him would melt.

Later that night they walked home on dark streets, silent except for the occasional passing car and the faint musical sound of wind chimes colliding in the cool night breeze. Impulsively, he pulled her close and kissed her passionately. He did not know how she would react. He knew from experience that any kind of reaction was possible with her. To his relief and satisfaction, Caroline's tongue responded sweetly in Ryan's mouth, and he knew then that they would get past this latest flash point in their relationship.

CHAPTER 8

He passed the newspaper stand on his way to work. Each newspaper that morning displayed a headline pertaining to the Cathy Wilet disappearance. The New York City dailies had latched on to the Albany-based story and had extensive coverage. The *New York Herald* had a photo of her with the word "Missing" emblazoned across the cover. It had been seven days since her disappearance. Ryan bought four newspapers, including the three New York City papers.

Wilet's father was offering a $50,000 reward for information leading to her discovery. However, the papers dutifully noted that there was no evidence the girl had been kidnapped for money. According to the papers, she had been last seen walking from the Colonie Center mall at 7:00 p.m. on Monday night. State and local police were focusing their search on a wooded area near the mall, using both dogs and helicopters. The newspapers stated Wilet did not own a car and it was open to speculation where she was headed on foot. Her roommates noted nothing eventful in her life; however, it was reported police were questioning several boyfriends, but none were considered a suspect. The newspapers also noted that she worked as an intern in the capitol. Ryan could not recall if he had ever seen her before.

Ryan studiously read the reporting in Somatos's assembly office. If he had in fact seen her at 7:30, it would alter the focus of the police search and possibly the investigation. Ryan for the first time also realized that if the girl did not own a car, there was no way, without being driven, that she could have been by the capitol at 7:30 p.m. Ryan considered two possibilities: one, he had not seen her, was mistaken in his identification, or two, that his watch had malfunctioned and was wrong. He checked his timepiece against the office clock; both corresponded. Ryan was fastidious about time to a fault. He measured his life in increments of days and hours lost. He would even time his sexual activity.

He picked up the business card he received from Detective Brennan and called the number on it. To Ryan's surprise, Brennan answered the phone. Ryan cleared his throat. "Detective Brennan, this is . . ." Ryan trailed off; he could not recall the name that he had given. Brennan again repeated his name, and the gruff tone jogged Ryan's memory. "Detective Brennan, this is Michael Baker."

"Mr. Baker, how are you?" Brennan sounded preoccupied. He recalled that the kid named Michael Baker had some story that was not very useful.

"I was just calling to see if there has been any further information that would confirm my sighting of Cathy Wilet?"

"Oh yes, well, we are receiving hundreds of leads, if not thousands of leads at this point. Your sighting just doesn't fit our pattern."

"How do you mean?"

"Your timing is off. Every lead we have places Ms. Wilet in the Colonie area at seven o'clock and even later. Yours is the only sighting we have near the capitol."

"Detective, it is reported that she was a capitol intern. Maybe she came back to work to pick something up."

"We appreciate your help, Mr. Baker. We are following these leads. Thanks so much for calling." The detective was off the line.

Ryan stared at his wristwatch. "I'm sure it was seven thirty," Ryan murmured to himself. He picked up the phone and called the chief clerk's office.

"Can you check for me the time the assembly adjourned following the death penalty debate on Monday."

The clerk paused. "Somatos's office, right?" The clerk had a device on his phone that displayed the origin of the incoming call.

"Yes, this is Ryan McNeil."

Ryan waited for about three minutes. "Mr. McNeil, the death penalty debate according to the official transcript ended at eight ten and the assembly adjourned at eight fourteen p.m."

Ryan asked the clerk to check again. The clerk, somewhat annoyed, repeated the information. Ryan had never checked a transcript before. Perhaps it was not accurate. At any rate, this information did not corroborate Ryan's account of events.

When Somatos entered the office, he found Ryan staring in mid-space with his desk scattered with newspapers clippings all bearing the story of Cathy Wilet's disappearance. Somatos did not say anything. He entered his office, closed the door, and two minutes later asked Ryan to come inside. Ryan entered and Somatos motioned for him to shut the door.

"You went to the police, didn't you."

Ryan grinned and nodded.

"I'm proud of you. You exercised good civic responsibility," said Somatos with obvious sarcasm.

"The transcript time is wrong," stated Ryan pointedly.

"What transcript?"

"The death penalty transcript. The journal transcript shows the assembly adjourning at eight fifteen p.m."

Somatos looked at Ryan bewildered. "So what?"

"I'm certain it ended at before seven thirty, because I saw the Wilet girl at seven thirty."

Somatos frowned deeply. "Does it really make a difference? What does the fact that the transcript may be off mean, anyway? You told the police you saw her. That's fine. Don't play detective. You're a damn good legislative aide and the best damn speechwriter in town, so please stick with what you're good at."

Ryan nodded in agreement and appreciated Somatos's backhanded compliment.

"Leave the door open and stop worrying about this matter. Justice works in mysterious ways; it doesn't depend solely on Ryan McNeil."

Ryan dropped the matter and diverted his attention back to work. It was several hours later that the invective was flowing loudly from Somatos's office. Somatos had just taken a call from the governor's office.

"The bastard. Governor Promo. That self-promoting bastard. Promo is not with us."

Somatos was fuming as he asked Ryan to shut the door. Ryan was acutely aware of the fact that "Promo," as in self-promoter, was Somatos's nickname for the honorable governor of New York, who as happenstance would have it was in the same political party as Somatos, a fact that caused Somatos endless political and personal anguish.

Ryan inquired what "Promo" had done and was told that Somatos had just received word that the governor had vetoed Somatos's genetic testing bill that had overwhelmingly passed the legislature. Ryan crafted a major portion of it, and if not for his preoccupied state of mind, the news would have had greater impact.

"Set up a meeting with Charles Green and see if we can't rally the Democrats to override the veto," Somatos snapped. "The governor is a hypocrite who causes blind hopes to live in the hearts of men," he bellowed in sudden eloquence and to Ryan's bewilderment.

Ryan quickly went to his phone to set up a lunch meeting with Majority Leader Green in his office. Green's chief of staff, Seth Tantalus, was to attend, and Somatos wanted Ryan by his side.

They arrived punctual to the minute, and a young male intern sitting behind a reception desk in Green's outer office greeted them. Despite their punctuality, Ryan and Somatos were forced to wait. Two leather couches lined either wall, but both Ryan and Somatos remained standing in the small reception area. Ryan eyed the surroundings of honorary plaques and framed art, while Somatos impatiently tapped his scuffed shoe, irritated at the indignity of a delay. After several minutes, Seth Tantalus, dressed in a dark suit and haughty yellow tie, emerged from behind a closed door and greeted them both with a cordial smile and the bulk of his handshake. He then led both into Green's inner office.

Assemblyman Green rose like a stern emperor behind his desk and, without any verbal pleasantries, motioned for them to sit on several chairs arranged around a conference table. Green's office was more elaborate than Somatos's, given Green's leadership status with the legislature. His oversize desk and credenza were finely crafted mahogany pieces in contrast to Somatos's veneer desk crafted by the inmates at Attica Correctional Facility. Beyond the disparity in furnishing was the ostentatious display of plaques and photos that graced every inch of Green's office walls: photos with the governor, president, mayors, teachers, union leaders, corporate leaders, Hollywood actors. Somatos's office had approximately twenty photos, all of constituents who happened to be community leaders, none of any notable fame.

Both of the young aides viewed the other with seemingly inexplicable antagonism. To the casual observer, their mutual maternal Irish lineage and love of politics should have been a source of implicit solidarity between them. Perhaps it was the competitive position of their mentors or an instinctual recognition of physical and temperamental differences, but for whatever ill-defined and innate reasons, a mutual antipathy between them existed.

Even in his dark suit, Seth Tantalus had the imposing broad physique of a football lineman and was twice the size of Ryan. The suit did little to cloak him in a professional appearance, for it only seemed to constrain the bearlike lumbering of his movement. To Ryan, Tantalus looked every inch like one of those loud, bragging fraternity boys who drank beer in gallons through a funnel implanted down his their throat. He was the kind of man that Ryan had outwitted and evaded throughout his life.

Conversely, Tantalus regarded Ryan as a lightweight; the kind of man he was used to intimidating on and off the football field. Seth Tantalus, of Northport, Long Island, had drunk many gallons of beer through a funnel implanted in his mouth by the fraternity at Notre Dame. He loved women, he loved politics, and he loved beer and by natural animal instinct in reverse order. He had no collegial affinity for his youthful colleague who now sat across from him. In point of fact, he sensed condescension from Ryan that was rooted in reality.

Catered sandwiches were brought in by an aide and solicitously unwrapped before them on porcelain plates. Assemblyman Green pushed aside the sandwich platter before him on the conference table. His preference was to discuss business over a finely prepared meal in an elegant restaurant, but that was not possible in this situation. Given the sensitive nature of this discussion, Green wished to avoid being seen or worse yet overheard; it was a mutual concern for Somatos. Assemblyman Somatos also abstained from the food before him while Ryan, panged by hunger, took a small bite of a ham sandwich. With a sign of distaste on his patrician face, Green watched as Tantalus, with unrestrained appetite, devoured in several bites the sandwich before him and then began shoveling potato salad into his mouth.

Ryan observed the visibly awkward interplay between Assemblyman Green and his chief of staff, speculating on the affinity between them. Unknown to Ryan, Assemblyman Green was grateful for Tantalus's willingness to tackle unpleasant tasks. Green felt that he needed a man like Tantalus. He did not like him on a personal level, at times he detested him, but he recognized the intrinsic value of audacious youth, loyal only to Green's ambition.

Green leaned back in his chair and spoke expansively, gesticulating with arms wide. "I can't help you, Nick. A veto override on this would be tantamount to mutiny; it would do long-term damage to the governor and weaken him for the Republicans."

"How do expect me to justify the governor's veto; I simply can't," snapped Somatos, leaning forward over his food.

"Nick, you're just going to have to accept this."

"Have you read his veto message?" Somatos noted dismissively. "He called this legislation foolish, feeble, misguided, implausible, and detrimental to the public interest. He has a hundred damn disparaging adjectives in this veto."

"Our esteemed governor has a way with adjectives," remarked Green.

"Well, I'll tell you," Somatos said with a wide wolfish grin, "I have a way with verbs."

"Assemblyman Somatos, you need to face the fact," said Tantalus, "that you just don't have the clout on this issue. You—"

Tantalus was cut off in midsentence by a burst of profanity from Somatos.

"Excuse me," said Somatos loudly while Tantalus was speaking. "Just who the fuck do you think you are?"

Tantalus was startled. Green smiled and explained, "My young aide has not yet learned diplomacy. That is not his specialty."

Diplomacy was the specialty of Charles Everett Green. He was part of an affluent five-generation family from the north shore of Long Island known as Locust Valley. He was gray haired and tall, with an erect bearing that accentuated his height, and he had chiseled Anglo-Saxon features and steel gray-blue eyes that dually conveyed intelligence and an arrogant aristocratic demeanor. Set on substantial acres of manicured land, Green's house, designed by a famed architect, was a stone mansion, built in 1929, with a sixty-foot pool, a driving range, greenhouse, two tennis courts, and terraced gardens leading luxuriously down to the tranquil waters of the Long Island Sound where his yacht was moored. The material trappings of his wealth were largely inherited, and his election to the state assembly was a product of his pedigree, since his father had held the seat until his death twelve years ago.

Somatos had one summer attended a Democratic fundraiser at Green's Long Island estate. The front door of the house was a good quarter mile from the road. When Somatos, from the gated entrance, saw the rich cream columns of Charles Everett Green's palatial house in the distance, an exclamation of profanity slipped in awe from his lips. He remembered the evening as possessing a kind of opulent glamour he usually associated with Hollywood or the movies in general. Affluent Democrats, some famous, some not famous, some believing in their own fame, lingered by an illuminated cerulean pool and in Green's twilight gardens and terraces, for this occasion festooned with pastel lights.

Memorably, under a setting sun, a bay breeze from the inland sea was sweetened by the wafting perfume and cologne of the crowd. Young, long-legged women wobbled in high heels on the arms of much older men, their thin dresses held in place by thin strings. Under a starlit night, Charles Everett Green's munificence and grandiosity was spread before him while piano key strokes and a wailing violin harmonized and sustained the party. Somatos abstained from the banquet feast and instead ate grapes and in moderation sipped champagne. That evening Nikolas Somatos, though outwardly cool and cordial, like the sea beyond Charles Green's gates, was internally seething with the disdain and envy of wealth. The elevated luxury of Green's world hovered beyond his reach. Somatos felt an unspoken hostility to Assemblyman Green ever since.

Now, Green's obstinate refusal to accede to Somatos's request rekindled that vexing memory and further irritated his own insatiable ambition. The discussion continued until it became evident that the meeting was a formal declination. Green had no intention of helping Somatos override the governor's veto. Upon that realization, Somatos abruptly stood up from the conference table and thanked Green and Tantalus for their time.

As Ryan strode down the hall, he could see the anger evident in Somatos's face. Somatos cleared his throat and uttered his observation in a voice so low that no one but Ryan could hear him.

"People with power are not smarter or luckier than us; the truth is most of them just popped out of a gilded pussy. Someday that bastard is going to come groveling to me for a favor, and he'll learn that, like the governor, I never forget."

CHAPTER 9

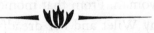

Ryan tried to call Caroline from Somatos's office. At first, he called the law office where she was working. They politely told him that she had called in sick. He then tried the house, but the phone was not answered. He tried her cell phone, calling every half hour, then every fifteen minutes, but his calls went to voice mail. Panic descended on him like a crushing weight. He became ambushed by the irrational fear she was abducted. He left work early in a frenzy and caught a cab for the quick ride home. Arriving home, he was stunned.

Her belongings were gone. Only a few personal items remained. Ryan was astounded. He searched for a note and found none. He sat dejected in the bedroom, staring with paralyzed bewilderment at the empty closet where her clothes had once filled the space, the strange void still faintly emitting her perfumed scent. The front door opened and Caroline came bounding up the steps, looking cheerful.

"Caroline, what's going on?"

She incongruously smiled and said, with a casual indifference, she was leaving. She handed her keys to Ryan, who felt struck by an electrified force, like lightning. An ineffable, heart-pounding rage rose within him.

"You met someone else? Who is it?" demanded Ryan, bitterly.

The smile erased, as she turned and glared at him, "It's you. You're the reason I'm leaving." Her voice was sharp, her demeanor churlish, and there was no further explanation as she abruptly left.

She was gone. Ryan for the first time in his life felt panic and anguish over a woman. From that moment forward in his mind, thoughts of Cathy Wilet and her dreadful fate were eclipsed by thoughts of Caroline Tierney and her sudden, inexplicable desertion of him. He wanted to shrug it off, tough it out, but everywhere he turned he was reminded of Caroline in fragmented and illusory visions. The flowery scent of a strange woman's perfume evoked the familiar redolence of Caroline. The lively chortle of a young girl on the street made him spin. A luxurious mane of blonde hair fluttered his heart. She was everywhere and nowhere. For seconds he could glimpse her behind glass in a restaurant and darting into taxis, only to realize it was not her. His mind latched on to her vision and tore at him. Ceaselessly, inexorably, he was compelled to search out her presence. Ryan McNeil was surprised and humiliated by the depths of his anguish. The tormenting pain of losing her would not relent.

A week after Caroline had left, Assemblyman Caluzzi asked his twenty-year-old intern to stay late with him, alone, to work on a legislative project involving educational allocation formulas. The young intern, who had been with his office for only six weeks, consented to the assemblyman's request even though she was already uncomfortable with his persistent sexual advances. She, in fact, was already working through the Assembly Intern Committee office to secure a position with another representative, preferably a woman. She had not communicated this fact to Assemblyman Caluzzi, and she wanted to pleasantly appease him before she left. She already learned it was better not to offend any politician, even a distastefully lecherous politician.

At eight in the evening, alone with him, behind the closed door of his office, she found herself again fending off his unwanted sexual advances. Caluzzi at one point pulled her close, and before she was cognizant of what he was doing, he had his tongue in her mouth, like a snake. His hands quickly moved over her breasts. In a frenzy of panic, she kicked him hard in the groin and ran for the locked door of the office, but she was unable to open the door. Her screams were loud but could not be heard before he removed his tie and savagely wrapped it around her throat.

"You stuck-up bitch," said the assemblyman as he pulled the tie tightly around her throat to suppress her screaming and subdue her. Caluzzi forced his intern around by the throat and then looked directly into her panicked eyes. The young girl could not scream or breathe. There was a sense of unreality. This was a legislative office; he was an assemblyman; she was just twenty. She could not possibly die this way.

She was being strangled, and forced backward over his desk. The intern, in a frenzied panic, reached out, frantically grabbing whatever weapon she could reach—a heavy marble bust of Lincoln that sat on his desk. With the heavy object in hand she swung her arm toward him, as if she were throwing a pitch, forcefully striking Caluzzi's head sideways, splitting his scalp open. The white marble bust was coated with a bright red splash of blood from the head of the Assemblyman. He instantaneously released his grip on the tie and fell forward, with his head in his hands bowed before her. Without hesitation, she struck him forcefully again, this time across the back of his skull. She recoiled as a sudden spray of blood hit her in the face and splattered the wall behind her. She held the statute with trembling hands but then saw a ghastly glob of blood and flesh that clung to Lincoln's face. She dropped it in revulsion, screaming for help.

His hands now went to the back of his head; there was a tactile thunderclap of pain, and the back of his head felt raw and slippery.

Collapsing from the blow, he crumpled meekly to the floor, balancing on one knee. She was ready to run for the door, but then she heard an ominous thud. A hefty piece of black metal—a gun—slipped from Caluzzi's suit jacket and fell to the floor. She saw the gun and quickly grabbed for it before he could retrieve it. In pain and balanced on his knee, he realized that his gun had fallen, and he was ready to lunge like a wounded beast. According to the subsequent police report, the intern, whose identity was not publicly revealed, with gun in hand, accidentally discharged the weapon, shooting Caluzzi through the heart at virtually point-blank range. The assemblyman died on the spot.

Ryan was sitting in a recliner chair, drinking a beer and bemoaning his beloved, when the local news interrupted the scheduled programming. The news anchor grimly reported the death of Assemblyman Caluzzi in his office by a gun used by his intern, who alleged she was fending off a sexual assault. The news report seemed outlandish to Ryan and yet somehow predictable, given the rumors of Caluzzi's corruption. An Albany police captain was interviewed and asked if the attack by Assemblyman Caluzzi and disappearance of Cathy Wilet were connected. Ryan turned the volume up on the television.

"We are not sure. Given that Ms. Wilet worked at the state legislature and given that tonight's incident entailed a young woman being attacked by Assemblyman Caluzzi, we believe that there may be a connection we will have to explore." The captain waved away any further questions or speculations.

Ryan started to pace the living room. He went out onto the patio, beer in hand, and watched the nighttime crowd of college students. Ryan considered the death of Caluzzi and its possible relation to the Wilet disappearance. Perhaps Somatos was right, Ryan thought; maybe justice does work in mysterious ways.

That night Ryan paced his apartment in an agitated state for over an hour. Finally, he decided to call the number that Caroline had left for him. She answered. There was static and interference on the line, some kind of weak cellular signal.

"Did you hear the news about Caluzzi?"

"No. What news?" she inquired with seeming disinterest.

"He tried to kill his intern; she apparently shot him," Ryan said nonchalantly.

"Is he dead?"

"The news said so. They are speculating that Caluzzi could have abducted Cathy Wilet. Perhaps he was driving the car I saw." Ryan paused. "Caroline, come back."

"I'm sorry, Ryan. I really am, but we both know that there were limits to our relationship. You seem to also forget you were trying to pick up Cathy Wilet. Remember? That says it all. You can't feel too deeply about me." She spoke coldly, without any emotional intonation in her voice.

Ryan emotionally choked on her last remark with a pang of enormous guilt.

"I'll talk to you another time," he said somberly as he hung up.

He decided to go for a run. He changed into shorts. He briskly ran down his steps and out his front door, sprinting down Western Avenue on an unusually warm night capped by a full moon. On the streets, SUNY students were in a Friday night state of revelry, drunk, loud, and obnoxious, cluttering the sidewalk in front of several bars. Ryan passed at a rapid clip through them and down the peaceful side streets, traversing Washington park lawn toward the capitol. He needed to run; to clear his mind. The park was deserted. Ryan, in a burst of angry energy, charged down a dirt path, dimly lit, with high bushes bordering the trail, but he felt eminently safe given the speed of his movement and the fact that crime was virtually unknown in this park at any hour.

Surprisingly, he could hear the peel of a police car wail, invisibly piercing the night, and then another distinct wail from a different direction, and then another that was proximate. The chorus of sirens soon turned into a crescendo that seemed to be converging. He was sweating profusely, breathing hard, and his eyes began to sting. The air seemed hot and pungent with the smell of smoke. Ryan halted his run and looked upward toward the Empire State Plaza. Catching his breath, he paused in bewilderment. In the distance was a bright scarf of scarlet flame draping the upper floors of a governmental office tower and flagging into the night. Between the Caluzzi shooting, the skyward inferno before him, the missing girl, and his own personal upheaval and tribulations, Ryan sensed a growing, insidious calamity all around him. He felt his once carefree life was about to end.

CHAPTER 10

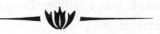

Seven Years Later, Fairfax, Virginia

Annie McNeil had been divorced for three years when she met Ryan. Her ex-husband was a Washington, DC, lawyer who had taken up an affair with another lawyer. They had moved to Texas, and the only contact she had with her ex-husband was confined to an envelope that came the first week of every month with a child support and alimony check. Occasionally, a picture or scrawled note was enclosed, though Annie was uncertain as to the purpose. Usually it revealed her ex-husband and his new girlfriend in some exotic location, as at the top of a snowcapped mountain or stretched on a pristine beach by aquamarine water. Despite the fact that her ex-husband was seven-year-old Jessica's father, Annie would usually toss these mementos in the garbage.

Jessica was only two years old when her father left. The little girl now rarely inquired as to his presence or expressed any interest in him, except around Christmastime when she deciphered that she could benefit by the added bonus of a biological and surrogate father. Ryan married Annie three years ago when Jessica was four, and the little girl now regarded Ryan for all purposes as her true father.

Annie had met Ryan through a dating website. It was her advertisement. She was looking for sincerity and stability. Annie was a deeply religious born-again Protestant. Her only prior sexual experience was with her husband. She regarded divorce as a personal failure on her part. It was a failure she quickly wanted to remedy with another marriage.

Ryan, whose hectic job as chief of staff to Congressman Nickolas Somatos, was becoming weary of the frantic and mostly frivolous single life he was leading. He was captured by the appeal of an immediate family, its comforts and structure. And of course the immediate acceptance and love of Jessica had led Ryan to conclude that he had discovered his true calling as a surrogate father.

Annie had many compelling reasons to marry Ryan. There were bills, so many bills that had piled up before, during, and after the divorce. Though she had a college degree, she had never worked for a sustained period of time at one job. Ryan appeared as a godsend. He had a good job with a bright future. She was attracted to his boyish good looks, his full head of sandy brown hair and bright blue eyes, and an almost feminine mouth that proclaimed sincerity, with no hint of guile or deceit.

However, they both now were facing problems in the marriage. There was a miscarriage in the night. To Ryan, it was a traumatic truncation of his paternal hope. By contrast, Annie recovered from the loss with a swiftness that to Ryan almost seemed to border on emotional relief. The event seemed to catalyze a change in her. Since then, Annie became more practical and efficient and denuded of passion. Her seeming aversion to sex had progressed to a stage that reduced their lovemaking to a rare, perfunctory process of sexual release, devoid of romance or passion. Ryan, who, in his past with Caroline deemed the act of making love to be a sublime joy, felt a mechanical pleasure, devoid of fully charged emotion. Sex with Annie had become routine and dull, but he developed enough diversions that allowed him to be sexually fulfilled and thereby also allowed him to fulfill the greatest obligation he felt as a stepfather.

After three years of marriage, Annie felt a simplistic contentment. She never felt any overwhelming sense of romantic bliss with Ryan, nor with any other man for that matter. To the best of her knowledge, the altitude of her emotions could not rise to that particular plane. Marriage was, to her, a practical, economical institution. Annie was unsure whether her attitude was part of her character or the result of her upbringing. She assumed, however, it was the result of her parents being emotionally distant from each other, and as a consequence she came to view men through a myopic lens of cynicism and detachment. At least, that is what her psychoanalyst told her.

While Annie was tucking Jessica into bed for the night, Ryan was reading the Sunday paper, and his attention drifted toward an article on the inside cover page:

Police Intensify Search for Missing Woman

Police in Fairfax County have requested the assistance of neighboring jurisdictions and FBI specialists in their search for Leslie Warren, 27. Ms. Warren disappeared one week ago after having dinner with friends in Old Town Fairfax. Police believe that Ms. Warren has been abducted, a conclusion they reached after locating her car in Old Town. Friends described her as cheerful and outgoing. She worked part-time at a souvenir shop in the old town area and the store owner said, "She is a terrific person; her life is ahead of her." Ms. Warren is a native of Canton, Pennsylvania, but police have been unable to locate any family. Police are also investigating that Ms. Warren may have recently come into a large inheritance that they believe may be related to the absence of any known family and the circumstances of her disappearance.

Ryan put the paper down. Whenever he read about such cases, he invariably thought back to Cathy Wilet. A vivid spring memory of her: young, vibrant, smiling at Ryan on a street corner seven years ago. Of course, he realized, he could never be sure that it was her he had seen. He had left Albany five years ago, and to the best of his knowledge she never surfaced, the case never solved, no suspect discovered, her body gone: a tangible existence now nothing more than an enigma of faded memory.

Annie was in the bedroom, preparing for bed. He had to gauge her emotional state to consider the prospects for sexual relations.

"I hope you remembered to take the garbage out," her disembodied voice came from the bathroom.

"No, I left it in your closet," Ryan said sarcastically.

"Remember, you need to take Jessica to soccer practice next Saturday. And the dentist afterward."

Ryan made the mental list; his life with her was reduced to a domesticated series of chores: garbage out, check; soccer, check; dentist, check; even sex when she granted it, check.

The eleven o'clock news had come on and led with two crime stories. Ryan felt safe in his neighborhood. There had been little crime of note in the years since they moved into the house.

"I'm so scared," said Annie as she emerged from the bathroom.

"Of what?" asked Ryan dismissively.

"There is so much crime now, and that Leslie Wheaton girl is missing."

Ryan corrected her: "Leslie Warren."

"How do you know her name?" she inquired with a seriousness that seemed to irrationally border on suspicion.

"It's here in the paper," said Ryan loudly.

The television news was on, and the report was also about the missing woman.

"Police are reportedly at a dead end for leads in the search for Leslie Warren. Warren, twenty-seven years old, has been missing for a week now after having dinner at the Red Rooster Pub in Old Town Fairfax. An FBI task force is working with Fairfax Police to generate new leads." The reporter signed off from Fairfax Police headquarters.

"I hope they execute the man that took her," Annie remarked as she pulled the covers back and entered the bed.

"How do you know that she is dead or that a man took her?"

"You know how I feel about capital punishment. The Bible supports it; murderers have no right to live. What if, God forbid, someone took Jessica? Don't tell me you would not want him executed."

"How can you be so sure that if they catch a person for the abduction that it is the right person? You could wind up executing an innocent man," said Ryan.

"So what?" she remarked righteously, without hesitation.

Ryan could not argue logic with Annie on this issue. She would emotionalize every discussion. The talk about missing girls, capital punishment, and the submerged tension in their marriage effectively dampened Ryan's passion. After the television was shut off, both pulled the covers up, and without further words or intimate touch between them, they mutually slipped into the abyss of deep sleep.

CHAPTER 11

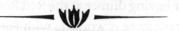

A lowered cream-colored shade suffused the bedroom with opalescent light. Ryan's dreams, a sentimental, sand creation of his sleep, were wrecked and crumbling now as a tide of awakening swept over him. Last night he had a dream of Caroline.

In the dream, he was walking down Western Ave in Albany away from the capitol. He could feel the spring air and could see vividly the trees of Washington park. He walked past the Cathy Wilet girl and instead this time he ran back, in a heart-pounding frenzy, because, in this particular loop of a dream, the girl who was disappearing into a dark sedan was Caroline Tierney, his beloved.

He turned on his side. Annie's head rested toward him, sideways on a pillow. Her thick mane of dark hair framed her pale face. Her mouth seemed slightly twisted in sleep. The silky folds and satin frill of her nightgown veiled the bulging contours of her breasts; the shallow rise in her breathing was imperceptible. When her arm moved above the cover, he realized she was awake. Her emerald eyes focused on him.

"What time is it?"

"It's about six thirty."

"Are you going to work today?" she asked as she turned away from him on the pillow. He was usually up by 6:00 a.m.

"Let's make love."

Annie slowly lifted herself up slightly in bed, feigning feminine interest. He knew that she was not one to fancy whimsical propositions, especially in the morning. And the rarity of his proposition was such that it required verbalized consent to act.

"I have to take Jessica to school," she said dreamily as she slid out of bed.

The chaste refusal to oblige and the offhand indifference to his proposition silently infuriated him. He had a sudden urge to impose his will upon her as he watched her disappear into the bathroom. Instead, he reined himself in and in response to this frustration contemplated his plans for the evening.

He sat in traffic that morning, listening to the radio and contemplating the limitations of his life. He had achieved his ambition to go with Somatos to Congress and become his congressional chief of staff. But his life now was curiously lacking in zest. He had thought little of Caroline these last few years. However, last night's dream left him disconcerted. He wondered whether dreaming had dimmed his daylight perspective and cast a shadow spell upon him.

CHAPTER 12

Congressman Nickolas Somatos of New York City wore a particularly dapper double-breasted pin-striped suit that Monday morning, with the flourish of a bright red tie and a perfectly adorned handkerchief in the breast pocket. The congressman's finely tailored suit complemented a striking photogenic tan. He told Ryan that he had spent much of the weekend on the Chesapeake in a boat, courtesy of a political donor. The hefty gold of his medallion cuff links and the waft of expensive cologne were consistent with his radiating aura of success.

Somatos, like many of his new peers, had been physically and sartorially transformed by the Congress. Unmistakable power emanated from a tiny official blue-and-gold pin worn on the lapel of his expensive suit, denoting his official status for the omnipresent security personnel, permitting entry into places for only the privileged few. He had lost weight, stopped smoking, and his hair was now maturely gray above the temples and immaculately styled.

These were the obvious changes. More subtly visible to Ryan, the caustic side of Somatos's language now seemed calculated. He could even be charming. Somatos in Albany had confined his charm to the ladies, but now in Washington, DC, he found it necessary to exercise charm on the men as well, especially the Democratic leadership that controlled the House and the fate of his legislative program and perhaps his political future. However, as Ryan knew, the wolf side of his persona never left, but he was more careful now, calculating his moves with greater precision.

With Somatos's newfound stature and influence, Ryan had collaterally benefited. His income had nearly tripled, and both Ryan and his wife lived comfortably in the most affluent community in the United States. Both Congressman Nick Somatos and his chief of staff, Ryan McNeil, were well regarded on the Hill. However, Ryan once thought of himself as almost indispensable to Somatos, but Somatos had developed his own skills. He seemed to have assimilated every line that Ryan ever crafted for him so that he could now, with the greatest of public ease, improvise a speech or a quote for any occasion. More importantly, Somatos had mastered the art of the quid pro quo. Ryan marveled at the elaborateness of Somatos's congressional deal making, exchanging votes like golden barter among the governing elite. Somatos had secured a million-dollar youth center in his district in exchange for his vote in support of a tobacco subsidy bill. Ryan had questioned the wisdom of the vote on ethical grounds, but Somatos said: "Those kids need a safe place to smoke." Ryan knew the congressman was being his usual flippant, irreverent self, but the essential truth was that for Somatos, the tangible was far more important than the principle. He wanted more cops, better schools, health insurance for kids. He would not hesitate to sacrifice a vote on principle for any of these tangible gains. He would deal with the devil if necessary. Ryan watched his mentor and considered it sound, practical politics. Ryan's job was to imbue it all with the flavor of high idealism. He handled the press, the speeches, and the legislation. Somatos cut the deals. For all of Ryan's insecurity, Somatos still valued his skill and, of course, his loyalty.

Ryan had long ago relinquished without regret any political aspiration he might have held. He had struck in his mind the perfect balance: he was in his element, had carved the proper niche. He had seen the burden of public office and decided that the lifestyle was, in fact, no real life at all. For as far as Ryan could determine, Somatos had no life but politics. Every meal, every event, every friendship, every acquaintance, every minute of his life was premeditated and programmed to relate to something political. He lived, slept, ate, drank, and maybe even screwed with politics in mind. Somatos the wolf was, to the visceral core of his existence, a cunning political animal, and he seemed to want it that way and relish every moment.

Notwithstanding his current tan and weekend boat excursion, Congressman Somatos invariably shuttled every week by commercial airplane between New York City and Washington. In the Bronx he maintained a small apartment residence. Ryan had seen it once. The place was a mess, scattered with newspapers and books and largely unkempt. A typical bachelor abode. In Washington, he rented another apartment that was three blocks from the Capitol. Ryan had never seen that domicile, but he envisioned that it was more of the same. This dual itinerant lifestyle was an onerous but nevertheless necessary demand of the office. In the district he would attend the park festivals, kiss the babies, placate the seniors, cut the ribbons, and hold his town hall meetings. Through it all he would offer a patient, sympathetic ear to the positions and problems of his constituents.

Somatos was walking briskly with Ryan through the marble-floored halls of the Longworth House Office Building.

"I'd like you to attend that business council reception tonight."

The receptionist congenially smiled at Somatos. He reciprocated with a wide wolfish grin. They both picked up a full wad of phone messages and went into Somatos's office. He sat down in his chair with suit jacket on. His office complex consisted of three high-ceilinged rooms divided by cubicles and two private offices, one of which was Somatos's, the other Ryan's. The highly prized offices had panoramic views of the Capitol, but Somatos's window faced a courtyard with the Capitol dome only obliquely visible at the very corner. Ryan's office was an office only in the sense that it contained a door and enough room for a desk and a small conference table.

"Congressman Green called to inquire about lunch," chuckled Somatos as he thumbed through his messages.

"He was lucky to win that special election."

"He's going to find it difficult to accept the fact that you are now more senior than him," said Ryan, grinning across the desk from Somatos.

"You know I want you to be especially cooperative with him; go out of your way to assist him and his aide. What was his name?"

"Seth Tantalus. You may finally get the chance to return that favor he did not do for you on the health bill," observed Ryan.

"Oh, would I do a thing like that?" With a smirk, Somatos leaned back in his chair behind his sturdy oak desk and for a moment seemed to savor the vicissitudes of political life.

CHAPTER 13

S ometimes the discreet business of American politics is transacted between sips of rose-colored wine, Chablis and cabernet sauvignon, and over fine china plates laden with great pink piles of chilled shrimp and crabmeat, seasoned squid, and seared salmon. The congressional reception was after work in the foyer of the Rayburn House Office Building. Ryan went because Somatos asked him to attend, because the host organization made large political contributions, and because he was yearning deep in his heart to see if Ms. Amber White would be there.

The crowd swirled noisily with lobbyists, Hill staffers, and dapper congressmen and the occasional congresswoman. In the middle of the room, an elaborately carved ice sculpture of a swan slowly melted. Around the swan was set a frilled table clothed buffet of hors d'oeuvres meticulously stacked on silver platters. Lobbyists wandered fraternally and yet purposefully among the elected officials and staff, eagerly exchanging handshakes and cordial conversation.

Meanwhile, in this congenial setting, not a gentleman or gentlewoman in the room shed a drop of perspiration. For the workings here were not so much a labor as they were an affable exchange of etiquette and information. The subtle gesture, the whisper, the laugh, the handshake or intonation could all determine the fate of legislation and with it the fate of a nation. For the lobbyists eager to entice a legislator to a cause, the alcohol lubricated the intricate machinery of the legislative process. To the casual observer, the event was nothing more than a celebratory gathering; to a seasoned political observer, the incestuous but lawful commingling of business and government was in inebriated, elegant motion.

Ryan's reception badge identified him as a congressional chief of staff, and lobbyists descended like vultures with broad smiles and open, hearty handshakes. Ryan disliked these events, but his mere presence cultivated good feelings with the lobbyists whose political action committee funds filled the coffers of the Somatos campaign war chest. All Ryan had to do was feign some interest in the cause de jour; seem articulate, sympathetic, informed; and exit.

At one group he recognized newly elected Congressman Green. Green had not changed much since Albany. Looking tan, haughty, and poised, he gestured dramatically as he spoke to a group of admirers.

"Congressman Green, it is good to see you again," offered Ryan with an open handshake. "I'm AA to Congressman Somatos, Ryan McNeil."

Green shook Ryan's hand firmly, with a beaming, perfunctory smile and a trite response.

"Somatos is a first-class legislator. I look forward to working with him again. Perhaps you should chat with Seth." Eager to extricate himself from the encounter with Ryan, Green looked across the room and, almost comically to Ryan, signaled to his aide. Ryan glanced over in the direction Green had motioned and immediately recognized Seth Tantalus by his towering presence among several likely lobbyists clustered around him.

Ryan, feeling dismissed by Green's pomposity, strutted over to

Tantalus, who was engaged in conversation with what looked like two standard-issue DC lobbyists.

"Ryan McNeil, you may not remember me. We met back in Albany."

Tantalus turned toward him and offered a hand that seemed twice the size of Ryan's. Seth Tantalus looked the same as Ryan had remembered. He was huge, easily over six feet, and in constant agitated motion. Something about the kinetic energy of his looming presence made Ryan immediately uncomfortable. He wished that Tantalus had never made it to Washington, DC.

"I remember you, yes," said Tantalus.

Two tall gentlemen, with perfectly trim haircuts, brightly striped ties, and dark suits, stood silent and expressionless as they eyed Ryan's name badge. Their right hands held drinks inside folded napkins, but they both deftly shifted these to the other hand to exchange affable introductions with Ryan. Ryan eyed their badges.

"I'm Mark Danzig with the Athena Government Relations Group, and this is Steven Heflon, vice president of government relations for Dorus Genetic Corporation."

Ryan recognized the company and glanced over to Tantalus, who looked suddenly concerned and nervous. Ryan felt a sudden awkwardness among the group. Eager to ingratiate himself with the seemingly aloof lobbyists before him, he offered a point of recollection and affiliation.

"You may not remember me, but I worked with Nick Somatos in Albany. Seven years ago, he had your genetic testing provision in his bill that was vetoed by the governor."

To Ryan, the company vice president Heflon looked immediately perplexed, and the lobbyist Danzig looked eager to move on.

"Sir, I'm sorry. I think you're confused. The governor signed our provision, thanks to Tantalus here. That bill was critical to the future of our company. Without the bill there would have been no

IPO or jobs created," stated Heflon simply. He quite clearly had no knowledge of any veto, as Ryan had suggested.

Danzig interjected to change the subject. "Dorus Corporation is concerned about the amendment that Congressman Somatos is contemplating for introduction to the health care finance bill coming before the health policy subcommittee in about a month."

Ryan ignored Danzig's attempt to transition the conversation.

"I believe the governor vetoed the genetics bill," affirmed Ryan, focusing on the company executive and then glancing over to Tantalus, who physically intruded to block Ryan's efforts at further conversation with Heflon.

In symmetrical choreography, like a dance partner, Danzig interposed himself as well, pulling his business card from the breast pocket of his suit and handing it to Ryan. "If you ever need anything, Ryan." He then diplomatically departed with his client, Heflon, in sudden, confused, but deferential tow.

"What the hell, Tantalus?" Ryan scowled. "That provision was vetoed by the governor. In fact I think the last time we met, Somatos and I were sitting with you and Green to urge a veto override. You and your boss had no interest then. When did you pass that provision?" To Ryan, Tantalus had the evasive look of a robber caught in the act.

Tantalus, who had first twisted and turned, now dropped his pretense of civility, leaning forward into Ryan's face.

"I can't recall, Ryan. I worked on a lot of issues. It's all a blur, you know." He poked his huge finger into Ryan's lapel. With this contemptuous utterance and intimidating gesture, Tantalus departed the conversation, briskly moving away into the swirling crowd.

Ryan mingled for another twenty minutes and was ready to leave, crestfallen that Amber White was not apparently in attendance. He then heard her distinctive voice. She always got a little too drunk at these receptions, and her voice would become silky, with a distinct, perceptible southern note of flirtation dancing in her words. Her auburn hair was pulled tightly up in a bun, and her black dress clung to her alluring curves. Even with the huge diamond wedding ring that flashed on her hand, Ryan could see men humiliating themselves to get close to her. She could still attract men and hold them like amber. Ryan always speculated that her name was a precursor of her talent for sensuous entrapment.

She was twenty-nine years old and married. She told Ryan that her husband was a lawyer at Bennington, Wandall and Reed. According to Amber, they had been married for five years and had no children. Evidently, Mr. White, of Princeton and Columbia Law School, was consumed and exhausted by extensive litigation. As a result, Ms. White's voracious sexual appetite was largely unfilled. It was an obligation that Ryan in the past year had assumed on several occasions.

Ryan came up to Amber's side, and she pretended not to see him as she chatted away. Ryan confidently knew that the conversation was feigned and forced, perhaps even for his benefit. He thrust his hand forward and introduced himself. A moment later he asked to borrow her for an "urgent matter."

"You're positively uncivil," she said as he escorted her through the crowd.

"And your positively sexy," he whispered in her ear. She turned to face him. "You know you're talking to a married woman."

"I know, and you're talking to a married man."

She bit her lower lip seductively and gave a glance of surveillance around the room. She then whispered in his ear, "Meet me by the statute of Rayburn in the lobby."

Ryan smiled and looked at his watch. He did some quick mental calculations and responded, "How long?"

"Ten, maybe fifteen," she said as she walked away.

They met in the lobby twenty-five minutes later. The room was empty except for two idle security guards, responsible for entry into the building and operating the metal detectors. The lobby was quiet. Ryan put his arm around Amber and they hurriedly headed for the exit, their heels clicking on the marble floor. The security guards watched them as they pushed open the front door into the sultry night. They left the building and quickly hailed a cab. Once inside the cab, they in unison directed the driver to the Hotel Washington. Amber's mouth immediately came to Ryan's, and he ran his hand up her nylon-sheathed leg, which she had swung over him. Sensuously, she tasted of champagne.

"I need to talk to you about the Connelly bill."

Ryan was breathing heavy. "What?" he asked as he groped her breasts through the dress.

"I need to talk to you about the Connelly bill," repeated Amber as she squeezed his erection through his pants.

"Amber, please don't lobby me in the cab," mumbled Ryan.

Amber pulled back. "Why Ryan, I do some of my best lobbying in cabs," she said softly while she tried to straddle him in the back seat.

"I'm sure you do," Ryan said as he tried to restrain her. He could see the driver watching them in his rearview mirror. This was probably nothing new for him, thought Ryan.

As soon as the hotel room door shut, they both began passionate groping, to the point of frenzy. Amber in her bra and panties pushed Ryan back till he sat on the bed. She then went for her handbag and produced two handcuffs and a vibrator.

"What can I say, Ryan. Tools of my lobbyist trade. I wish I had a bigger bag," she said with a mischievous glint in her eyes.

Ryan felt the animal rise up in him.

CHAPTER 14

After his hotel rendezvous, Ryan retrieved his car from work and then drove home through the rain. It started drizzling as he left the hotel, but now the rain was fierce and, despite the vigorous sweeping arc of his wipers, obscured his vision and the dark road ahead. He was pushing the speed limit so that at times he sensed he was losing control of the car; a feeling that seemed to manifest his sense of the moment. When he was three blocks away from home, he looked at the dashboard's digital clock that read 11:40 p.m. He figured that anything past midnight was unequivocally suspect, downright incriminating.

In his mind he could rationalize his infidelity by the loss of passion in his marriage. Nevertheless, he needed to maintain a cool facade of fidelity and exercise prudent discretion to avoid the inevitable crash that would occur. Undetected infidelity was like driving above the speed limit, Ryan thought; unchallenged it provided a great high, a pulse-pounding sense of sensual excitement, but a crash would bring sudden scrutiny, if not conclusive catastrophe.

He noticed the minivan as he turned onto his block. There was nothing overtly alarming, except that it was rare and suspicious to see a car parked in front of his house this time of night. He then noticed, in the glare of his headlights, that the rear license plate seemed obliterated, illegible. He had the instinctive sense that the van was trouble. He swung his car into the driveway and noticed that the garage door was fully up. Through the rain, his car's headlights illuminated the garage. Annie's car was parked, seemingly undisturbed. Ryan could not see any movement. He opened his car door, and the violent roar of rain filled the air. Leaving the headlights on and motor running, he stepped out of the car and was immediately drenched by the cold storm shower. He walked slowly, apprehensively, toward the garage. The garage light was off.

For a moment he stood in front of the open headlight illuminated garage and could see no movement and nothing amiss except for the fact that the door was up. *Could Annie have inadvertently left the garage door up*, he wondered. He looked around. The nearby gutters off the roof gushed rain like an open spigot, flooding the driveway and lawn. Rather than enter through the garage, he decided to approach through the front door. Under the shelter of his front entrance, he pulled his house keys from his pocket, but they clumsily slipped through his wet hands. Quickly, he retrieved the fallen keys and then opened the door.

The house was dark and quiet and still. He left the front door open. He put his house keys and phone down on the entry table. His hair was wet, and he wiped the water from his eyes. His mind began to flash vivid unknown horrors. He turned on a light and called out loud, "Annie. Annie." No sound issued back. He called again: "Annie, Jessica."

He bolted up the stairs, and some instinct pulled him first to Jessica's room. He turned left at the top of the stairs. Jessica's door was open and her light was on. Entering her room, he immediately saw the child's bed empty and her cover sprawled on the floor. Then he heard what he thought to be the front door slam loudly. The intruder had his daughter and fled, he feared. Outside, he could hear the grinding sound of a car engine being started. The sound of the engine energized him, like a starter's pistol, so that he bolted back down the stairs, pulled open the front door, and dashed out into the storm.

He heard the screech of tires before he saw the minivan swerving in a semicircle in front of his house. A strong gust of wind blasted rain into his face, and he screamed Jessica's name. He had only a few seconds to choose between going back for his cell phone or giving chase. His car was to his immediate right, lights still on and engine beckoning.

Splashing through the marshy grass, he raced for his car. He slammed the door shut, shifted into reverse, and careened out into the street. He depressed the accelerator and sped after the van. The rain was thick as a curtain, obscuring his vision. Ryan cursed the fact that he did not have a phone in his car and began to second-guess his decision not to call the police immediately. Speeding through three intersections, he ignored the stop signs when at the fourth one he thought he could discern the red taillight configuration of the van. Quickly, he turned the car left in pursuit.

The van appeared to be traveling at a normal rate of speed as Ryan's car closed the gap between them. Perhaps this was not the right car, he thought. He was cursing out loud and pounding the wheel in frustration. If he had chased the wrong car he was wasting precious time and his stepdaughter was slipping away into some inconceivable horror. He was directly behind the minivan when it sped through a red light, and Ryan knew then that this was the car.

The road was mostly empty, and the two cars accelerated through several red lights. Suddenly, the van lurched right and accelerated again, fleeing onto a highway entrance ramp. It flew onto the dark highway with the speed of a night creature, the bright red eyes of its taillights only visible.

Concentrating on not losing control of his car, Ryan followed blindly and soon both vehicles were racing at high speed on Potomac Highway. The two-lane highway traversed public parkland for miles without an exit. He hoped that the police were stationed at their usual checkpoints. The two vehicles had the rain-swept road to themselves. Checking the speedometer, he saw he was pushing eighty-five. The bright beam of his headlights kept a steady fix on the van. If he kept up the chase, maybe a police cruiser would intercept them for speeding. It seemed his best hope. The dark, narrow road was a submerged surface. Pooling water had rendered the lane demarcations wholly invisible. Also indistinguishable now in the darkness and rain were those perilous sections of highway, abutted by stone barriers that precariously guarded the steep cliffs above the Potomac River.

The van ahead created a virtual watery wake in its path. Into this treacherous wake, Ryan depressed his accelerator until he was five car lengths behind the van. Water churned from the van's rear wheels and blew fiercely into Ryan's windshield. His grip on the steering wheel tightened. He pushed the accelerator again. The air was saturated and a film of condensation kept forming on the windshield. He repeatedly wiped it away with his hands. Through it all, the red taillights of the van were still visible. There was no plan but pursuit—frantic, reckless, close pursuit. Rain and night and fog flew past him with greater and greater velocity. The car momentarily lost traction with the road. There was a sense of skidding, hydroplaning. The action forced him several times to apply brakes and then reaccelerate. He wondered how long he could keep up this frantic chase.

He had been following for about seven miles when he saw her flying out the window. Suddenly, his headlights caught it brightly in midair, a white, wet flash of clothes that fluttered directly in front of his car. He had only seconds to envision Jessica vulnerably sprawled on the road in front of him. Slamming on his brakes, he reflexively jerked his steering wheel toward the right, hoping to avoid any crushing contact. He depressed his brakes fully, but the car skidded and then swerved uncontrollably off the shoulder of the road, breaking through a feeble border of brush. The car then became airborne on a downward trajectory, into the blackness of the woods below. Ryan, in a sudden swirl of nausea, braced himself on the steering wheel. The ground in front of him momentarily disappeared from headlight illumination.

Crashing back to earth and into a rocky ravine, the vehicle careened violently over boulders and fallen trees, nearly toppling on its front end. The car's uncontrolled motion continued downhill until a loud collision of finality at the base of an oak tree, crumpling metal and shattering glass. Ryan was swung forcefully forward and felt the painful constriction of the seat belt. Then the sudden, explosive, powdery burst of the airbag shot into his face and chest. This dual action forced the wind from his body as he rebounded into the seat. Within seconds, the bag deflated like a punctured balloon in his lap. Ryan's tongue tasted the acrid, powdery film, like talcum, that filled the air of the vehicle. He spit out saliva and opened and shut his eyes several times to regain orientation. He felt the painful infliction of bruises, his ribs and face hurt, a trickle of blood here and there, but he felt intact. He could feel and move his legs and arms. He realized he had been knocked unconscious for a few seconds and that his windshield was now a spider web of glass.

He tried to push open the door, but it was mutilated and wedged tightly shut. My God, he thought, Jessica is lying wounded on the road, far from his car. The car's headlights were now shattered and extinguished. From what he could judge, the car was at least fifty yards from the road, at an almost forty-five-degree declination lodged into a ditch beneath a large tree. Fierce gusts of rain blew in the darkness, wave after wave, cascading over the immobilized wreck of the car. He unclasped the seat belt and attempted his own extrication, but the dashboard, doors, and roof had crumpled on all sides, wedging him into the seat. He felt for a point of leverage to lift himself from the seat. He contorted and twisted his body with several efforts that were futile. He kept up the attempt to break free. Within minutes, he was relieved when he saw the blue-and-red strobe of police cars lighting up the woods around him and then heard the insistent high-decibel sound of unseen sirens. Miraculously to Ryan, a policeman with flashlight in hand quickly appeared at the opening in the driver-side window. "My daughter's been kidnapped; she's lying on the road," Ryan yelled out.

It took almost twenty minutes, but three firemen eventually opened the mutilated door. Once outside the car, he was gingerly placed on a stretcher and carried up a muddy hill, with strenuous effort by several firemen, while a paramedic took his vitals. Ryan demanded that the paramedic turn his attention to Jessica, and several times over he inquired about her condition. On the road, a police officer into his shirt-collar microphone relayed Ryan's description of the van while questioning him further to elicit more information: "Sir, do you have identification?" "Sir, what kind of minivan were you chasing?" "Are you sure there is another victim?"

"Is she all right?" Ryan asked repeatedly, to no avail. He wanted immediately to rush to Jessica, but the police and ambulance crew gently constrained him. They carried his stretcher to the inside of an ambulance, where his injuries were evaluated. After an initial evaluation, Ryan was permitted to sit up in the back of the ambulance. He then watched through the open rear door while the police searched outside. A contingent of policemen appeared from numerous cars, and they moved with the proficient speed of their profession. Cloaked in long rain jackets, they methodically inspected the road with powerful portable lights, slashing through the mist and rain and darkness and into the murky woods that abutted the road.

They ran back and forth, yelling commands, searching for the little girl that Ryan thought was sprawled somewhere on the road. Ryan sat despondently in the back of the ambulance, thinking of his stepdaughter's plight, while shards of glass were removed from his head and bandages were wrapped around his chest and applied to his forehead. The police and emergency crews brought order to the scene by placing flares and directing the occasional traffic, and the sound of sirens was calmed gradually and replaced by the cryptic chatter of police communication.

His blood pressure was being checked for the third time. Abruptly, the steady fall of rain eased and the night scene emerged into illuminated headlight clarity. A young-looking, white-shirted police lieutenant was before him.

"Mr. McNeil."

"Is Jessica all right?" Ryan demanded.

"Mr. McNeil, the paramedics have evaluated you, and you apparently have no major injuries except for several contusions and lacerations, but they are recommending that you be transported to Fairfax Hospital for an evaluation. We've checked the road and found no other body. We have dispatched a cruiser to your home."

Ryan took the news solemnly. There was no relief by the fact that his stepdaughter was not found. He felt like a lifeguard that had lost a victim to the drowning depths. An agonizing knot of terror tightened in his chest. The paramedic taking his pulse felt the elevation of pressure in his wrist. From the back of the ambulance, Ryan gazed at the ghostly road down which the van had sped and his stepdaughter had vanished. Along the road, the kaleidoscope colors of the police and emergency car lights lit the wet night.

"I need to get home," said Ryan emphatically as he began to exit the ambulance. As he gingerly stepped down, he saw the wreck of his car lying sprawled in a ditch with a tow truck working on an extraction that would be of no value to him.

The lieutenant stepped forward to gently block him.

"Your leaving against medical advice?"

"I need to get home."

The medical personnel shrugged and handed Ryan a waiver form, which he promptly signed.

"Let's drive him back," said the lieutenant. "We may have to evaluate his home for crime scene evidence."

Ryan sat in the back of a police car, thinking for the first time of his wife. Events had unfurled so quickly that he had not coherently integrated what had transpired until this moment. The police car sped swiftly but silently, with its strobe light illuminated. Despite the speed of the car, the ride home seemed painfully protracted. By the time they arrived at Ryan's house, two other police cruisers were present. But the officers outside seemed strangely relaxed and conversed with smiles. Ryan began to feel a growing hostility to the police as he wondered what could explain such a lackadaisical attitude.

Ryan walked in his front door escorted by an officer. There was a plainclothes police officer standing in the living room, talking with his wife. On the living room couch, Jessica was sitting, looking tiny and sick but miraculously intact and unharmed.

"What we have here, Mr. McNeil, is thankfully not a kidnapping but more likely a burglary of some kind."

Ryan wasn't listening; he was emotionally embracing his wife and stepdaughter.

"Jessica was in the bedroom with me; she got sick in the night," said Annie. "I guess being with her in the bathroom I didn't hear the garage being opened."

Ryan felt foolish relief. The problem of an aborted burglary was inconsequential compared to the horrors he had ominously projected.

"Thank you, Officers," Ryan said as he went to shake the detective's hand.

The uniformed officer spoke: "We'll come back tomorrow to take a closer look at the garage and ask you some more questions. We're going to secure the area with crime tape and station a unit here until the CSU makes a full evaluation."

Ryan smiled happily at the officer.

"Mr. McNeil." The detective looking at Ryan wasn't smiling. "Can you explain the clothes that were found on the road?"

Ryan looked straight at the detective. "What clothes?" he asked as he tried to focus on the officer's question. "Clothes?"

CHAPTER 15

The digital clock read 12:45 p.m. He rose gingerly and went to the bedroom window. Squinting into the afternoon glare, he took comfort from the absence of crowds, police, vans, or anything extraordinary. The suburban street was tranquil; his house was quiet. The transition to normalcy was reassuring and yet, in juxtaposition, made the prior night seem like a grotesquely absurd dream. Nevertheless, a glance in the mirror at his discolored ribs, bruised forehead, and bandages were a tangible reminder of his impetuous car chase in the night.

A note from Annie indicated that she would be picking Jessica up at school and should be home at about 3:00 p.m. Ryan called Somatos's office. The congressman was not in, and Ryan laconically described to an office colleague that he had been in a car accident and the extent of his injuries. He indicated that he would try to make it into the office the following day. He showered and dressed with discomfort.

At 2:00 p.m., the doorbell rang and Ryan walked slowly to the door. Looking through the peephole, he recognized one of the detectives from the night before. He opened the door and was greeted by the detective and another well-dressed man.

"Mr. McNeil, hi. You may remember me from last night. Detective Lars Hestrom. We want to fill in some of the details from last night. By the way, this is Mike Anglus with the Federal Bureau of Investigation."

Ryan looked warily at the FBI agent's identification. Agent Anglus was athletically slim in a suit and had a crew-cut look of efficiency.

"Detective Hestrom and I are assigned to the Fairfax County Joint Task Force investigating the abduction of a young woman. We would just like to ask you a few questions."

Ryan cordially invited them into the living room as he tried to sort out the motive for their presence.

"I'm really sorry for all the confusion last night. I thought it appeared that this was a kidnapping and not an attempted burglary," explained Ryan.

"We understand. Can you describe the van for us again, please?" asked Detective Hestrom with a supercilious smile as the FBI agent curiously paced the room and looked at the photographs that were scattered about.

Ryan described the van as best he could given the limited visibility in the rain. He felt somewhat annoyed since he had engaged in this same exercise four or five times before.

"Mr. McNeil, can you tell us where you were from seven p.m. to eleven thirty p.m.?" The FBI agent, Mike Anglus, had stopped his movements and was standing at the far end of the living room, looking directly at Ryan. Ryan immediately resented his officious posture.

"I don't see any relevance here to the status of the van," Ryan shot back, annoyed and defensive. He was being pushed into a defensive stance that posed risks, and he knew it.

"I suggest it would be in your best interest to cooperate at this time unless you want to assume the status of a suspect." Hestrom spoke stiffly, with no trace of the smile he had flashed moments before.

"Suspect to what?" Ryan asked as he wondered where all this was headed.

"A suspect in Leslie Warren's disappearance."

"Leslie Warren, the missing girl?" Ryan's heart palpably accelerated in his chest. "Why the hell would I be a suspect?"

The FBI agent methodically proceeded to elaborate as Ryan stood motionless, with his hands unconsciously clenching into fists.

"Mr. McNeil, let us consider fact one that you were found by a police cruiser at 12:04 a.m. skidded out on the shoulder of Potomac Highway after a cruiser clocked you speeding twenty-five miles over the limit. Fact two, Mr. McNeil, the cruiser did not see any van, and we found no evidence to support your contention that there was a van that you claim you were chasing. All on the mistaken presumption your daughter had been kidnapped. And fact three, Mr. McNeil, in your car we found a pair of handcuffs below the front seat, which is an unusual item to have in a car. And fact four, most importantly, at the scene of your car wreck was found a bundle of female clothes which were stained with what preliminary results show to be blood. We are not sure exactly whose blood until we get the results from the FBI crime lab, but we have this morning confirmed that the clothes were worn by Leslie Warren the night of her disappearance."

Ryan's mouth formed words but no audible voice issued. In a matter of hours his life had careened out of control, and Ryan again felt like he was lying bloodied in a ditch.

CHAPTER 16

Ryan left in Annie's car to call Amber White away from the house on his cell phone.

"Hello, Amber White." Her pleasing voice was sweet at the other end. Ryan wished this call were for another reason.

"It's Ryan. What did you do? Did you put those handcuffs in my coat?"

"Why are you calling me? No. I put them in your suit jacket. Did your wife find them?" She giggled impishly.

"No. The police found them. I was in a car accident and they found them. It's a difficult item to explain away." Ryan was speaking quickly and breathing fast. "Listen, the police are going to ask if I was with you the other night, and—"

"What? Are you crazy?" she interrupted him with shrill indignation.

"I was in a car accident and the police are questioning my whereabouts that evening. I had to tell them about us. Nothing will come of it. I promise it's just a little investigation."

"Ryan, a little investigation by the police is like being a little bit pregnant. It just doesn't work that way."

Before he could offer a rejoinder, she slammed down the receiver on her end. He did not bother to call back. He had given her fair warning.

"Ryan, why were you so quick to run out into the storm without checking the house first?" Annie asked, as she was about to enter the bed for the evening.

"I just saw Jessica's blanket on the floor and I didn't hear her, or see you, and I thought I needed to move fast," said Ryan as he too entered the bed and shut the light off.

"Didn't you think to check on me?" she asked in the dark.

"Like I said, I just felt I needed to act quickly. I wasn't thinking it through."

Hours later, tossing and turning, he could not find peace. His bruises ached. He simply could not succumb to sleep that evening. The digital clock read 2:20 a.m. Phantom fears multiplied in the dark. He had not related the afternoon visit from the police to Annie. He took extra doses of his sedative he had been prescribed, but that only seemed to render a claustrophobic feeling of his world closing in and suffocating his plans, ambitions, and his life. He finally surrendered his futile fight for sleep and rose from the bed.

He sat in a chair in the dark room and for several minutes watched his wife slumbering with the quiet, even breathing of untroubled unconsciousness. He decided to check on Jessica. He carefully rose from the chair and made his way down the carpeted dark hall to Jessica's room. He softly pushed open her door. In the motionless moonlight of her room, he could discern her fetal-like outline on the bed. Her sleeping breath soughed softly, like a purring kitten. An unconscious paternal pride caused Ryan to smile lovingly. He began to close her door and turn back down the hall when he was startled by a shadowed figure.

Annie was standing still in the hall, watching. Her presence in itself seemed to denote an accusatory posture. He walked back down the hall toward her.

"What are you doing?" she whispered urgently.

"Checking on her," he whispered back defensively, sensing his wife's protective paranoia. "Insomnia. Can't sleep."

"Take some pills and close your eyes," said his wife harshly as she turned and led him back, in obligatory fashion, by his hand toward the bedroom.

"If I close my eyes I see nothing. Just nothing at all."

CHAPTER 17

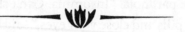

Annie drove Ryan to the Metro that morning. He kissed her before he exited the car, but he did not look back as he descended the escalator into the cavern of the Metro station.

Ryan took the Orange Line. It had been a while since he commuted via the Metro, and now he was silently amused by the distinctly decorous crowd that herded together into the carpeted compartments of the train. Ryan ruminated on the fact that the Metro was unlike any other mass-transit system in America, based on the volume of reading material being assimilated by erudite, harried commuters. Then he noticed something more disturbing—a headline in the *Washington Daily* that read, "New Leads in the Leslie Warren Case."

The reality of the police interview came to him in a rush of fear. He could be identified as a possible suspect in a case to which he was utterly unconnected. By nature of his political instinct, he began to construct headlines in his head: "Capitol Hill Aide Found with Leslie Warren's Clothes: For Alibi Claims Tryst with Married Woman." The art of idly postulating headlines consumed his conscious thoughts until his station arrived.

Ryan entered the office and was immediately faced with the Congressman. Somatos winced at Ryan's bruised face

"I'd give you a hug, but I'm not sure where you hurt. I hope you weren't DWI on this crash, Ryan," Somatos said with a chuckle. Ryan knew he was half serious about the DWI.

"Take comfort, Congressman. I was stone sober."

"Well then, you must be one hell of a lousy driver, because your wife didn't mention another car in that accident."

"You spoke with Annie?"

"Of course. She is concerned about you."

"She didn't tell me that she called you."

Ryan sat down in front of his office computer and pondered the notepad before him. The pad contained a reminder list of items for his follow-up. His eyes focused on the line that read, "Seth Tantalus, Rep. Green Financial Disclosures, and Dorus Genetic Corporation?"

CHAPTER 18

Annie McNeil stood in her kitchen and was hastily preparing lunch for Jessica while golden sunlight poured in through a skylight, polishing the immaculate surfaces to reflective brightness. She set the food down in front of Jessica, who fiddled with it playfully.

"Mommy, is Daddy going to jail?" Jessica's casual question stunned Annie so that she spun quickly on her heels to turn toward her daughter.

"No, of course not. Why would you think that, honey?" Annie pulled a chair up close to Jessica, hoping to attain some measure of clarity.

"Just with all the policemen that were here the other night. Did he do something wrong?"

"Jessica honey, I thought I explained that he got in a car accident because he thought we were in danger and so he thought he was chasing after us."

"He thought we were both in danger?"

"Yes, darling"

"Oh. I see. Can I go downstairs and watch TV there?"

Annie could not tell if she had allayed Jessica's childish fears, but she was willing to let the matter rest. "OK, sure."

The little girl flitted away so fast that Annie wondered whether she was quickly retreating from a mistaken trespass on adult territory.

Annie was standing by the window when she noticed the car drive up. She recognized the detective from the prior night emerge with another grim-faced gentleman dressed in a sharp suit and dark sunglasses. She was at the door by the time they rang the bell. She opened the door with a smile and a residual tinge of gratitude for their work.

"Ms. McNeil, you may remember I'm Detective Hestrom with the Fairfax Police Department, and this is Special Agent Mike Anglus with the Federal Bureau of Investigation."

The FBI agent removed his shades and smiled politely.

Annie apprehensively recoiled at the mention of the FBI.

"Ms. McNeil, do you mind if we come in?"

"Sure, I'm sorry. Would you like some iced tea?"

Both men accepted the offer. Annie left them in the living room and went to the kitchen. While she was away, the men began browsing the living room, scrutinizing books and pictures and the starkly white decor set with glass furnishings. Very clean, very modern, and very fragile. A framed abstract painting created a shocking splash of crimson color on one wall. The life of every family could be inferred from their surroundings. These men were trained in that craft. They could see no apparent disarray here, but, to their trained eyes, the decor seemed to have an element of instability.

She entered with their drinks. Both cordially accepted, and the sound of ice rolling in their glasses filled a momentary silence. Annie smiled blankly, wondering about the nature of their business.

The Fairfax detective spoke after he took a sip. "Freshly brewed. Very sweet. Almost as good as my wife's."

"I always add pomegranate," said Annie mindlessly.

The officers looked at each other. It was time for business.

"Certain questions have been raised in our investigation of the incident the other night. We thought that maybe you could help clarify some issues for us."

Annie encouraged them to sit down. They sat at opposite sides of the room, with Annie in another corner. Almost immediately they placed their glasses down.

"Do you know where you husband was until eleven thirty p.m.?"

Annie pondered the question before she answered it. "I assume he was working late. He does that frequently."

The FBI agent frowned. "You say your husband is frequently absent and you are not sure where he is?"

"I presume I know where he is. I don't keep track of his movements. No."

"He does own a cell phone?"

"Why yes, but he keeps it mostly off to stay in control."

"Control?" they asked in unison.

"Well, it is not off entirely," she said almost defensively. "I just can't always reach him on it. You understand?"

"Does your husband keep secrets from you, Ms. McNeil?"

The question elicited a coy laugh from her. What a preposterous question, she thought.

"Mr. Hestrom, if there were secrets how would I know?"

"Sometimes wives know things that their husbands presume they do not know."

She began to regard both of the officers with growing hostility.

"Do you have something to ask me"—she paused—"or tell me?" She leaned back in the chair, bracing for bad news.

The officers looked at each other, and with an implicit signal the FBI agent spoke.

"Do you own a set of handcuffs or do you know what your husband might be doing with such an item in your car?"

Annie unconsciously mouthed the word: handcuff.

"A set of handcuffs?" Annie angrily searched for a logical

explanation. She kept coming back to one ineluctable conclusion that was now putting a visible sanguine hue in her cheeks.

"Ms. McNeil, do you know a woman named Amber White?"

"No" was the terse response. Annie's eyes were beginning to sting.

"Well apparently she is your husband's alibi for between seven and eleven p.m." He in fact claims the handcuffs are hers."

"I don't need to hear any more." She was on her feet, nervously. She felt as if she was being publicly humiliated.

"Has your husband spoken to you at all about the Leslie Warren abduction case?"

Annie had turned her back and she wasn't even sure which gentleman had asked the question, but she turned quickly.

"Did you say the Leslie Warren case? Yes, he has mentioned it to me," said Annie as she felt a tinge of queasiness.

"We don't have a search warrant, but do you mind if we search through your husband's possessions?" asked Anglus.

"Go right ahead. Go upstairs." She was relieved when they headed up the steps.

After several minutes of reining in her acute anger, she regained her composure and went up the steps to check on the search.

They were looking in his dresser draws, inspecting his possessions, carefully making sure to not leave behind evidence of the search. She watched them silently for several minutes as they worked with quick, calibrated precision. They finished their inspection and then they looked at Annie as if for further guidance.

"Does your husband have a safe or trunk or boxes for special articles?"

Annie focused on the question and looked up toward the ceiling with a cold sense of trepidation. "He keeps a trunk in the attic."

The two investigators looked at each other without expression. "Could we see it?"

Annie went out into the hall and pulled down the attic stairs. The detectives followed her up the stairs. She asked for one of them to flick a light switch in the hallway. A naked bulb hung from the ceiling and now dimly illuminated the space. The attic was hot, musty, and strewn haphazardly with relics from their prior lives. Particles of dust seem suspended in the stagnant air. The detectives combed the articles until they found the trunk that Annie pointed out.

Before the FBI agent could open the trunk, the Fairfax detective gently blocked him. "We can't open it." Both detectives looked at each other for a moment, then seemed to pull back, seemingly thwarted.

"What's wrong?" Annie asked, mystified.

"*Carey v. US*, Ms. McNeil. The search would be of dubious constitutionality. We do not have probable cause or reasonable suspicion." Both men knelt before the trunk, pondering its inscrutable contents, sweat and frustration beating on their brows.

"What if I opened it?" offered Annie graciously. Curiosity now burned within her as well.

The two men looked at each other. "I don't see a problem with that," the FBI agent said officiously.

Annie inspected the box. The lock was secure and would not open. Annie looked around the attic and spotted a screwdriver. With the tool in hand, she wedged it into the lock and pulled back to no avail at first. The officers watched, eagerly, as Annie again pulled the screwdriver back with determination to break the lock open. She twisted the tool with full force on the lock until the metal yielded and snapped and the box opened. Inside were yearbooks, photos, letters, envelopes. They rummaged through the trove. In a large manila envelope, Hestrom pulled open some fragile yellowed newspaper clippings. In the dusty light, the agents and Annie silently read the collected newspaper accounts of a missing twenty-year-old girl in Albany, New York, seven years ago. A faded newsprint photo of Cathy Wilet was neatly folded into the stack of clippings. There was a heart-throbbing silence in the dank, dim light that seemed to accentuate the horrible implication of the clippings.

The first words were from Annie. "Oh my God," she said as she covered the gape of her mouth with her left hand. Her exquisite diamond wedding ring flashed under the light from the hanging bare bulb above them.

"Ms. McNeil, I'm sorry, but I suggest that you may want to take some precautions for yourself and your daughter." Annie did not hear or understand the comment by the officer because she was already crying and trembling with a terrible chill in the stale heat pool of her attic.

CHAPTER 19

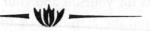

"Ryan, you have a call. It's the Fairfax Police," said Somatos's secretary.

Ryan, who was already on the phone in front of one the legislative interns, swung around in his swivel chair, nodded to the harried secretary, and then verbally extricated himself from the business at hand to take the call in his office with the door shut.

"Ryan McNeil here."

"Mr. McNeil, this is Detective Hestrom with Fairfax Police. I wonder if you could come to the station after work. We could send a car for you."

Ryan did not like the ominous sound of a police car being sent for his travel.

"What? Why do you need me to come down there?" Ryan asked, annoyed and then alarmed at a suspicious pause at the other end.

"We have a few more questions for you."

"All right, I'll meet your car at four thirty in the front of the Longworth Building."

"We'll see you later, Mr. McNeil."

As soon as he hung up, he regretted his decision. He scribbled on a yellow legal pad the word "lawyer." He contemplated for several minutes the pros and cons of retaining legal counsel. The thought gave him pause. A lawyer meant a mountain of legal bills, and it also gave the appearance of something to hide.

At 4:30 p.m., Ryan exited the Longworth and was immediately greeted by a stern-looking gentleman in a suit. "Mr. McNeil, the car is over here." A dark and muddied four-door sedan was parked nearby. Ryan noted that another plainclothes officer was driving. Two policemen as escorts; this was a serious expenditure of manpower. Ryan grimaced and entered the back seat. Almost immediately he felt subjugated to the authoritative control of the police, a strange sensation of being officiously constrained.

Ryan thought several times during the drive of changing his mind and not voluntarily submitting to further questioning. Several times he vacillated about the prudence of permitting himself to be questioned without benefit of counsel. However, objecting to inquiry had a suspicious appearance of concealment and would naturally engender a police inference of guilt. He had, after all, nothing to hide, and innocence was its own virtue of protection. His feeling of omnipotent innocence was only solidified as the car passed over Memorial Bridge, past the inspirational edifices of the Lincoln Memorial and Washington Monument, and over the glinting channel waters of the Potomac.

The two officers were silent during the thirty-minute ride, but in the self-imposed claustrophobic captivity of the back seat, the grim demeanor of the officers did not seem awkward or particularly ominous. Faced with another police encounter, he sat quietly analyzing his position, speculating on lines of inquiry.

"Park over there," the officer in the passenger seat said to the driver, jolting Ryan from his reverie. The Fairfax Police Department in front of them was a sleek, modern four-story glass building in Old Town Fairfax. A historic county court with a modern annex and adjacent municipal building created a busy plaza of pedestrian activity. The officers ushered Ryan from the car and walked hurriedly through the sun-speckled plaza to the glass front entrance of the building. Inside the cool air of the building, Ryan was led to a small room with a table and several chairs and a mirror.

Here, unlike Albany, Ryan could see a video camera attached to the ceiling, recording the interaction. The room felt uncomfortably cold, and Ryan wondered if they intentionally lowered the air-conditioning. He thought again of not cooperating and requesting legal counsel, which he again dismissed as verging on paranoia.

From another door entered Detective Hestrom and Special Agent Anglus.

"Would you like a cup of coffee, Mr. McNeil?"

Ryan smiled and shook his head negatively; he wanted to expedite the matter at hand.

"Since the last time we met we now have the results of the DNA blood test of the clothes from the FBI crime lab and Dorus Genetics. We positively identified Leslie Warren's blood on the clothes." Hestrom paused, studying Ryan's reaction.

Ryan was purely expressionless; the conversation seemed surreal. He had to consciously focus on what the officer was saying and not drift into his own thoughts. Hestrom, discerning no reaction, proceeded with his questioning.

"We interviewed Ms. Amber White, and she corroborates that you were with her earlier on the evening in question."

With that news, Ryan's tension went down several notches.

"I hope we can avoid disclosing this information to my wife."

The officers seemingly ignored his request and proceeded with their script.

"However, your accounts of sexual activity involving handcuffs differ in that she says the handcuffs were your idea. She states that you have a, shall we say, proclivity to unusual sex that involves handcuffs and bondage."

"Now wait a second," Ryan interjected vehemently. "Those are her proclivities."

"Mr. McNeil, she was explicit."

Ryan shook his head and grimaced. At least she corroborated that they were together, he thought.

"Did you know that Ms. White is married to Henry Adams White?" asked Anglus.

Ryan glowered at Anglus. He could see the gold wedding band on the FBI agent's hand, and he sensed that there was an element of moral condemnation in the question.

"I knew she was married to some SOB who wasn't interested in sex."

"Well, Mr. White is sixty-four years old," said Anglus with a smile.

Ryan scowled. "What are you talking about? Amber is twenty-nine, I think."

Anglus nodded. "So what is your point?"

Ryan realized that while Amber had described the intimate details of her marriage, she never explicitly stated the age of her husband; he had just presumed his age.

"She's a gold digger, Ryan. She must have been sleeping with you for something." There was a slight smirk on Hestrom's face.

"Look, the handcuffs were Amber's," said Ryan defensively.

"Ryan, have you ever heard of Cathy Wilet?"

The name came like a sudden electric shock. Ryan visibly flinched. The two antagonistic officers could perceive Ryan's startled reaction to Hestrom's question.

"I've heard of Cathy Wilet, yes." Ryan's heart accelerated, and he was ready to bolt the room and demand legal counsel.

"What is your connection to Cathy Wilet?" asked Anglus casually as he removed a pack of cigarettes from his jacket. He laid the pack before Ryan. It was an implicit offer, which Ryan ignored because he did not smoke.

"She was abducted in Albany when I lived there. I have no personal connection to her. Why are you asking about Cathy Wilet?"

"Can you tell us why you would be interested in her case?"

"I have no idea," said Ryan bluntly.

"All right, let's go back to Leslie Warren. Did you know her at all?"

"No."

"Never met her here in town?" inquired Anglus.

Hestrom prodded, "Maybe an encounter like the one you had with Amber White?"

"No. Never."

"Ryan, you lived in Albany at one time, right?" Hestrom asked the question with his arms crossed.

Ryan nodded as his blue eyes shifted back and forth between the rapid-fire questions.

"Would you have any idea why Leslie Warren deposited a bank check some two months before she disappeared in the amount of $770,000? The check was from an Albany-based account."

Ryan frowned; he could not fathom why Warren would have received such a check.

The officers looked at Ryan without movement. Ryan was met straight on with the critical, aggressive eyes of two lawmen who were clawing at what they perceived to be their prey.

"I didn't know Leslie Warren and I have no idea where that money could have come from."

"We know you are a bright guy, Ryan, but no law degree, right?"

"Yes, no law degree."

Anglus leaned in to Ryan and spoke in a soft tone.

"Well, you may not know this, but Virginia does not have a corpus delicti requirement to file murder charges. In other words, we don't need her body to make a case against you."

Ryan rubbed his forehead, evaluating his predicament. The

officers had their sights locked on both cases, to Ryan's consternation. For the moment, Ryan could not comprehend a connection.

Now, feeling cornered, Ryan stood up. The officers remained seated. "I'm finished with this line of inquiry, gentlemen. I'm invoking my right to counsel. If you're not charging me, you can send your car to take me home."

Ryan began to head for the door, half expecting the officers to tackle and handcuff him. When he realized that he was at liberty to leave, he turned. "Look, just for your own clarification, I thought I may have been a witness to Cathy Wilet's abduction."

The officers stood at attention and pondered this information.

"Ryan, we're not accusing you—yet," said Anglus with a sly smirk. "But understand, we're just calculating the odds that you may have been the last person to see Cathy Wilet alive and the first person to find Leslie Warren's bloody clothes. You're a smart man, Mr. McNeil. You can objectively judge the incriminating nature of the circumstances."

As Ryan walked down the hall to leave, he suddenly realized the obvious question: How did they know about Cathy Wilet? Rather than inquire, he walked hurriedly down the hall, met his two police escorts, and exited the police station for the ride home.

CHAPTER 20

Perturbed by the police interview, Ryan sat grimly in the unmarked police car as it drove to his house. He analyzed the growing abyss of his predicament. How did they know about Cathy Wilet? This was a jagged mess, he thought. He was tired, and he longed to lie in bed in the calm, safe harbor of his marriage. No more affairs, Ryan pledged silently to himself.

As the unmarked police car pulled on to his block, Ryan heard the officers abruptly curse in exclamation. Ryan leaned forward from the back seat. A white unmarked van with an uncoiled pole, spiraling wire and a transmission disk was parked obtrusively at the curb in front of his house. Neighborhood children gathered on his green lawn, festively encircling the van, like magnetic filings drawn to a magnet. Ryan cursed. He only saw the one van, but he knew more reporters would follow. The newscast unfurled effortlessly in his mind: "Capital aide suspected as serial killer. Story at eleven."

"What do you want to do, Mr. McNeil?" the driver asked.

"I'll go in at the front door."

The officer swung the car into the driveway, and a tall, gangly brunette with a mask of makeup came straight at the car, bellowing questions.

"Mr. McNeil, why did you have Leslie Warren's bloody clothes?"

Ryan could see a video cameraman swinging his equipment over his shoulder and into action. Then into his face came a bright beacon of light, targeting him. Ryan swiftly exited from the back seat.

"Mr. McNeil, what is your role in the abduction?"

The reporter moved in with a microphone thrust into Ryan's face. The question startled him and, unconsciously, he flashed a bemused look at the inquiring reporter. As he looked directly into the dark, shark like eyes of the reporter, he could smell her hairspray, wafting thick in the air.

He composed his thoughts and spoke. "You have your facts entirely wrong. I was at the police station in regard to an attempted kidnapping of my stepdaughter. I am working with the police to capture whoever is responsible. If there is a link to the Leslie Warren case, you need to discuss it with the Fairfax Police. Thank you."

Ryan turned his back on the reporter, and she rapidly shot a flurry of questions to his back. "You did have her bloody clothes at twelve midnight. Does Congressman Somatos know about this?" With complete composure, he unlocked his front door and shut it gently behind him. Inside his entrance hall he breathed a sigh of relief.

Annie emerged. Ryan noticed she looked tense and angry.

"This is crazy," said Ryan.

"You haven't told me the whole truth," said Annie with tears in her eyes.

"The truth about what?" Given the growing dimensions of his personal crisis, he did not know where the explosive mines were scattered.

"How could you, Ryan. Who is Amber White? You're having an affair with an Amber White." Annie cried as she moved away from him and up the stairs. Her eyes were puffy and her cheeks mottled with the moist hue of humiliation and hurt.

"Wait a second, who told you that? The police?" He was following close, realizing fast that the police had talked with her, uncovering his omissions and, worse yet, his deceptions. For the first time Ryan had a broken-glass flash of his marriage, utterly shattered and irreparable.

Annie had retreated to the bedroom and now turned to launch her accusatory diatribe. "You're a liar. I don't know who I married. You cheated on me, and worse yet I don't know what you're up to. I found those clippings of the girl in Albany, and now the reporters are out there screaming that you're connected with Leslie Warren's disappearance."

"You had no right to go into that chest. You showed them the newspaper clippings? You've released nothing but trouble from that box."

Ryan came up and grabbed her shoulders with both hands, pulling her close. He was inches from her face as he spoke. "I had nothing to do with Leslie Warren. The girl in Albany was just a coincidence; I went to the police as a Good Samaritan because I thought I'd witnessed her abduction. I have no idea how Leslie Warren's bloody clothes were on the road with me."

Annie's face paled and her lip quivered. "Bloody clothes? What bloody clothes? Oh good God."

He knew he was deeply ensnared. There was too much circumstantial evidence. He could not clearly refute it all at once. He could maybe try to explain Amber White and her handcuffs. But then he had to explain Cathy Wilet and the newspaper clippings, and of course he had no explanation for Leslie Warren's bloody clothes. He released Annie from his tight grip and resigned himself to his immediate marital plight.

"I think you should leave. I need to think of Jessica's safety."

He went to the bedroom window and hostilely eyed the news

van and knot of reporters that had assembled. They were busy exchanging notes and speculation amid the moving shadows of the coming dusk. He knew that news interest would intensify in the immediate future. He knew as well that in a matter of hours his broad green lawn would be the idle backdrop for the intrusive alien light of the news cameras.

"I'll pack and go to a hotel for now. We need to talk."

Annie nodded quietly in assent and then went to Jessica, who was crying feebly in her room.

Ryan finished packing and surreptitiously exited. He walked out a rear door into the twilight dusk of his backyard. He wheeled two suitcases over his freshly mowed grass to what he now perceived to be the blue-green border of the yard. He turned to look back at the house and felt a rising well of emotion. He then trudged through a secluded dirt path that cut between the property lines, emerging at a nearby side street, a cul-de-sac, bordered by several glowing homes but with no traffic. There Ryan stood, isolated, deep in thought, while the shrill din of crickets grew louder as he waited for a cab.

For privacy, Annie had pulled shut all the drapes and shades of the house. With nightfall, as Ryan had knowingly predicted, his once quiet and leafy street was disrupted by a stirring, inquisitive brood of reporters, most accompanied by little camera comets of light that flared sporadically and then extinguished in the suburban darkness, creating trails of public notoriety across the property where Ryan McNeil once lived.

CHAPTER 21

H is body ached for comfort. He checked into the Hotel Washington without apparent notice. He entered his finely furnished room and felt a tranquil moment of reprieve from the chaos of the day. However, whatever feeling of escape he derived from his stealthy exit evaporated after he switched on the television.

The eleven o'clock news was on, and the TV anchors had a title caption that read "Abduction Mystery Deepens." He depressed the volume on the remote control and sat attentively on the edge of the bed. Ryan listened as the anchors relayed the story:

> "The Leslie Warren abduction story has taken a new
> twist with possible Capitol Hill implications. We
> turn now to Mary Downey in Fairfax."

Ryan could now see on the television the front of his lawn and the pasty-faced brunette from his earlier encounter.

"Police sources in Fairfax County have confirmed that they recovered Leslie Warren's clothes several days ago, following a traffic accident on Potomac Highway. The clothes were found with blood that the FBI crime lab has conclusively determined to be Leslie Warren's. Now the circumstances surrounding the recovery of the clothes are not clear, but apparently they were found at the scene of a car wreck involving Ryan McNeil of Fairfax, Virginia, who is the chief of staff to Congressman Nicholas Somatos of New York. I am in front of Mr. McNeil's house in Fairfax. Mr. McNeil claims that he was in a car chase with a person suspected of attempting a kidnapping of his stepdaughter. However, police sources have been unable to substantiate that account. Earlier we spoke briefly with Mr. McNeil as he returned home."

Ryan watched the clip of his encounter and began to get a sick feeling. He clicked the television off. He undressed in the bathroom and was reminded of his recent injuries. *I'm having a rough time*, he said to himself. *My life has turned to shit, but I'll get through this.*

He stepped into the shower and let the steaming water purge his pounding emotions, and when he toweled down he felt supreme fatigue. He slipped under the silky, tight hotel linen, and sleep effortlessly enveloped him.

The phone rang, startling Ryan awake. He reached for the phone and eyed the digital clock that read 7:42 a.m. Early-morning light filtered through the gauzy curtains.

"Hello," said Ryan, half awake.

"You're moving up in the world, getting a lot of publicity I see." It was Somatos on a cell phone with static in the background.

Ryan lifted himself up in bed. "Things aren't going well at all. How did you know I was here?"

"Annie told me. I called your house early. Well, at least you're hiding out in style." Somatos sounded breezy confident, and his confidence instilled a collateral feeling in Ryan.

"What do think, Congressman?"

"So you're not only a bad driver, you're a kidnapper and a possible murderer. Not the best image to project for a congressional chief of staff."

"Are you getting press calls?"

"Oh, let's see, I have invitations for *Hello NY*, *Good Morning USA*, *Breaking News*. You're a press bonanza. This isn't good at all."

Ryan breathed an audible sigh. "What do you think we should do?"

"I think you should not come into work." Ryan heard Somatos emphasize the "you" in the sentence.

"Do I still have a job?" Ryan asked with a growing measure of unease.

"I'll stand by you for now." Even through the static, Somatos's voice now sounded gravely serious. "I've received notice that the governor is going to release a statement calling upon me to fire you."

"What?" Ryan was taken aback by the immediate gravity of the situation. "The governor is involved?"

"They're going to use this to come after me. You know the *New York Herald* is going to blow this up."

"Shit." Ryan's exclamation expressed genuine consternation at the speed at which events were overtaking him.

"Don't come to Longworth. I'll have a limo and I'll meet you at front of the hotel at ten a.m. OK. Bye."

Ryan sat up still in bed and for several minutes tried to analyze the situation.

"I can get out of this. Somatos will help me out of this," he said out loud to himself. He began to pick up the phone to call Annie, and then he hesitatingly replaced the receiver and went to the shower instead.

CHAPTER 22

Ryan entered the lobby at precisely 10:00 a.m. A black limousine was outside, idling with its engine running. The tinted window rolled down. Somatos waved him into the car with a smile and moved to the left side. Ryan wondered if Somatos was paying for this extravagance from his own pocket. Unexpectedly, he felt nervous with Somatos, unsure whether to attribute it to the unusual setting for their meeting or the extraordinary circumstances.

"You're punctual as usual," observed Somatos.

"Where are we headed?"

"We'll drive around for a while."

"You're in luxurious style today," remarked Ryan.

"Well, in moments of crisis we all need our little luxuries," said Somatos with a wolfish grin and implicit reference to Ryan's temporary hotel abode. Somatos passed Ryan a copy of the *New York Herald*, folded open to page five.

Ryan read the story entitled, "Congress Aide Eyed as Suspect."

"This story will move to the front page if the governor gets involved," Ryan noted dryly.

Somatos looked out the window and murmured, "I hate that bastard. Unfortunately, he knows it all to keenly." He then turned to face Ryan. "Run through this whole episode with me from top to bottom."

Ryan recounted his tale in detail while Somatos fiddled with a pair of dark sunglasses he was holding. The limousine glided aimlessly around the monuments and National Mall, and Somatos occasionally turned to glance out the window, craning his head skyward as they passed the spire of the Washington Monument.

Ryan concluded his recitation of the facts and circumstances. "Well, what do you think?"

"There are no bodies uncovered and no one knows what happened to either girl, so what are they going to charge you with? Bad driving? Being a victim of an attempted burglary and possession of old newspaper clippings?"

Ryan was not relieved by this reassurance. "The police said they don't need a body. The bloody clothes have a DNA match, they said. They only need enough circumstantial evidence for a grand jury to indict."

"Don't believe this DNA match crap, Ryan," said Somatos. "I hear they screw up half the results. Besides, I'll check on Amber White's husband, Henry Adams White. His name sounds familiar to me. You were after all balling the old man's young wife right before the van appeared. Maybe he was having her followed and wanted to set you up. Secondly, Leslie Warren's clothes being thrown at you could have been an afterthought or it could have been part of an inadvertent setup. I'm presuming that no murderer has a particular grudge against you; maybe it was me they were trying to obliquely destroy by bringing you down."

Ryan nodded in thoughtful concurrence and stretched his legs. A long period of ruminating silence followed.

"There is one part of this that makes me think there is some connection to Cathy Wilet," Ryan finally said. "Leslie Warren's clothes had blood on them, and I would presume she has been either murdered or met with violence. Maybe I was targeted because of the Cathy Wilet connection."

Somatos frowned incredulously. "Who knows about your sighting of Cathy Wilet? She hasn't even been mentioned in these news reports. I think it was an unexpected and inadvertent bonus to whoever was trying to set you up. Besides, I know about your Cathy Wilet sighting. Am I a suspect, Ryan?"

An awkward moment hung between them.

Somatos dipped his face and peered at Ryan with two fierce eyes. Ryan for the first time felt an unexpected trepidation that even his friend and mentor could not be utterly trusted. An uneasy feeling of mutual distrust momentarily slid between them.

"There is something else. Apparently Leslie Warren had a connection to Albany that I learned from the police," said Ryan with a deliberate pause to gauge his mentor's reaction.

"Another link to Albany?" Somatos observed quizzically.

"The police told me that an Albany-based check for $770,000 had been deposited in Leslie Warren's account in the months before she disappeared."

Somatos whistled at the amount. "A hefty sum for a kid working a counter at a store. Sounds like a legal settlement."

"A legal settlement? Why not a payoff?"

"Because of the amount."

Ryan could not grasp the logic.

Somatos elaborated: "You see, the lawyer took one third of a million, say about $330,000. And of course the settlement would be sealed." Somatos smiled, brightened by a thought.

"What is it?"

"Well, Ryan, unless you or I are sitting on bank accounts with a million dollars in them, then I can't see how the police or anyone could consider you a suspect. I can't believe that the check and her abduction were coincidence. Right?"

"But they do have an Albany connection again," observed Ryan.

"But you know who would have that kind of money and not break a sweat writing that check? Our esteemed Congressman Green has that kind of dough. Even his protégé Seth Tantalus I heard bought a big house in Potomac or McLean."

"I'm glad you brought that up," exclaimed Ryan, ready to expound. "The night of the accident I was at a congressional reception and ran into Green and Tantalus. Tantalus was in a close conversation with a lobbyist and VP from Dorus Genetic Corporation."

"Dorus Genetics, the New York firm from seven years ago with the provision in my bill from the assembly?" Somatos asked, with deepening interest.

"Yeah, that firm. These two gentlemen seemed very cozy with Tantalus. And he seemed very nervous for me to see them together. With the accident and all, I almost forgot the entire episode, but I did an internet check and I accessed the records with the congressional financial disclosure office."

"Go on," prompted Somatos, intrigued.

"Did you know that the governor signed into law that exact same provision he vetoed in our bill? The provision allowed Dorus Corp to offer their genetic test to the public, and the company later took their stock public in an initial public offering that netted the officers millions. Some of that stock showed up in Tantalus's disclosures. About two million dollars' worth. That's why I think Tantalus was so edgy when I saw them all together."

"What about Green? Was Green holding Dorus stock?"

"Green's holdings are in a blind trust. He was probably smart enough to cash out. Tantalus being stubborn and idiotic probably held it."

Somatos nodded. "Or perhaps he held on to some and sold a chunk before coming here to DC. You know, under congressional rules what you're describing would be a crime," he observed. "However, I don't recall any Albany rules on stock ownership and conflict of interest, so I think Green and Tantalus technically are in the clear. I'll check with counsel on that."

"I think you're right except for the role of the governor. He may have been complicit. Why else would he veto one bill and then sign the same exact bill a year later."

"He could rationalize anything any way he wants," Somatos said. "You're not going to implicate him based on Green's or Tantalus's stock holdings. You see a connection with these missing girls and your situation?"

"Yes, I do, and I was thinking of going up to Albany to ask around."

"Why do you need to go there?"

"I've been researching on the internet," Ryan answered, "but you know Albany keeps its records hidden. Not the most transparent state government."

"Just be careful. Assume your phone at the hotel is tapped, and assume you are being watched." he cautioned and then paused. "Is it over between you and Annie?"

"I think so. You know, I feel a kind of relief. Things were not going well between us. It's really Jessica who I will miss. I don't know; I really don't feel like starting over."

"You're young. It will be fine. You know women and children can play in the sand; men have responsibilities in this world," Somatos said sagely.

The limousine pulled up to the curb of the hotel. "I'll call you after I've got some information. Try to stay out of trouble in the meantime," said Somatos.

Ryan shook Somatos's hand formally and then darted from the car into the hotel lobby. He felt unnerved by the meeting with his boss, but it stirred a recollection from years ago, a key fact from the Cathy Wilet case that he had almost forgotten. The alteration in the death penalty adjournment time the night of Cathy Wilet's abduction was now foremost in his mind.

CHAPTER 23

S omatos strode briskly through the Longworth Building toward his office, past the knots of enthralled tourists and congenial lobbyists who clogged the halls, stairs, and elevators. He had left his sunglasses on and was hoping to evade any stray reporter that might be out. Turning a corner in the corridor where his office was, he could see a camera crew and a pack of reporters, with pads open and at the ready. It was a clear press ambush in front of his office doorway. Don't break stride, look relaxed, Somatos thought to himself.

The reporters, many of whom knew Somatos on sight, quickly descended on him. He waved his hand. "I'll talk later, really. Joe, you're looking good." The reporters fired a volley of questions that lamely shot at him. Somatos entered his office and passed the receptionist and startled aides, who had momentarily stopped whatever they were doing to appraise the demeanor of their boss and thereby the gravity of the crisis.

"Sally, no calls, all right?" Somatos entered his office and shut the door. He took his shades off and massaged his temples. Shit, what a mess, he thought. Politically, the crisis presented several problems. If he cut Ryan loose, he could be portrayed as panicked and perhaps even complicit in Ryan's alleged crimes. If he stood by Ryan, he could be portrayed as manifesting a double standard on crime and demonstrating dubious ethics in office. He pondered his options until his line rang. "Yes, Sally," Somatos said with a snarl.

"Congressman Somatos, Tom Griffen with the governor's office is on the line and says it is urgent."

Somatos paused and then picked up the line. "Tom, so good of you to call."

"Nick, I've been asked by the governor to send you an advance copy of the statement that is going out, calling on you to either fire Mr. McNeil or suspend him without pay."

"Our governor has a very deep and abiding appreciation of our system of justice, does he," responded Somatos in a voice that dripped with sarcasm. He knew the conversation was a meaningless courtesy call.

"I'll send you a fax as soon as we conclude the call."

"Tom, send the fax and consider the call concluded," said Somatos as he slammed the receiver down.

As soon as the fax was transmitted, Sally walked it into Somatos's office. He took the fax and read it carefully for several minutes. It was three sanctimonious paragraphs and a direct attack on Somatos. He needed to respond quickly and decisively. He scratched some notes on a yellow legal pad, then asked Sally if any reporters were still outside, hovering in the corridor. He went to a mirror on the back of his door, ran a comb through his slick hair, checked his teeth, made a few minor cosmetic adjustments, and then stood behind his desk.

He directed Sally to allow the reporters in. The swarm entered Somatos's inner office, feeling somewhat privileged and shocked. They were not yet aware of the governor's statement and were betting that Somatos would be dodging them for the remainder of the day. The sudden candor by a politician under fire endeared them momentarily to Somatos, who issued an impassioned defense of his chief of staff. However, Somatos had few facts to offer them. Following his largely extemporized statement, he allowed questions.

"Congressman, in your mind is there any possibility that Ryan McNeil could be involved in the Leslie Warren abduction?"

Somatos paused. This was a tricky question.

"In my mind, based solely on my knowledge of Ryan McNeil, and of course I have no knowledge of the Leslie Warren case or any other case, no, emphatically no, Ryan McNeil is not a criminal." Somatos's confidence wavered, but he kept his smiling composure. He frantically wondered if they'd caught his faux pas. Somatos kept thinking: Did I say "any other case"?

———————————————

Tantalus paced excitedly outside Green's closed office door. He had inside news, exclusive information, and it was in these moments when he had the edge and felt eminently valuable to the congressman. Though Tantalus had just turned thirty-one, he had retained a boyish enthusiasm for his job that was not especially congruent with Green's generally aristocratic and restrained persona. But they had been through too much together and had forged a political link that, like Somatos and Ryan, could not be easily broken.

Green opened his door and Tantalus quickly approached.

"I've got a copy of the governor's statement." He passed the paper to Green, who removed a pair of glasses in his pocket to read it.

"The governor is really going after Somatos," said Tantalus, noting the obvious, to the annoyance of Green.

"Is this what you are so excited about?" demanded Green.

"Ryan McNeil knows about the windfall provision for the genetics lab," said Tantalus.

"So what," said Green, annoyed at his aide's sudden paranoia.

Green was sitting in his suit, prepared to divert his attention to other matters.

"You don't think there will be any fallout?" asked Tantalus.

"The governor has vetoed hundreds of bills that sometimes make it back as legislation. Not one press call ever inquired about this issue. I told the governor that this was something so esoteric, so obscure, that it would never have any public consequence. I've been right now for years. Somatos will not make anything of this." Green spoke with reassuring and haughty confidence. He then suddenly stood up behind his desk, turned his back to Tantalus, and looked out the window in a contemplative posture. His office faced a small courtyard. The view was limited and undesirable.

"You know, I understand that at the very corner of Somatos's window you can see the Capitol," said Green contemptuously.

Tantalus did not know how to answer that observation by his boss.

Green turned to Tantalus. "Imagine a delicatessen owner with a view like that, an office view of the Capitol." Green paused and Tantalus again wondered if he was being invited to respond.

Green looked at his young aide. Tantalus's face was flush red and he looked angry and agitated, as if he had been in a scrimmage. Green felt the need to allay his concerns.

"You more than anyone should know that there is an unseen level of politics that few people are aware of. Sometimes, there are"—Green paused for the fitting word—"scandals, and the press focuses. But largely things go unnoticed, unchecked. You know that. You've seen and participated in this level. Somatos understands this. Do you think he got to where he is by being a moral highbrow? He rose from the gutter, from the streets of the Bronx." Green's voice became elevated in agitation. He checked himself and spoke again, with the hot breath of contempt in a lowered voice.

"Those streets are not clean. This is not his concern. You and I have prospered, and we did it in a discreet and proper way. No one cares, and no one can ever discern anything illegal about it. It goes on all the time. The governor vetoed Somatos's bill and signed my legislation. Nothing illegal occurred," said Green with officious finality, dismissing Tantalus's concerns.

"What will the governor say if asked about the veto?" Tantalus inquired, pressing on to the discomfort of his boss. Green glowered at Tantalus, silently pondering his position for several moments.

"The governor is a man of eloquence. No shortage of words for him. He will offer a logical rationale. And Ryan McNeil will not press this issue; it would be impolitic, and I'm sure he will eventually be distracted by more pressing business. You can leave the door open," said Green, dismissing Tantalus and his concerns.

CHAPTER 24

R yan turned from the street in front of the hotel carrying several packages containing purchases he had made that afternoon. The clerk dutifully alerted him to the fact he had several voice mail messages and handed him a hotel envelope. Ryan thanked the clerk and noted the fact that none of the people at the front desk appeared to notice him. Perhaps being routinely exposed to the famous and infamous, they were now inured to whatever publicity they had seen regarding Ryan. Ryan did not open the envelope, and as he turned, he immediately saw both Anglus and Hestrom strutting toward him. He braced himself for what he thought to be imminent arrest.

Instead of arrest, Anglus casually and without great ceremony handed Ryan a search warrant for his house and his hotel room.

"Not under arrest?" asked Ryan.

"Not yet," said Hestrom, dampening Ryan's momentary elation. "Let's go up to your room."

Ryan took the elevator up to his floor and walked down the corridor to his room, escorted by the silent and plainly grim law enforcement officers.

He used an electronic key to open the door and stepped inside. The search of the hotel room seemed perfunctory to Ryan. He had feared they were going to start ripping apart pillows. He wanted to say something flip and outrageous but restrained himself, knowing that any remark at this point could be taken out of context and used against him. The search warrant officially conveyed the obvious: he was now a suspect. "Am I allowed to leave the room? Even leave town?"

"It would help to keep in touch with us during the course of the investigation, but you are not constrained in your movements at this time. You are not a suspect but what we call a person of interest," stated Hestrom.

Ryan suspected he was being placed under surveillance and his phones were probably tapped. Hestrom and Anglus, finding nothing suspicious in the room, completed their search. They both knew their earlier search of McNeil's home had revealed nothing incriminating. "All right, Ryan, stay out of trouble," said Hestrom as he pointed directly at Ryan's chest.

With relief he closed the door behind the two investigators. He sat down on the bed and opened the envelope. The cover sheet was from Somatos's office contained a scrawled note from the congressman, urging Ryan to call a particular lawyer, furnishing the number, and mentioning that he had given a press statement in support of Ryan. Attached to the cover sheet was the text of the governor's statement calling on Somatos to fire Ryan. Ryan read it with hostile fury.

He went to the phone and placed a call to Somatos's office. The receptionist recognized Ryan's voice and informed him that the congressman was out. She also began to convey the support of the office staff for him, but he was far too agitated to listen patiently. He abruptly ended the call, thought for a moment, and was reminded of his voice mail messages by a small, insistent blinking light on the phone.

The first message he retrieved was from Annie. She sounded emotional; she was calling because the police were in the house, executing a search warrant.

He saved the message and then retrieved his second voice mail. The female voice was immediately recognizable as Amber White. She was speaking in her sweetest southern accent. "Ryan, it's Amber. I am sorry, truly sorry, but I can't cover for you any longer. We both know the truth is I wasn't with you that night. I cannot be true to myself if I continue to lie for you. I needed to tell you. Ryan, I'm scared that if you continue to lie about us, harm will come to you. Take care."

Ryan stood up and replayed the message, listening carefully to the part that he interpreted as a not very implicit threat while he forlornly looked out the window. He dialed his house number and Annie answered the phone in a low, tired voice.

"They took the house apart," she noted abjectly. "If there is any other evidence, they need to just tell me where it is before they come back."

"Is Jessica all right?" Ryan asked with concern.

"She is traumatized. Not only another divorce I have to deal with, but how do I explain the police?"

"Tell her that I love her very much and will see her soon," said Ryan, emotionally choked. "Annie, please be very careful."

"It's a little late, Ryan," said Annie.

"Well, in case you need to reach me in an emergency . . . ." Ryan waited after saying the number, but there was a long pause at the other end. He assumed she was writing the number down.

"A woman called for you."

"Did she say who she was?"

"No. I assumed it was your mistress," Annie said bitterly. "It's over between us, you know that?"

Ryan paused and offered the best response he could. "I don't know; I simply don't know what is going on. I've got to go." He hung up the phone and drew in a deep breath.

He scanned his room wearily. He already felt imprisoned by circumstances, but the thought of living life in the purgatory of a prison, instead of the lavish comfort of a hotel room, made him sick with fear. He knew what happened to men in prison. *I need to drink, perhaps get drunk.* The thought momentarily lightened his heart. Maybe even pick up a woman, he mused. He was now, after all, separated physically and emotionally, and there would not be the concomitant guilt that burned into him after his past carnal visits with Amber.

Ryan changed into a suit in order to blend into the after-work crowd. He left the room, took the elevator down to the stirring lobby, and exited the hotel. The street was busy with pedestrians, released from the captivity of work, and commuters were streaming through the sun-washed streets. Exhilarated by the evening's possibilities, Ryan planned his itinerary.

CHAPTER 25

He was standing in a noisy, hot, and crowded bar, amid the lost fragments of conversation and the sharp shards of hilarity. He had patronized three bars and separately engaged three women in conversation. Ryan was forced to improvise at several points in his conversations and adeptly eschewed the usual Washingtonian emphasis on careers and current events. His efforts at seduction had not been successful. All three women had politely declined his more wanton and direct advances to return to his hotel room.

The initial extroverted ebullience induced by the alcohol could not sustain his evening. The cumulative impact of dimmed senses, combined with the knowledge that drove him to consume, now left him effectively warped out of the social interaction. He was standing alone, surrounded by swirls and eddies of inebriated patrons. There was only the vicarious indulgence of watching the counterfeit exchange of conversation, touch, and glances among the sexes. He knew he was drunk, and he began to contemplate returning to the hotel and lapsing into alcohol-induced sleep. Watching the women around him, a melancholy memory of Caroline came into his mind. He knew then that he needed to leave. He negotiated his way through the tumult of the crowd, stepped out into the warm metropolitan night, and hailed a cab.

By the time his cab discharged him at the hotel, he was feeling lethargic and less inebriated. The hotel lobby was almost devoid of activity, and Ryan walked briskly past the desk clerk, who called out "Mr. McNeil" and summoned him over with a wave of his hand. Ryan was surprised that the clerk recognized him now and wondered what new problem he would be confronted with.

"Mr. McNeil, there was a woman here for several hours waiting for you."

Ryan found himself squinting in incomprehension. "What woman?" He scanned the bright, elegant lobby and saw no woman.

"She was blonde, very beautiful." He pronounced the word "beautiful" with what sounded to Ryan like a foreign emphasis on every syllable.

"Did she have a southern accent?" He presumed it was Amber; she obviously knew he was at the hotel.

"Oh no, definitely not."

"Well, where is she now?"

"She was in the lobby, then the lobby bar. I don't see her now. But she did stow some items with the bellman."

Ryan was too tired to decipher who the woman was or where she was. "Well, I'll be in for the rest of the evening, so ring me if she is here again."

He strode over to the elevator and depressed the button. Somewhat agitated, he wondered what woman was looking for him. Feeling sexually frustrated, the thought of any woman at this point was appealing. The empty elevator opened and Ryan entered it and rang for his floor. He arrived at his floor, walked down the hall, and then entered his coded key in the door. The dark room was illuminated only by his window view of several buildings in the distance. He flicked on several lights and began to feel anew the oppressive loneliness of his plight.

He was washing his face in the bathroom, with the door closed from force of habit, when he thought he heard a pounding on the outside door. *Who would be at the door this late?* The threat mentioned in Amber's message resonated in his mind. He closed the faucet to stop the flow of water and looked at himself in the mirror. All was quiet, except for the susurration of water flowing in the pipes and then a complete silence. No sounds. *Was it the door? A maid? Room service?* Then, abruptly, there was again a violent pounding on the outside door, unmistakable. Ryan's heart accelerated and the blood roared through his body. He wiped his face with a towel, exited the bathroom, quickly put on a pair of pants, and went to the door. Silence.

"Who is it?" he called out, but no response issued back.

Ryan put his hand on the door lever and pulled it open. It took a moment to focus on the woman, but then his sight integrated the startling visual image with a deep pool of memory. It was Caroline.

"Hi. Can I come in?" She was smiling without any tentative sign of the seven years that had passed between them.

The superlative wash of emotions through Ryan's body was such that he was temporarily robbed of coherent thought or speech. He thus simply nodded dumbly and stepped back from the door. He looked at her as one would look at a ghost, doubting the reality of the vision.

Ryan was bewildered. "Caroline? How did you know I was here?"

Caroline stepped into the middle of the room, glanced around, and looked back at Ryan, beaming a radiant smile. In Ryan's perception, she was still beautiful and had not changed. The small room quickly filled with the potency of her perfumed presence.

"Your wife told me. I've been reading about you. It's in all the papers. You know the governor asked Somatos to fire you. It made the New York papers." Her voice had become breathless and quivered slightly so that Ryan judged that maybe she was as nervous as he was.

There was an uneasy and awkward posturing between them that Ryan felt powerless to overcome until her intentions were made clear. She was wearing a short, dark-blue skirt with white silk blouse; it was all stunning and seductive to Ryan. His eyes dropped to her ring finger and noted no diamond marriage ring; he was shocked. The last he had heard was that she was married to a successful Wall Street financier.

"You're in town for business?" Ryan asked, searching for a clue.

"No. Not exactly," she said coyly, savoring her mystery.

"Do you want a drink?" he asked, and for the first time he opened and peered into the minibar and noted that it contained few options. "I could order room service, or do you want a beer?"

"A beer is fine."

From the minibar he handed her an opened bottle of beer. She drank from it once and then set it down on a nearby table. "I know this must seem strange seeing me." She paused.

"Ryan, is time still important to you?"

The question made him uneasy. "Are you rushing somewhere, Caroline?" he asked softy, close to her.

"Yes, I am. I'm rushing right now." She paused to watch the hurt expression in his eyes. "I'm rushing to make up seven years very quickly." There was expressive silence as she stepped even closer to him so that her reality vividly imposed upon his overwhelmed senses.

"I missed you," she said. Her eyes sparkled and her face beckoned. The blood in his body roared again, this time rooted in a different primitive sensation. He lowered his face to her and kissed her deeply until he could taste her hot breath. The embrace was sustained, and she reciprocated passionately with a skilled tongue in his mouth.

She then drew back unexpectedly, with a serious look that Ryan could not interpret. He started to speak, but Caroline put a finger in front of her mouth and then gracefully knelt before him. She looked up at him, and Ryan felt ineffable wonder in the proximity of her beauty. She slowly ran her hands up both of his legs, and she then began to undo his belt.

The golden intimacy of her hair and the intoxicating aroma of her now brought him back into an almost forgotten dream that tranquilized his thoughts and for the moment consumed his body and his being.

CHAPTER 26

Ryan lay in bed, alert. The brightness of sunlight slanted into a corner of the room, between the gap of opaque curtains. A steady volume of cooling was blown by the hotel air-conditioning system. He could have risen and blocked out the intrusive sunlight by shutting the curtains entirely, had he the energy or inclination; instead he lolled in the moment and then made love. He could not have imagined a more salacious form of salvation.

They took a cab to Georgetown and then walked, hand in hand, down the narrow cobblestone streets to a restaurant abutting the bright blue ribbon of the Potomac. Forgoing the cool interior, they had Bloody Marys and brunch beneath an umbrella-shaded table, while a caressing breeze from the water stirred the otherwise languid air. He had occasionally thought of her these last few years, but the memory was so poignant as to be almost painful, even when assuaged by the passage of time. But now that pain had suddenly passed, obliterated. Ryan soaked in the pleasing glint of her, and the dark unpleasantness of the last few days was itself eclipsed by her radiant presence.

He made all the necessary intimate revelations to her about his life. He spoke of his failed marriage; how he had sought the security of a family, only to have it turned against him. He confessed his sins of infidelity while she listened attentively. In their conversation, Ryan reached a comfortable point of inquiring into her past and current state of affairs.

"Did you ever get married, Caroline? I had heard you married some Wall Street type."

"Yes, I was married for three years," she said ruefully. "He worked on Wall Street. Eventually he lost his job by doing too much cocaine and driving his car through a window of a restaurant. After that episode, I left him."

"Of course," said Ryan as he toasted her with his Bloody Mary. He gave her a long look and then asked, "What is it about money, Caroline? Is that why you left me?"

"Beauty is fleeting, but money is forever," she obliquely responded.

Ryan failed to grasp the concept. "What does that mean?"

"I can't live on idealism. You didn't have any money then, and you didn't care about money."

Ryan sighed with exasperation. He relented on the issue. She would never change, so instead he changed the subject.

"You know, Caroline, I feel that I am being finally punished for not stepping forward in the Cathy Wilet case."

"Ryan, that is just baseless Catholic guilt. You went to the police; you did the right thing. You don't really believe that this Leslie . . . Leslie . . ."

"Leslie Warren," Ryan filled in her blank.

"You think this Leslie Warren case is connected to Cathy Wilet. Why would you think such a thing? You always believe too easily in conspiracies. Besides, I thought that it was Assemblyman Caluzzi, the one who was killed when he was sexually assaulting his intern.

Maybe he could have been involved. I thought when you called me that night that was what you were thinking."

Ryan nodded in agreement but then proceeded to reject her speculation. "I thought that too for a while, but you know, Caluzzi could not have done it because I remembered that the assembly transcript time was altered. Only a Democrat could have done that."

Caroline looked at Ryan, puzzled, while she swept some of her fair hair back.

"What transcript change?"

"I thought I told you that the assembly adjournment time was changed the night that Cathy Wilet disappeared."

Caroline looked concerned and confused. "You never mentioned that to me."

Ryan tried to recollect. "I thought I did."

"Ryan, why are we even thinking about Cathy Wilet? What does this have to do with your present problems?"

"Caroline, I believe that whomever tried to drop Leslie Warren's bloody clothes at my house was trying to set me up and knew about the Cathy Wilet case and the fact that I may have seen her."

"Why do you think that?"

"Because the police now think of me as a suspect in both cases," said Ryan emphatically.

"Coincidence," retorted Caroline confidently. She picked up a wet wedge of orange, sucked the pulp, and squinted into the bright afternoon.

"No, it is not coincidence. There is also another link that the police told me."

Ryan paused, reticent to share all his information with Caroline.

"What?" Caroline leaned forward, intrigued.

Ryan relinquished his knowledge. "Leslie Warren apparently had recently received a $770,000 check from an Albany-based bank account."

"Seven hundred and seventy thousand dollars," Caroline repeated as she enviously contemplated the magnitude of the sum.

"So you see I am going up to Albany Monday, because I need some answers. I don't even know if they ever found her body."

"Ryan, why are you always playing policeman?" said Caroline with an annoyed intonation that for Ryan elicited a sharp, acerbic recollection.

He decided to change the subject. "As I said, my wife threw me out. Divorce is coming." He paused in almost tentative adolescent-like awkwardness. "Caroline, do you regret leaving me?"

Caroline looked out over the narrow channel of water, squinting in mental reflection. She pondered the question to a point that made Ryan uncomfortable; he had expected an easy affirmation of her love.

"Yes," she said finally with a smile as she reached out to touch Ryan's hand across the table to his obvious relief.

It was at that moment, thirty yards away, and unknown to both Ryan McNeil and Caroline Tierney, that FBI Special Agent Mike Anglus, concealed by a pillar, clicked the shutter of his telescopic camera for the twelfth time in the last fifteen minutes.

CHAPTER 27

In the five years since Ryan had last seen Albany, it had not visibly changed. In the cab ride from the airport the traffic was sparse, and the cityscape was as he remembered. After cruising down past the modern shopping malls into the center of town, the suburban traffic thinned. The wide stretch of streets narrowed into a slice of urban dreariness between dilapidated housing and grimy retail establishments with the occasional forlorn pedestrians, indistinguishable from the roaming homeless. Aside from the business of government, there was no business to speak of in Albany.

He remembered Albany as perpetually cold. However, now the heat and humidity seemed intense. The dilapidated cab was not equipped with air-conditioning, or it had been rendered inoperable. Fresh air blew through the open window. The green border of Washington Park appeared, and Ryan mentally noted the spot where Cathy Wilet had vanished. Past the park, the modern monoliths of state government submerged the streets in shadow, and brisk groups of pedestrians appeared, here looking less forlorn and more prosperous. The cab turned a corner, the towering gothic center of

Albany—the capitol—emerged, and Ryan felt a sudden chill in the heat of summer. The governor's call for Ryan's termination meant that a potent and possibly sinister animus lurked behind those walls. He could almost envision the governor darkly roaming this colossal palace, plotting against Ryan and Somatos.

Ryan had made a written list of several items: Joe Houseman, Clerk; Death Penalty Transcript; Cathy Wilet, newspapers; financial disclosures for Green and Tantalus; and employment records. The first item was to meet with Joe Houseman, who was the clerk of the state assembly. Houseman had held the position when Ryan was serving as Somatos's aide in the assembly. In fact, he had held the position through a secession of four Speakers, continuing in his role uninterrupted for twenty-two years.

Houseman's office was on the second floor of the capitol, not far from the ornate cathedral-like assembly chamber. Ryan entered the capitol and walked up the grand interior staircase. As he walked up the heavily worn granite steps, he noted the indelible faces carved into the stone walls that now imparted an ominous and evil look. One hundred years ago, these haunting visages had been carved by stoneworkers given the artistic discretion to depict whatever they wanted. Ryan had never before noticed the depictions, but now with a fresh eye and a mind open to the intricacies of corruption and evil, he saw this craft from a different perspective.

On the second floor, Ryan saw two erect flags and five uniformed capitol police officers, officiously guarding the seat of power—the Office of the Governor. Behind a huge wooden door, emblazoned with the great seal of New York, was a complex of offices that led to one grand office. Ryan quickly turned right and walked the hallway past the assembly chamber and to the office of the clerk of the assembly.

Houseman was African-American and hailed from Buffalo. He was steeped in the daily process-based intricacies of the assembly. With an affable smile, he recognized Ryan as he entered the office.

Based on the enthusiasm of his greeting, Ryan surmised that he was unaware of his troubles.

"Mr. McNeil, good to see you. How is Assemblyman, I mean Congressman Somatos?" Houseman waved Ryan into his office with a smile. He then sat back down in his leather chair. There was no session that day, and he was dressed casually in an open dress shirt. His desk was bare except for a copy of that morning's *Albany Times Dispatch* spread open to the sport page.

"Nick is fine and he sends his warm regards," replied Ryan with weary pleasantry. He was pleased that Houseman, who could be temperamental, seemed in a very relaxed, expansive mode.

"Joe, I'm here doing some research, and I need your help."

Houseman's face grew serious, and he leaned back in his chair. "How can I help you, Ryan?"

"Is it possible for leadership to alter a transcript time of adjournment?"

Houseman looked puzzled. "I'm not sure what you mean."

"Look, let's say that an assembly debate ends at seven thirty p.m. Could leadership alter the time to reflect the debate ending at, say, eight fifteen?"

Houseman contemplated the question with visibly intense calculation. Ryan could not tell if he was trying to formulate an accurate response or a politic response or was just wondering what the hell Ryan was doing posing such a far-fetched question.

Houseman leaned forward in his chair slowly so that the cracking sound of leather shifting under his weight could be heard. By tacit understanding, Ryan leaned forward to receive the official response.

"The best way I can respond to your question is to tell you what you already know. The transcript of the assembly proceedings is an official record of the legislative body. It can be entered as evidence of legislative intent in a court of law. However, as you know, the Speaker, and only the Speaker, can, under Rule 52, supersede the record to reflect such minor nonsubstantive, technical adjustments as he sees fit."

"Only the Speaker has the authority?" Ryan asked.

"Yes."

Ryan was cognizant of the Speaker's broad authority, but he was probing as to how much latitude may have been granted other leaders. He decided to offer his speculation.

"What about Deputy Majority Leader Green?"

"You mean Congressman Green?" Houseman smiled. "No. No way. Green did not have the authority, and I can tell you as well, that Speaker Mariano would never have done anything like that for Green."

Ryan discerned no equivocation in Houseman's response. There were several possibilities that Ryan considered: he was perhaps mistaken in the time of adjournment the night he thought he had seen Cathy Wilet, or that the time of the adjournment was in error by accident and not by design, or lastly that Speaker Mariano had been induced to alter the record. Knowing full well the nature of Speaker Mariano, Ryan considered the last possibility as the least likely. Mariano from Brooklyn was a tough man to extract a favor from under any circumstances. He was in the habit of asking for favors, not performing them. In any event, the mystery could not be solved since Mariano had died of a heart attack almost two years ago.

"Thanks, Joe. You've been very helpful. By the way, could I get a copy of the following transcript?"

Ryan stood up and handed Houseman a slip of paper containing the date of the assembly debate the night Cathy Wilet disappeared.

"I will also need the financial disclosure forms for these two individuals in these years." Ryan slid the names across the desk to Houseman.

Houseman looked at the paper and grimaced.

"It could take a couple of hours," said Houseman, mulling the requested information in his mind and wondering what possible significance the debate transcript and the financial disclosure information could have to Ryan.

The men shook hands, and Ryan left the office. He walked briskly down the hall, past the state assembly library and archive. He paused for a moment and then pulled open the door.

The library was deserted except for reference staff. Ryan asked for the microfilm of the *Albany Times Dispatch* for the days following Wilet's disappearance. He had kept many of the subsequent clippings, but he had not saved the initial accounts of her disappearance.

Within minutes an efficient staffer handed him a microfilm container. Ryan threaded the film into a machine and advanced the copy to the day after Wilet disappeared. He immediately spotted the article by the photo of her. Ryan was always troubled by the photo. After her disappearance, he had spent hours mentally trying to superimpose this stilted image with his animated memory of her walking on that spring day. There would be moments when he doubted that the girl he had seen and the haunting photo were one and the same.

Ryan read the story and then the subsequent article published on the following day. The byline was the same, but the story had moved from page three to the front page. He was about to move on to the following day when he noted a discrepancy in the two articles. The first article reported that Wilet was an intern in the Office of the Governor. The second article reported that she was an intern in House Operations.

Ryan had never seen Wilet working in House Operations, but back then he rarely would meet anyone that worked in that department. The office for House Operations was located in the tower complex of offices adjacent to the capitol and the Legislative Office Building. Most of the work was conducted separate and apart from legislative activity. Ryan wondered why the same reporter had changed the fact of her internship. Did Wilet work for the governor or did she work for House Operations?

A hand was on his shoulder, and Ryan, startled, jumped from the seat.

"Ryan McNeil?"

It took Ryan a moment to recognize the vaguely familiar bearded face. "Tom?"

They exchanged an enthusiastic handshake. Ryan had not seen Tom Bronfman since he had last been in Albany. Bronfman had gained weight, and even his eyelids had become heavy, as if he hadn't slept in months. His dark beard was now supported by thick jowls.

"This is the last place I'd expect to find you," said Bronfman with a look of surprise. "I hope the governor doesn't find you hiding out in here." Bronfman had obviously been keeping up with the news.

"Well, I haven't seen him yet. Does he still roam the halls like Darth Vader?" asked Ryan humorously.

"You bet. He's getting scarier every day."

The two spent some time exchanging pleasantries until Bronfman could no longer suppress his curiosity.

"What kind of research are you doing here, Ryan?"

"I'm looking for background on the Cathy Wilet case," said Ryan casually.

"Who?" Bronfman was a blank.

"Cathy Wilet, the intern, the one who went missing," said Ryan.

Bronfman frowned and thought back in time. "Oh yes. I don't want to appear curious, but don't you have enough troubles with a missing woman down in Washington?"

"I think there is a connection."

Bronfman drew back incredulously, wondering whether Ryan McNeil had lost some sanity in the last five years.

"A connection between the girl missing in Washington, the one the governor says you are a suspect in, and the Wilet girl that was missing here, almost eight years ago?"

Ryan could tell from Bronfman's face that his story sounded absurd. He stood up and was about to move on when he paused and reluctantly asked for a favor. "Tom, could you check around into who she worked with back then?"

"You mean Cathy Wilet?"

"If you could, Tom, and one more thing. Could you check to see if there are any employment records for Leslie Warren in New York state government?"

"Who?"

It was obvious that Bronfman did not know the particular name associated with Ryan's current dilemma. Ryan wrote the name on a piece of paper and passed it to Bronfman.

To Ryan's surprise, Bronfman nodded yes. "I'll dig around and meet you at Western Tavern at five thirty. I've got to get going. Remember, five thirty."

Bronfman stood up to leave.

"Tom, do you have a card, a business card?"

Bronfman nodded and fumbled through his wallet, handing Ryan a blue-and-gold embossed card with the seal of New York. Ryan looked at the card: "Tom Bronfman, Special Assistant to the Assembly Speaker." Bronfman shook Ryan's hand and left.

"Thanks." Ryan wondered if his old colleague was sincere. He replaced the microfilm of the newspapers and asked the reference librarian for the location of House Operations.

"Tower Two, twenty-second floor."

Ryan left the library and walked through the nearly empty labyrinth of the capitol. He headed down a chiseled stone stairwell encased with ornate carvings and cryptic depictions and passed through an underground tunnel into the subterranean part of the Empire State Plaza. State workers milled about, dallying on errands. He strode preoccupied through the crowds. He had begun to walk toward the elevator for Tower Two when he noticed the capitol police station. He then changed direction and headed for the door of the police station. He hesitated for a moment before he pulled it open.

The anteroom was exactly as he remembered it: nothing had changed, the paint was still peeling, and the same picture of the governor still hung, now slightly yellowed. Ryan was about to talk to the desk sergeant when he looked over to the bulletin board and noticed the standard poster of Cathy Wilet he had seen years ago. A major difference was apparent in that this one was emblazoned with the words "Still Missing." Before the officer had time to inquire as to his business, Ryan turned and exited with a "never mind." He walked across the mall to an elevator inside Tower Two.

At the twenty-second floor, Ryan pulled open a glass door inscribed "Assembly House Operations." The entry to the complex of offices was secured. A receptionist was stationed there to ask people for identification and the nature of their business.

"Can I help you?" said a smiling female clerk in her fifties.

"Yes, I would like to see the House Operations materials worked on by a former intern named Cathy Wilet." Ryan knew he would be stymied in the request, and he was beginning to improvise.

"Press inquiries go to the Speaker's office," said the clerk.

"No, I'm with the Speaker," said Ryan.

"The Speaker?" asked the clerk while trying to place Ryan's face. "You are?"

"Tom Bronfman," said Ryan as he handed the clerk the card.

The clerk read the card, looking befuddled. "I'm sorry, Mr. Bronfman, I've been here a short time." She started to go into the back, then paused to reach for a phone. Ryan tapped impatiently on the reception desk.

"Mr. Harding, this is Emily. Mr. Bronfman is at the front desk looking for a House Operations file. OK. Yes."

The clerk smiled at Ryan, seemingly reassured, and then hung up the phone. "I'll be right back, Mr. Bronfman."

Ryan paced the reception area and impatiently waited. The clerk appeared with a smile and a manila folder that looked to Ryan to be virtually empty. "Here is Ms. Wilet's work folder."

Ryan sat down and opened the folder. There was a written memo from the Office of the Governor Ombudsman Division, which read that Wilet was assigned to the division. The only other piece of paper was a huge red index card marked "Missing: Fire Recovery." Ryan sat for several minutes trying to decipher the card's meaning. *Missing. Is that a reference to Wilet or the file?* Ryan pondered the point. He doubted whether the bumbling clerk would be able to clarify the mystery. He stood up to return the folder.

"Emily, what does this card mean?"

Emily looked at the card and to Ryan's surprise answered quickly. "It's a fire card."

"Wilet was fired?"

"No, no," said Emily. "The record was never found; it was destroyed in the fire. There was a fire about eight years ago, and many of the records were destroyed. The DA's office and the assembly Speaker asked us to identify missing records with these cards."

Ryan's mind reeled like a video in reverse. He began to remember that frenzied jog the week that Caroline left him. He had run through the park and stopped, awed, before the scarlet flame that hung from Tower Two. He had never connected the inferno to Wilet, but now there seemed a relation in timing that could be reasonably inferred. Ryan could almost feel the sensation of a pulse beating on his brain.

CHAPTER 28

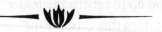

“Caroline, Caroline. It's good to see you,” said Somatos as he stood up and embraced her.

“Nick, you look great,” responded Caroline sweetly. “It's been too long.”

Somatos eyed the effect of age on Caroline. She was still beautiful in a summer dress, but her youthful spring softness had faded. He could see the hard edges of life prematurely etching creases into her face and around her eyes, now concealed with makeup and mascara.

He motioned for her to sit next to him in the enclosed booth at the Apollo Restaurant. The restaurant was popular with elegantly tailored lobbyists and their clients. The front part of the restaurant contained richly upholstered seats and was bathed in discreet, brassy light. In the middle of the interior was a gilded sphere fountain, with jets of waters rushing over rocks and into a perimeter pool of aquatic blue tiles. Aesthetically, the fountain was designed to evoke the ambiance of the Mediterranean Sea. Functionally, the decibel level of the cascading waters concealed the conversations of the surrounding patrons for whom privacy in conversation was paramount. For those more interested in not being seen, there was the rear of the restaurant, beyond the fountain. Here they sat secluded, discreetly hidden from view, swathed in shadow, illuminated only by the light emitting from the centered candle on the table.

"I'm glad you called, Nick," said Caroline as she took his hand.

"How is our boy doing?" inquired Somatos.

"He's up in Albany, tracking down Cathy Wilet leads."

"I hope the two you of you shared some blissful moments at least," said Somatos as he licked his lips and continued to hold her hand.

"Nick, you know that any moment alone with me is blissful," said Caroline with a smile of pure seduction.

"Yes. That is certainly true." Somatos pulled his hand back and waved for a waiter. He then ordered a bottle of expensive wine and began to study the menu.

"Nick, he's asking about the transcript time," said Caroline sheepishly.

Somatos looked up from the menu. "What. What did you say?"

Caroline leaned forward and lowered her voice. "Ryan is in Albany checking on the adjournment time of the death penalty debate the night Wilet disappeared. I'm concerned."

Somatos's eyes settled low, below Caroline's neck.

"Caroline, sweet Caroline," Somatos said with his wolfish grin. "Try some of the olive spread appetizer." Caroline could not be distracted by the food.

"Look, Caroline. Ryan has got enough problems with this Leslie Warren abduction case. An assembly adjournment time from seven years ago is irrelevant."

Caroline reached her hand out to his shoulder to focus his attention and to look directly into his furrowed brown eyes. "Nick. Are you sure that it is irrelevant? Are you being honest with me?"

"Of course I'm being honest," said Somatos sarcastically as he puffed himself up in his seat. "Why, Caroline, I am a United States congressman, and I can tell you categorically that the assembly adjournment time of the death penalty debate has nothing to do with Cathy Wilet's disappearance in Albany, which has nothing to do with this Leslie Warren case, which I am sure has nothing to do with Ryan McNeil. These missing women and politics are unrelated, so can we decide what to order here."

"Everything is a coincidence, right, Nick?" said Caroline, seeking reassurance.

"Politics requires a degree of paranoia," said Somatos sagely. "We have enemies everywhere. God knows I have enemies. So not everything is a coincidence, but the transcript change was something that is unrelated."

The waiter arrived and presented the wine to Somatos, who gestured acceptance with a wave of his hand. Rosy wine splashed with a flourish into two large fluted glasses. Somatos took a sip and expressed his pleasure. He then looked over at Caroline, who stared morosely at her glass.

"Drink up, my dear. It'll smooth the rough edges. I need a favor."

"I thought my coming here was a favor."

Somatos smiled. "I need another favor. I need you to pay a visit to Seth Tantalus's house and get to know him. Here is the address." He passed her a piece of paper with the information neatly typed out.

"You know him, don't you? Congressman Green's chief of staff," asked Somatos as he bit into a bread roll. Caroline shook her head negatively.

"Size him up, so to speak," said Somatos with a smirk at his own unintended innuendo.

Caroline grimaced distastefully. "Are you my pimp now?"

"Don't belittle yourself. You would be helping Ryan. This missing girl in Virginia, I don't know why he would be involved in that. So see what you could find out, OK?"

"Who am I helping, Nick? Ryan or you?" asked Caroline,

lingering on the subject of her distress. "What about the $770,000 check to Leslie Warren?"

"You have an unhealthy preoccupation with money, Caroline." Somatos paused and seemed stuck in thought. "Yes, somebody was paying her off. But I've got nothing to do with that."

Caroline looked at Somatos quizzically. "I didn't say that you had anything to do with the $770,000. I was just asking about the origin of that money."

"It's coincidence. You know the problem with corruption in New York, Caroline." Somatos leaned in whispering, as if he were confiding a hushed secret with her. "It's an orgy; every dirty deed is incestuously intertwined. Everybody's got some action going on. And you tape some corrupt rich bastard's calls and it leads to another corrupt rich bastard. How ironic given that only the poor go to jail."

"You don't have to make a speech for my benefit, Nick."

"No, I suppose not. That's one thing I don't have to do for your benefit, right, Caroline?" said Somatos with a wink and a smirk.

The waiter arrived dutifully with menu pad in hand. Somatos breathed a sigh and then, with a sly smile and wolf's ravenous hunger, asked the waiter to recite the specials.

CHAPTER 29

He needed to walk in the open air to think things clearly through. He was faced with multiple strands of information, none of which seemed to integrate coherently. Ryan exited the dim air-conditioned underground of the capitol complex and strode out into the effulgence of the open plaza. He was blinded by sunlight. Around him now was the grandiose design of a prior governor: a modern plaza framed by four sleek office towers, sheathed in steel and glass, an architecturally awkward civic theater shaped like a tilted egg, and, at the far end, a five-story uninspiring library archive.

Across the vista of the plaza, the day's heat was blown in palpable waves, like the flare from a blast furnace, making a desert of this governmental domain. As he strolled beside a hundred-yard-long rectangular pool of reflecting water, Ryan was quickly soaked with perspiration. Except for Ryan, the plaza was unoccupied. He looked up at the glass office tower called Tower Two, now reflecting the dense flame of the sun. The nighttime fire in Tower Two seven years ago, he thought, seemed to be an act of cover-up, an intentional destruction of evidence. If this were the case, it could mean that

Wilet might have been abducted or killed to conceal something political or criminal. On the other hand, the fire could have been set to conceal the tracks of whoever killed her. He could have dismissed the fire altogether as coincidental, but he had the keen, intuitive feeling that it tied together.

The obvious part of the puzzle that he could not fit in his mind, jutted grotesquely out, and made a mockery of this line of reasoning was of course Leslie Warren and her bloody clothes. Again, he could rationalize two plausible explanations. One relatively benign explanation was that Warren's abductor had decided to frame Ryan without knowing the Wilet connection. The more devious and sinister explanation was that Wilet's abductor had seen Ryan talk to Wilet right before he had taken her and now, having committed the Warren abduction, thought Ryan to be an obvious suspect to mislead the police.

The most unfortunate aspect, Ryan recognized, was that these theories were all entirely products of his speculative mind, without any firm grounding in evidence. The police would be no more than amused, and none of this could, in any way, exculpate him as a suspect in both cases. The faster his thoughts turned, the more he felt propelled to walk. He had become oblivious to the heat and the sweat that trickled down under his shirt. He began to walk fervently away from the plaza toward Washington Park.

He would not have noticed the spot had it not been for the little girl running toward him. To his relief, he saw an attentive mother following closely. Suddenly, he had a somber realization of his loss, prompted by the fact that he was standing at the corner where he saw Cathy Wilet vanish. Here, the pavement was coated, almost ceremoniously, with pink, yellow, and white petals, shed like pastel tears from the flowering trees around him.

Like the rest of Albany, the corner seemed immutable, forever caught in a moment of time that did not change, except for the passing of seasons. He stared at the corner and visualized Cathy

Wilet. He remembered the limousine. Ryan knew now the car was not driven by a pervert seeking random victims. Whoever abducted Wilet had to be a member of the legislature and was responsible for altering the transcript time to provide an irrefutable alibi.

For months after the incident, he solaced himself with the notion that Assemblyman Caluzzi could have been responsible. Caluzzi, after all, had tried to rape and murder his intern. But Caluzzi was a Republican, and the Democrats controlled the assembly. He could never have gotten the transcript adjournment time altered. Besides, Caluzzi had been dead for seven years. Leslie Warren's disappearance and her mysterious $770, 000 payment meant the abductor of Cathy Wilet was still alive, he thought. The fire, the adjournment time change, the abduction, and the $770,000—it all somehow tied together.

CHAPTER 30

Tom Bronfman entered the pub. A small after-work crowd had merrily coalesced at the front, and Bronfman picked his way through them to discover Ryan sitting farther back in a booth with a bottle of beer in front of him. Ryan's eyes were pensively focused on the bottle, as if the object itself presented some puzzle that required a fixation of thought. Consequently, he did not notice Bronfman until his looming presence stood at the edge of the table.

"Are you all right?" inquired Bronfman with serious solicitude.

"Tom, I'm sorry. Sit down; I was just lost in thought," responded Ryan with a self-deprecating chuckle.

Bronfman removed his suit jacket and slid into the seat across from Ryan. He noticed a large stack of bundled papers on the table. "What's that?" Bronfman benignly inquired.

"It's a transcript of the death penalty debate the night Cathy Wilet disappeared."

A young waitress came to the table and with a pronounced Irish accent asked Bronfman what he wanted to order. Bronfman ordered a beer for himself and another for Ryan.

"You know, Ryan, I think your obsession with the Wilet case is unhealthy given your present troubles."

"You're not the only person to think that," responded Ryan dryly.

"You know, most people wrote this Cathy Wilet thing off when it happened, but I always suspected that there was more to it than a missing girl."

Bronfman's remark caught Ryan as he was gulping down the beer. For a moment Ryan peered at him, weighing his motives and innuendo.

"What made you think that, Tom?"

Bronfman paused but was now ready to offer Ryan his knowledge.

"At the same time that Wilet disappeared, there was an investigation going on by the Albany DA into the governor's ombudsman office. Most people don't remember it, but the governor was pretty concerned, as I understand it. Wilet, even as an intern, had access to the governor's files that documented the hiring and illegal use of state workers for political purposes. After Wilet disappeared, the investigation floundered, went nowhere."

"The fire also may have impeded the inquiry," interjected Ryan.

"Yes, of course, the fire," said Bronfman as he peered circumspectly around.

"You think it was arson?" asked Ryan with fervent curiosity.

"I know it was arson," said Bronfman gravely, in a whisper, "and I also think I know who set it."

As if on cue, the music of the jukebox came on, having been triggered by several quarters of a patron. The percussion throbbed from a speaker attached to the ceiling several feet away.

"Who do you think set it, Tom?"

"Seth Tantalus," answered Bronfman, who then seemed to wash down his seemingly definitive answer with a long gulp of beer.

"Why do you think it was Seth Tantalus?"

Bronfman sighed. Enough years had passed and only now,

Bronfman felt he could unburden himself without constraint upon his career.

"It's like this, Ryan. I did tell the fire investigators that I saw Tantalus that night. I was working late, really late. You remember what House Operations was like with the hours we put in. What I didn't tell them was that Tantalus that night told me not to hang around much longer. At first I laughed at him because he had no real rank to suggest that I go home, but then I remember the look on his face and I felt that it . . ." Bronfman paused with a deep look of confession. "I felt that it was a threat and if I stayed something would happen and I needed to leave."

"I don't understand, Tom. If you told the investigators that you saw Tantalus, they must have questioned him. Checked video surveillance, whatever. Why didn't you tell them the full story that you felt it was a threat to you to stay?"

"Ryan, it was just an inference on my part. I was starting my career in the legislature. I didn't want to make a false accusation against the majority leader's key staffer. I did tell them I saw Tantalus. I just never told them that he basically seemed to know that the building would burn that night. Ryan, you understand about wanting to be circumspect."

Ryan thought back to his own interaction with the police following the Cathy Wilet abduction. He had never even provided his real name to the officer out of fear of damaging his career. He wondered in retrospect if he had been as candid and convincing as he should have been in conveying his story to the police.

"To be honest with you, Ryan, I don't know anything about Tantalus only to the extent that I believe he set the fire in Tower Two."

Ryan grimaced. "Well, presumably on the direction of someone. I mean, I don't think that is something you do on your own initiative. He was working for Green at the time."

"I believe so," said Bronfman. "You don't think that Tantalus was involved with the Cathy Wilet abduction, do you? I mean, it is one thing to set a fire in an empty building late at night. It is a bit of a jump to murder a young woman. I mean, he did warn me not to stay. He may have been an arsonist, but murderer doesn't fit."

Ryan did not see the gulf between arson and murder as being as formidable as Bronfman was suggesting. He could not see Green committing murder or abduction; it was much easier to visualize the overpowering, hyperkinetic Tantalus losing control and committing violence.

"The only thing I know, Tom, is that this all somehow ties together."

"Oh, I almost forgot," said Bronfman. "I checked on that name you gave me, Leslie Warren, and I found no woman with that name ever employed by the legislature, the executive, or any agency of the state here in Albany."

"Just my luck."

The volume of music and cacophony from the bar crowd had drowned out Ryan's remark. Bronfman leaned forward with his hand to his ear, indicating that he had not heard Ryan's observation. Ryan repeated himself and then, shifting his analysis, moving away from Leslie Warren and back to Cathy Wilet, realized he needed further clarification in an area.

"Tom, why was the governor's office concerned about with the ombudsman inquiry?"

Bronfman's eyebrows elevated slightly and he was about to speak when the waitress brought him his beer. Bronfman smiled at her and then gulped some beer. He considered for a moment whether to share what he knew.

"Tom? You were about to say?"

Bronfman grimaced, looked round the bar, and proceeded "The DA was investigating whether the governor was using his political appointee power for personal gain. You see, the governor was establishing in every county a so-called ombudsman that reported directly to the governor." As Bronfman spoke, he began to nervously peel off the label of his beer bottle.

"These individuals really were not conducting any state government business, but they were on the state government payroll. In many cases they were no-show jobs for the sons and daughters of Democratic county chairmen, political favors."

"Wilet worked reviewing their case files?" inquired Ryan intently.

"Yes, she was an intern in the screening office. She could have seen confidential memos that substantiated the unlawful nature of the jobs and perhaps the governor's direct involvement."

"How could an intern been given that access?"

Bronfman smiled. "Welcome to Albany."

Ryan chuckled and nodded his head in assent. They implicitly knew the very faulty workings of the state government. Ryan could plausibly see how an intern could be handed confidential files, perhaps even intentionally since the intern would be presumed to be naive enough to trust with the content and implications of the files.

For several minutes Ryan sat quietly, contemplating Bronfman's information as he finished his beer. Recognizing the import of his information, Bronfman refrained from further discussion, finishing his beer as well. There was, however, one last piece of information that Ryan wanted his opinion on.

"Can you think of a reason why the governor would veto a bill and then years later sign it into law?"

Bronfman rubbed his beard thoughtfully. "Well, there might have been some overriding political consideration that dictated a veto—say it was a Republican bill and he wanted a Democrat to receive credit, or it may have been an ego thing. You know how the governor is."

"Have you ever seen a case like that?"

"No. Not verbatim. The governor must have been doing someone a big favor."

"Theoretically, imagine a piece of legislation with substantial financial ramifications for one particular company," said Ryan. "The governor vetoes it even though it passes the legislature overwhelmingly."

Bronfman nodded in understanding.

"However, if one knew that the veto was a ruse, a simple delay tactic," posited Ryan with a glimmer of wily admiration, "then conceivably couldn't a legislator take personal financial advantage by investing in the very company he knows will benefit when the legislation is ultimately signed into law, a sort of windfall benefit?"

"That is an interesting concept. It would have to be some obscure provision, though; otherwise the press would have a field day and uncover the apparent inconsistency. You know," Bronfman further mulled, "the interesting aspect to what you're suggesting, and I don't know the context, is that it is certainly unethical, but I don't think it is illegal. Criminal intent on the part of the governor, if he did not receive any personal financial benefit, would be virtually impossible to prove. Do you want to be more specific?"

"Not really. Sorry," stated Ryan as he glanced at his watch. "I need to catch a plane back to DC. You've been helpful."

Ryan began to gather his papers. As he stood up, Bronfman offered his hand.

"I hope things work out for you."

They began to cut their way through the crowd to the front door.

"It's too bad you don't know whether she dated Tantalus," said Bronfman to the distracted Ryan.

Ryan looked at Bronfman quizzically. "What?"

"That would fit in your puzzle if you could determine if Tantalus dated Wilet."

Ryan stood still in the bar and considered this line of reasoning. "Except for one thing, Tom: I don't think Tantalus is a serial killer. Even if he is somehow connected with Cathy Wilet, I'm still left with Leslie Warren and her bloody clothes."

Together they left the air-conditioned commotion of the bar.

The street outside was warm and serene. Birds were flapping about, picking at the food scraps from the tavern's garbage.

"Do you need a lift to the airport?" Bronfman offered.

Ryan could see an empty cab idling nearby. "No, thanks again. Take care, Tom."

Ryan opened the door to the cab and was seating himself when he heard Bronfman yelling something. Ryan stuck his head out the window. "What?"

"Good luck finding the connection between Wilet and Warren. Both names do end in W."

Ryan smiled blankly. "Sure. Thanks."

"Where to, sir?" the cabbie asked.

"Airport," stated Ryan as the cab quickly pulled away from the curb.

The cab followed a different route than the one that Ryan had entered Albany. Heading up Western Avenue, Ryan watched the suburban streets yield to the expansively manicured lawn of the State University of New York. The cab moved at bullet speed past the four-story dormitories and then past the huge structure of the central campus building. As the cab began to turn onto the highway, Ryan had an inspiration. "Change direction and head back to the SUNY campus."

The cab driver could not clearly hear Ryan over the blast of his air conditioner. Ryan reiterated his request and checked his watch. He would make a later flight.

As he sat in the university library, his first reaction was shock. For several moments he could not correspond his memory of Cathy Wilet with the yearbook photo now spread on the broad graffiti-etched table before him. Aside from his brief personal encounter, his mind was indelibly ingrained with her memory exclusively in the form of the photo in her missing poster. Indeed, it was that photo that was used ubiquitously in every poster, news story, and television coverage of the case that he had ever seen.

Now he had before him a photo that presented her in a dramatically different light. He had to mentally readjust his lines of perspective. Here she was smiling, in almost Mona Lisa fashion, quite different from the pouty, almost pensive image that was used in the posters. After the initial shock of this new image ingrained on him, he began to reconcile it with his memory. *This is the girl I saw*, he again thought confidently. He curiously thumbed the yearbook to the "T" section but found no Seth Tantalus. He turned the book to the "W" section, but there was no Leslie Warren. The "W" connection that Bronfman had suggested didn't pan out. Ryan shut the book with a loud crack and brought it back to the reference assistant.

"Can I purchase the yearbook?"

His flight from Albany was at dusk. It was in moments of plane flight that he felt profoundly alone. His feeling of solitude seemed to be more poignant and intensified by flights that occurred at night. He attributed this disconcerting sensation to that morose and harried night flight from college to return home following the death of his parents. A car accident had claimed them, and Ryan, hurled back into loss, realized somberly on the fight that he was alone, catapulted into destiny without the comfort or support of a mother or father.

From the portal of his plane window, he followed the slipping earth below and then watched the arc of flight give a short reprieve to a submerging filament of sun. Soon, however, the orange glow sank and in its wake, a wispy fan of iridescence painted the sky and was itself gradually dissolved into darkness.

The cabin to the plane was nearly empty, devoid of distractions, and Ryan's mind focused on his recent tribulations. A mental picture of Jessica laughing and rushing into his arms brought a sentimental and lachrymose quiver to his being. With some ambivalence, he also missed the orderly, reassuring comfort of his wife sleeping beside him. This vaporous trail of thought enervated his consciousness so that under the monotonous roar of engines and the constrained courtesies of flight, he was lulled to sleep.

By the time he awoke, the blackness outside his window had transformed into an opaque surface that reflected his image back on him. He reached upward and turned off his passenger light. The altitude of flight had shifted slightly into a declination, and the cabin seemed to now possess an inhospitable and discomforting chill. He began to yearn for the raw sexual warmth of Caroline to certify and embrace his existence. How fortuitous had been her arrival at this stage in his life, he thought; maybe, her presence was itself a manifestation of some providence that was safely guiding his destiny.

Following three chimes, the pilot announced that the plane would be landing shortly. Looking out, he could see the incandescent network constituting the capital and its surrounding metropolis majestically floating below. Ryan realized his palms were prickly with a suppressed sense of what he could best determine to be a sudden rush of anxiety or maybe even claustrophobic panic. He was subsumed suddenly with desperation to be back on the ground and out of the cold sea of darkness that extends from familiar earth out into the unfathomable universe.

CHAPTER 31

66"How was your trip?" asked Caroline while she stretched languorously on the bed beneath covers. Ryan paused in visible appreciation of her. She clicked off the television and turned on her side. For Ryan, there was something intensely gratifying in arriving back to her. As far as he could discern, she was undressed, awaiting him and eagerly attuned to his current desires.

"It went very well," remarked Ryan as he bent down to kiss her and to drink from his well of passion. "I'm going to take a quick shower," he said as he quickly undressed and entered the bathroom.

While the stream of hot water fogged the bathroom and cleansed the foulness of the summer heat from Ryan, Caroline furtively thumbed through the papers that he had brought back from Albany. By the time Ryan emerged, with a towel wrapped around his waist, Caroline had returned to the bed. Their lovemaking had an erotic intensity, an atavistic ferocity that forced sounds from Caroline that Ryan had not heard from her before. She found herself losing her grip on her usually detached and calculated sexual being. Their lovemaking continued sporadically throughout the night so that by morning their intertwined bodies were limp and weak and their appetites ravenously whetted.

"You were a complete animal," Caroline rasped, "and I loved every minute of it. Let's order breakfast in."

Ryan nodded in hungry concurrence and dialed for hotel room service. They both began to dress to a modicum of decency in order to allow room service entry.

"I think it's going to rain today," said Caroline almost abjectly as she glanced at the window, wrapping herself momentarily behind the sheath of curtains. The gray light of the day fluttered in the room as the curtains fell back into place.

As Caroline turned her back to Ryan to put on one of his shirts, Ryan for the first time noticed several jagged scars on her arm and shoulder. He could not understand how he had not noticed this before. The immediate thought was to inquire about it, but discreetly he opted to wait for another time. He pulled on shorts and a T-shirt. Ryan looked at Caroline, a long, deliberative look that made Caroline self-consciously smile.

"What is it?" she asked.

"I love you; you know that," said Ryan.

"You've just had too little sleep and too much good sex," she said with a smile that twitched slightly. She wanted to regard his statement as impetuous.

"No, I mean it, Caroline. I've always loved you," said Ryan again with more confidence.

Caroline did not know how to respond. He had told her when they were living together seven years ago that he loved her, but that was in the past, another life for her.

There was a knock on the door, and both Caroline and to a certain extent Ryan were thankful for the interruption.

An elaborate breakfast was wheeled in, and they pulled chairs over to the serving table. With voracious focus they began to feast on eggs, bacon, sausage, pancakes, coffee, and croissants. Neither spoke until a substantial portion of the food was consumed and their hunger satiated. It was while Caroline was dreamily sipping coffee and nibbling on a croissant that Ryan began to recount what he had learned in Albany.

"I believe the fire was deliberately set," stated Ryan nonchalantly.

"You're obsessed," countered Caroline. "You're off on an absurd tangent." She glowered at Ryan across a table littered with the remains of their breakfast.

"You're trying to implicate the governor of New York, a nationally renowned politician, when a missing girl's bloody clothes were found with your car, along with a set of handcuffs I might add. Your story is not credible. Nobody will believe you," she said with red-faced finality.

Ryan was startled by this harangue, and, with baiting purpose, he asked, "Do you believe me?"

"I don't know what to believe," answered Caroline with obvious frustration.

Ryan stood up, agitated, and began to pace the room. He then turned to Caroline and expounded fluently on his theory, constructing the logic of what he painfully could feel had the appearance of a far-fetched tale.

"Let's assume that Cathy Wilet was going to the Albany DA to reveal information that would be damaging to the governor. Perhaps Assemblyman Green or his aide Seth Tantalus decided to approach her, talk her out of going to the DA. Maybe she resists. Maybe there is a violent confrontation and as a result she is killed. In order to provide an irrefutable alibi, the assembly adjournment time is altered. Tantalus then sets a fire to conveniently destroy her records and to obliterate any record of the killer and the governor's malfeasance. In return, the governor agrees to perform a favor for Green. Specifically, he vetoes Somatos's health care bill to allow Green and Tantalus time to profit by investing in Dorus Genetic

Corporation. All they needed to do was cash out when the bill was finally signed."

Ryan removed a stack of papers from a manila envelope and spread them on the bed.

"Look, here is the Somatos health bill that the governor vetoed."

Caroline nodded in dumbfounded agreement.

"Now here is the bill the governor eventually signed. The legislation is identical except for this one provision that exempted a certain large genetic laboratory from the requirements. I checked the financial disclosure forms in Albany. Both Green and Tantalus had bought stock in the one company that profited from the exemption after Somatos's bill was vetoed. The stock went up tenfold. They both made millions. Green had already cut the deal with the governor to exempt that company."

Caroline interrupted Ryan's monologue. "All right, Ryan. For the sake of argument, let's assume you're correct." Caroline was smiling in a way that Ryan interpreted as overt indulgence. "How does all this relate to Leslie Warren's bloody clothes being found by your car? So what if she got a check for $770,000 from Albany."

"Caroline, I'm sure that check came from Green or Tantalus. If either of them had driven the dark sedan that took Wilet the night she vanished, they most likely saw me talking to her. Green is elected to Congress several weeks before Warren disappears . . ."

Ryan paused blankly. The crystal of his thought melted. He was visibly groping for the inexplicable truth of the matter.

"You see, Ryan, your motive doesn't make sense. There is no connection between Leslie Warren and Cathy Wilet except for you," stated Caroline with exasperation. "Unless you're insinuating that either Congressman Green or Tantalus are serial killers, which is not congruent with the motive you're proposing, there is no motive for either of them for abducting or killing Warren. No motive at all."

"Unless it was to frame me," he tentatively postulated.

"Oh, come on, Ryan. Just because Tantalus made a ton of money off the governor's veto of Somatos's bill. There is no plausible connection between Warren and Tantalus."

Ryan was thwarted. "Look, I see your point. But I am certain of one thing. The transcript time was changed. And I believe the reason it was changed was to provide an alibi for someone at the legislature."

Caroline's lips tightened, her eyes misted, and she shook her head in disagreement.

Ryan knelt down in front of her to argue his case. "Just think of it. A murder concealed by a debate on the death penalty. The audacity of it. The hypocrisy in it. How could I see the abductor if he was a legislator who was at the session and the session ended after I saw her getting into the limousine? That was the reason for the time change. We need to check the transcript to see if the adjournment time was altered. That will settle the matter for me."

"How are you going to figure out the adjournment time from the transcript if it has been altered?"

"By reading it out loud and timing it. You and I could take turns reading it."

Caroline grimaced. "You're kidding, right?"

"No. We just need to time the death penalty debate," said Ryan flatly.

"That's absurd. We don't know how fast the legislators were speaking," stated Caroline.

"All New York legislators talk fast."

"This is a complete waste of time, Ryan. I'm not doing it," said Caroline as she crossed her arms obstinately in the chair and pouted. He came close to her.

"Caroline, come on; it will be fun," he coaxed softly.

"I'm not doing it."

"Why?" asked Ryan, annoyed.

Caroline stood up. Her face filled with tears. She shook her head no, turned from Ryan, and looked down at the floor. "I don't want you to be upset with me."

"What is it?" asked Ryan, acutely curious now.

"The adjournment time was altered by the Speaker. They did adjourn before seven thirty that night." She avoided eye contact with Ryan.

Ryan was bewildered by her assertion.

"Caroline, how do you know that?" Ryan asked as he sensed an imminent confession of betrayal.

For a moment she did not dare to utter the truth. She feared the truth would pull her in an uncomfortable direction. After some hesitation, she said, "Because I had the time changed by Speaker Mariano."

Ryan could not intelligently respond to her statement. His mind was racing like a loop of film spun wildly from a reel.

"Mariano changed the time because I asked him to," reiterated Caroline. "You never said anything to me in Albany about the adjournment time and Wilet's disappearance. I swear."

"I thought I did," mumbled Ryan, confused, "but why did you ask Mariano to change the transcript time?"

The answer to that question was overtly painful for Caroline. "Because Somatos asked me to."

"I don't understand why Somatos would ask you to do such a thing. Why would . . ." Ryan's voice trailed off.

"I don't know why; he just did."

"This doesn't make any sense, Caroline," said Ryan, baffled. "Why would Speaker Mariano change the time for you?"

There was no immediate response to the question. Ryan was shocked to see tears, and her lips were pouting pitifully. She stood up and walked away from him, dressed only in his shirt.

"You slept with Speaker Mariano?" asked Ryan incredulously.

"No," she said indignantly, "it was just oral sex."

Ryan laughed mockingly and his voice rose in anger. "You're fucking unbelievable, and were you sleeping with Somatos too?"

"Only before I met you."

"Good God," exclaimed Ryan, aghast. "You're a whore. Who didn't you sleep with or give a blow job to?"

The remark incensed Caroline; she did not expect such a brutal condemnation of her conduct from Ryan. "You knew about me when we got together. You used to take vicarious delight in prying into my sexual history. You should know that Mariano's blow job wasn't personal; it was just politics."

"Politics? I guess that makes it all right? Now if you had said business I would know what you are," taunted Ryan.

"How dare you." Caroline moved to strike him, but then, in restraint of this physical urge, she looked around the room for her belongings to gather.

"You rapacious cunt," he said harshly. "What about our sex life, Caroline? What column does that fall under?"

"It falls, Ryan, under the category of *over*," she screamed back at him. She again moved toward Ryan to crack him across the face, but he blocked her. He grabbed her strongly, catching her thin wrist as it flailed through the air to strike him. He held her wrist tightly as she twisted it, feeling its mad pulse, looking directly into the angry sea of her blue eyes. The anger in him subsided. He feared the argument had gone too far. Breathing hard, she glared at him, and then she too gathered her composure. He released her, with the ambivalence of hating her at that moment and yet still wanting to hold her in his arms.

"I'll just get my stuff together and leave right now."

Ryan collapsed in a chair and watched as Caroline frantically pulled her clothes and belongings together and packed them into a suitcase. He contemplated grabbing her and throwing her back on the bed with a different psychological motivation. Instead, he resisted that confused urge and watched silently as she dressed.

Caroline eyes were no longer brimming, and Ryan wondered how much of her display was pure histrionics. She had expected Ryan to intervene before she left his room, but with no effort on his part, it was now a matter of pride for her to depart. The moment Caroline left and the door to his room shut, Ryan cracked his fist hard against the wall.

CHAPTER 32

Ryan strode rapidly through the high-ceilinged historic halls of the Longworth House Office Building. Propelled by Caroline's revelations of betrayal and her disclosures regarding Somatos's actions, he moved with an angry swagger and a surge of adrenaline pumping in his system. As he turned into Somatos's office, he brushed against and sent tottering a New York State flag officiously planted beside the front door entrance.

A startled receptionist looked up. "Mr. McNeil. We didn't know you were coming in today."

"Is he in?" inquired Ryan without pausing for a response. He rapidly passed through a row of startled aides and office visitors. He opened the door to Somatos's inner office without the deference of a knock. Somatos was not there; the office was empty.

"Ryan, he is not in," stated an aide to the congressman.

Ryan turned angrily on his heels. "Message him. Page him now."

"We've been pinging him for the past hour. He hasn't called in yet."

Ryan glowered at the collection of office staff, his colleagues, who were watching him with a kind of apprehensive look.

"Ryan, is everything all right?" one of them asked.

"Have him call me ASAP," ordered Ryan as he beat a hasty retreat from the office.

Ryan depressed the accelerator of his rented car as it cruised the highway toward Virginia. It was late morning now, and rush hour traffic had dissipated. A few heavy drops of rain pelted the windshield. Ryan drove with mindless abandon, weaving in and out of lanes, but with no particular sense of destination. The exit to his former home beckoned. Ryan took the turnoff after hesitating considerably, almost to the point that the exit had passed.

Ryan parked the car directly across the street from his former home. He turned off the ignition. He sat solemnly in his car with a bystander perspective on his former life. Across the street was his lawn, his front door, his living room. Inside was his wife, his stepdaughter, shared memories. A transparent but impervious perimeter now hemmed him out.

Charcoal-colored clouds loomed massively in midair; a thunderstorm was evolving. He lowered his car window and felt the hot, moist breath of summer air, compressed by the impending storm. A warm wind stirred the suburban landscape, and the nearby tall trees rippled in green, leafy waves. Still no rain fell; only the threat of rain quivered in the air.

Unexpectedly, Ryan noticed a car parked in the driveway that he did not recognize. He fixed his sight on the car and then noticed a man moving across the front lawn. He was balding, stout, enormously built, with the physical swagger of a quarterback, though past his prime. The first notion to enter Ryan's mind was that the man was a police officer. He was dressed in a polo shirt and jeans.

Ryan watched the man with a mixture of apprehension and annoyance. Jessica suddenly emerged from the shadows. Her little figure moved rapidly across the lawn toward the man, who strutted toward her. He then peremptorily grabbed her by the hand, leading her to the car. Annie was not in sight, and the scene seemed strange to Ryan. The car did not look like a police car. Ryan discerned a certain gruffness in the man's movements. He then saw Jessica forcibly flinch and resist entering the car. The man appeared to coax her by bending down, then taking her hand again while she appeared to flinch. Something was not right here, Ryan thought. He opened his car door and began to jog over to the scene.

As soon as the man saw Ryan approaching, a complexion of sanguine rage suffused his face. He appeared to recognize Ryan. "Come over here, you sick bastard," he yelled at Ryan. The man's two hands belligerently balled into massive fists. Ryan had intended to avoid a physical confrontation, but the man was approaching him now, threateningly.

Within three feet he charged, sending a fist flying in the general direction of Ryan's face. Ryan parried the blow, but then came a quick succession of punches. Ryan hammered with his fist into the man's enormous gut, but a blow struck Ryan down and the salty taste of blood was on his lips from an open gash. The exchange of fists was no more than a minute, but by now they both could hear Annie screaming. She was rushing from the front door and yelling emphatically for both men to stop.

"John, leave him alone. Ryan, stop it."

"What are you doing, Ryan?" Annie glared at him in reproach.

Ryan rose from the grass and steadied himself in a crouching position. Jessica was crying profusely and clutching her mother.

"What am I doing?" gasped Ryan. "Who the hell is he?" he asked as he straightened up and spit a froth of blood onto the trim green grass.

"I'm Jessica's father, you pervert murderer," said John acidly. "You stay the hell away from my daughter."

Ryan looked again at the man who had just attacked him. The man's face was fully contorted in a loathsome expression that Ryan couldn't correspond with the photo he remembered of Annie's former husband suntanned, insouciant, and cavorting in the Caribbean.

"You keep making the same mistakes over and over again," Annie stated with condemnation in her voice.

Ryan looked at Annie and then to her ex-husband. "It appears you have the same problem."

"She told me about you, Ryan. You sick bastard. You took a girl in Albany and now here in DC. The police will nail you. Stay the hell away from my daughter."

Ryan glowered at John and decided to ignore the provocation. He spoke directly to Annie: "I thought she was in danger." As he spoke the words, he couldn't ignore the validity of Annie's condemnation. It was the second time he had acted blindly thinking that Jessica was in danger. Nevertheless, he could not understand how this altruistic and purely paternal impulse could be a basis for a personal indictment of his behavior. The absurdity of it all forced a sigh of humiliation from Ryan. However, the sad, confused face of his stepdaughter elicited a strong pang of guilt. His actions were incomprehensible to her, if not frightening.

"Jessica, I'm sorry. I didn't mean to scare you."

She hid meekly behind Annie. Ryan's apology had no effect on her.

"I'm going," stated Ryan, defeated.

"Don't come back to save us again," said John with sarcastic animosity.

"Ryan, please don't come back," said Annie. "It's hurting Jessica."

Ryan wanted to respond, but instead he turned to walk slowly back to his car.

"I'm glad you were here, John," said Annie. "I think he is dangerous."

John watched Ryan return to the car. "Don't worry. I'll make sure you're protected against that nut."

There was a faint pulse of light in the distance and then the ominous throb of thunder high in the atmosphere. Ryan looked up. The cloud canyons were building directly above him. He had an immediate desire for the rain to come.

As he sat back in the car, he reached for a recently purchased cell phone. He called Somatos's office. The receptionist told him that Somatos had checked in and would call Ryan back at the hotel.

It was on the highway drive back that the rain began to fall. Within minutes, it became a torrential downpour. It reminded him of the night he had slept with Amber at the same hotel and driven home to his fateful rendezvous with the van. Now, he thought, the reel of events was spinning sickeningly in reverse. He looked at his lower lip in the rearview mirror. It was swollen, and a blood smear had formed. More injuries, emotional and physical, to contend with, he thought wearily.

As the rain formed a flood on the highway, the traffic slowed and a multitude of red brake lights illuminated. Traffic soon ceased to move, and Ryan impatiently tapped his steering wheel. He switched on the radio. The bombardment of rain on the roof of the car was a sustained roar. He drove back to the hotel while great gashes of lightning and the resonance of thunder punctuated the ride.

He wanted a valet to park the car, but all available space under the awning was occupied by numerous cars that seemed intent on remaining immobile. Impatient again, he exited his car yards away from shelter so that in a few seconds he was drenched in the deluge. He tossed his car key to the valet, who shrugged his shoulders at Ryan.

Back in his room, he changed from his wet clothes and applied ice in a towel to his lower lip. The drapes and shades had been opened by room service, but the room was dark. Ryan switched on a lamp and looked out the window on a city so darkened by rain that the streetlights were lit but barely visible in the downpour. He checked the message light on the phone, but it was dark. He had expected either Somatos or Caroline to have called.

Ryan picked up the transcript of the death penalty debate that lay on a glass table. Beneath the transcript was the yearbook from the State University of New York. He put down the transcript and began to thumb through the yearbook. He sat down in a chair. He turned again to the page with Cathy Wilet's photo. Then Ryan began thumbing through the photos until he saw one that had the mental impact of a surging electric current.

"Oh my God," he said out loud to no one. "How can this be?"

He was dumbstruck. He stood up with the book still tightly gripped in his hands.

He pulled out his phone and searched the internet for the name "Cindy Ambrose" in New York and then Canton, Pennsylvania The internet search was inconclusive.

He then searched for the SUNY Albany registrar's Office phoned number. He called the number.

"Yes, I want to confirm the past enrollment of a young woman." Ryan now held the first tangible evidence that his theory had been right all along. His next call would be to the Fairfax Police Department to convey his finding and his speculation regarding Seth Tantalus.

CHAPTER 33

Congressman Somatos was on the phone with a reporter when Ryan entered. He noticed immediately that Ryan looked rather soaked and his lip was swollen. He also noticed that Ryan was carrying a manila envelope, mottled from the rain. Somatos motioned for Ryan to sit on the couch while he continued his interview. Ryan did not sit down but looked like a man ready to explode. Somatos, while conducting the call, considered how to deal with his distraught aide.

"I would characterize the governor's position as overzealous," Somatos said to the reporter. "Mr. McNeil is on leave, and I have full confidence that it will be shown that he is the victim of an unfortunate occurrence, or perhaps even a deliberate attempt to implicate him in a crime." He placed his hand over the receiver and said something to Ryan that was inaudible.

Finally, Ryan sat down on the leather couch and impatiently waited for Somatos to finish the call. He nervously tapped the manila envelope on his lap. Across the room, Ryan noted a newly placed photo of Somatos and the governor, a handshake between them and two broad smiles. The room was shrouded in gray light from the window behind Somatos. Rainwater cascaded down the windowpanes.

"Yes. Yes. OK, thank you, Michael," stated Somatos as he concluded the call. He put the receiver down and leaned back in his chair.

"I understand you showed up here earlier a bit agitated. It looks like your lip got you in some trouble," Somatos stated with a wink.

Ryan fingered his cut and smiled lamely at Somatos. "Just a scratch, nothing irreparable. I see you've put up a new photo."

Somatos smirked and looked over to the wall. "No meaning implied. Every congressman needs a photo of the governor." Somatos cleared his throat. "Well, what's up, Ryan? You obviously wanted to speak with me. God, it's dark in here. Hell of a storm."

Ryan had several hours to contemplate his line of attack. He decided to be direct and candid with his mentor. "Caroline told me you had the transcript time changed."

"What transcript?" asked Somatos, feigning ignorance with a sly smile.

"Don't bullshit me, Nick. The death penalty adjournment time the night Wilet disappeared."

"All right. All right. Yes, I did," stated Somatos plainly.

"I told you about the transcript change and the connection to Wilet. Why would you do such a thing?" asked Ryan toughly.

"Do you think I was involved in her abduction? Is that what you think, Ryan, after all these years we've worked together?"

"That change in the transcript adjournment time was an alibi. Whoever needed that change is a murderer. You tell me, Congressman."

"You think I killed Wilet and Warren too?" asked Somatos with a chuckle. "God, it's dark in here; I can barely see you. Flick that couch light on."

"Well?" asked Ryan as he leaned over to the lamp.

"Well, I'll tell you, Ryan. No, I didn't abduct anyone. You think

I kiss babies and old ladies on Sunday and then go out and commit murder and mayhem on Monday? Is that what you think, you ingrate?" Somatos was not smiling now; he appeared dead serious and chagrined.

Ryan pressed on, not intimidated or deterred. "The transcript change?"

Somatos leaned forward in his chair and placed his arms on his desk. His dark eyes peered directly at Ryan. "Yes. Yes. I asked Caroline to use her influence with Speaker Mariano to make the change in adjournment from 7:26 p.m. to 8:12. Yes."

"Why?"

"Because, Ryan, I was performing a political favor. You understand those things."

"A political favor for whom?"

"For Assemblyman Green."

Ryan absorbed the information. He was now confronted with a dual plausible hypothesis.

"Why did Green ask you to change the time?"

"I don't know, nor did I care," snarled Somatos.

"Didn't you think it was a bit odd?"

"No, I didn't. It was no odder than the hundreds of favors I get asked for."

"So you went to Caroline?"

"Caroline had more influence with the Speaker than I. I think you understand how that was possible. I don't want to be indelicate with your feelings, Ryan, but she had, shall we say, influence."

"So let me understand this," Ryan said. "Green asks you for this favor, you don't question why he wanted the adjournment time altered, you ask Caroline, and she gets it done. Well, weren't you suspicious of Green's motive when I told you about the Wilet disappearance and the time difference? You didn't think the two were related?"

"No. No. Green was an elected member of the New York

State Assembly. He is now an elected member of the United States Congress. I am not going to presume he is a murderer."

"Or an accessory to murder? Maybe a jury should determine that fact," stated Ryan pointedly.

"Green has already been tried," stated Somatos as he rose from his chair. "He was tried first by a jury that elected him to his assembly seat, and then he was tried again by constituents that elected him to his congressional seat. He was found by that jury, Ryan, to be of moral character. Qualified to walk these halls and sit in that hallowed chamber. I'm not going to second-guess the judgment of the electorate. If a jury of qualified voters elected him and he is in my political party, I'm going to give him a strong presumption of innocence."

A cannon explosion of thunder jarred them. Startled, Somatos turned toward the window.

Ryan caught his breath. "Obviously there were facts that the electorate were not aware of."

"You think juries are perfect, Ryan. Their full of prejudices and subjective judgments."

"Nick, I think you're missing the point. Politics and justice are two separate things."

"No, Ryan, you're missing the point," stated Somatos hotly. "Do you expect me to believe that Green was involved in the Wilet case or even the Warren case? I don't like the guy. But I cannot make that jump. I like you, Ryan. I trust you. But it would be easier for me to believe that you were involved before I believed Green was involved."

Ryan was visibly stung. "I didn't have a motive."

"What the hell motive would Green have?"

Ryan decided to avoid the bait at this juncture. "Why should I believe your story, Nick?"

Somatos paused. "All right, Ryan. Remember the bill that the governor vetoed?"

"Yes. When we went to Green's office to seek an override."

"Right. Well, why the hell did you think I went to Green? I went to Green precisely because he owed me. He told me that the transcript change was a big deal for him and that he would return the favor, but when I went with you to see him, Green reneged. Why else would I have gone to him?"

Ryan contemplated this defense. There was logic to it. He looked out at the brightening window. A period of silence filled the room. Outside, the deluge of rain ceased, and in the ephemeral manner of summer storms, strong sunlight now abruptly slashed into the room.

"Ryan, the fact is you're obsessed with this Wilet case. You had the ill fortune to have some psycho dump his trail of evidence at your house or your car. There is no connection to Wilet. The police found those clippings in your attic. So what? If you didn't have those damn clippings, there would be no connection to Wilet. This whole thing is in your mind. Maybe you should get some help."

Ryan sat quietly, bemused with Somatos's counsel.

"Ryan, look," said Somatos as he sat down again in a leather chair by the couch where Ryan sat. "I understand your upset about Caroline. Maybe I should have told you about her, but don't go off the deep end on this Wilet-Warren thing. There is no connection."

"What if there was a connection? Would you reconsider your position regarding Green?" asked Ryan.

Somatos scratched his brow. "Yes. Sure. Maybe."

Ryan reached for the manila envelope he had brought with him and opened it. Inside was the SUNY yearbook. Somatos furrowed his brow quizzically. Ryan opened the yearbook to the photo of Cathy Wilet and passed it to Somatos.

Somatos looked at the photo for a minute, and then he looked at the entire page of smiling graduates "So what is your point? It is a photo of Wilet. So what?"

"Look at the other page I marked," stated Ryan dramatically.

Somatos turned the book to the "A" section and scanned the

photos. One was a sorority photo with a dozen girls. One face and caption with the name Cindy Ambrose was circled.

"I don't understand," said Somatos, confused.

Ryan handed Somatos a newspaper photo of Leslie Warren he had downloaded from the internet.

"That is a photo of Leslie Warren. Cindy Ambrose and Leslie Warren are the same person. She lived in Albany, went to school with Wilet, and she changed her name after Albany."

Somatos froze and looked up at Ryan in amazement. "Why would she change her name? Is it her?" Somatos asked, seemingly stunned.

"I checked with the college registrar. Do you know who Cindy Ambrose, a.k.a. Leslie Warren, roomed with her freshman year?"

Somatos scowled incredulously. "Cathy Wilet?"

"Yes, Cathy Wilet."

"They knew each other, and therefore the killer is likely the same person."

Somatos looked at the photo for several more minutes and then handed the book back to Ryan. He then opened the breast pocket of his suit, withdrew a cigarette from his gold cigarette holder, and positioned an ashtray in front of him.

"I thought you quit?"

Somatos grimaced and lit his cigarette. "You think Warren knew Wilet? You told the police?"

Ryan responded with a grin and a nod. "And I told them about Seth."

Somatos furrowed his brow, and blew a billow of smoke between them.

CHAPTER 34

It was 9:00 p.m. Seth Tantalus looked at his frontal naked image in the mirror. He was proud of his physique. The upper torso was well developed and defined from years of weight conditioning. His arm and shoulder muscles flexed thickly. The eagle tattoo on his right arm had wings now that spread broadly. He had not only survived, his body had outwardly flourished, but nevertheless, there was the constant, unrelenting threat that lurked in every cough, in every chill, in every midnight awakening of apprehension that soaked his sheets in sweat. He was superstitious that some omniscient God, by some means, would hold him accountable. During the day he was confident, but in the night, a judgmental guillotine of guilt occasionally descended.

In the exercise room in the basement of his house, he strode over to the steel-laden weight machine and began again more calibrated tuning of his arms. The heavy clang of metal rang repetitively in the air. This continued for some time until the great mass of his arms ached. Mindless lifting and pulling, a grueling regimen that he imagined had fortified him against the nightmare of his crimes—two young girls dead by his brutish hands. After a time, his muscles exhausted, he rose, conceitedly eyed his form again in the full-length mirror, and headed for his downstairs shower.

He loved the polished Romanesque opulence of his house. He had prospered to luxurious heights. The bathroom was enshrined from floor to ceiling with black-veined white marble. With clouds of condensation in the air, the jet of warm water from the shower relaxed him. He began to contemplate the prospect of sex. It had been a while. He had deliberately kept a low profile, but he needed the outlet of a compliant woman to serve his needs. While he toweled down, he mentally settled on a midnight excursion to the Arlington Brew House. He would take the sports car rather than the luxury SUV.

He wiped a clear surface on the fogged mirror and began to shave. He felt tired and for a moment, Tantalus thought he could discern a ring of weariness beneath his eyes. A small nick from his razor sent a trickle of blood down his chin and into the sink. Tantalus watched his blood run, fascinated. He stanched the flow with a small piece of toilet tissue and, wrapped in a towel, went up the stairs to the main level and then up a larger staircase to his upstairs bedroom bath. Several lines of cocaine were neatly set on a mirror. In several mighty inhalations he consumed it, following it with a glass of water. He was now inured to the process of being high. Cocaine, oxycodone, ecstasy—he had consumed it all with gusto. Tonight, he would dress, catch the baseball game on TV, and then head out.

The night was warm. He turned the ignition of his sports car, and the efficient purring of the engine seemed melodious and powerful. He pulled out of his garage, down his driveway, and was off with a sense of exhilaration.

The Arlington Brew House was crowded, and he eyed the

women with a predatory sense of purpose. Too many shrill college students, thought Tantalus as his blue eyes restlessly roved the scene before him. He shouldered his way through the crowd with an air of sophisticated superiority. He was losing tolerance for their immature exuberance. His presence was appealing enough to attract the attention of several young women, but Tantalus was bored.

"You looked bored," said a mature-looking, elegant blonde in her thirties, with a smile that was entirely flirtatious and seemingly sympathetic. She was wearing a tight black dress that concealed her flesh but left no doubt as to the erotic curves of her figure. She seemed incongruous in the crowd of jean-clad college students.

Tantalus appraised the blonde. "I am no longer bored," said Tantalus, reciprocating with a receptive smile. She was petite, almost a foot and a half smaller than him, but he liked that.

"You can buy me a drink. My name is Caroline."

"What would that be?" inquired Tantalus.

"Whisky on the rocks," she said as she looked straight into Tantalus's harsh eyes.

For several minutes they engaged in polite conversation. It had been a while since Tantalus had a woman of this caliber. He knew that he wanted her in the first few minutes of their contact. He inferred a sexual audacity that he felt would be an exhilarating challenge to tame and bend to his will. He felt she implicitly understood what he needed and wanted. He directed her to a booth nearby that had just emptied.

"So, Caroline, you're in town for business and what business might that be?"

"Market analyst. But tell me about yourself. Are you in government?"

"Do I look like I'm in government?"

"No. You look like a cop," she said with a smirk.

Tantalus responded with a look of disgust. "No, I'm not a cop."

"You've got something against cops? You've been arrested, right?"

Tantalus laughed an insolent, arrogant laugh. "First I look like a cop; now I look like a criminal."

"There's not much difference, is there?" teased Caroline. "I can't stand them. You know, I was falsely arrested once for grand theft auto. I just borrowed a friend's car, and they nearly killed me. Barbarians." The din of the bar nearly drowned out her words.

"Yeah, I was arrested once in high school, but my father had the charges expunged," said Tantalus as he took a swig of a whisky shot.

"What were you arrested for?"

Tantalus scowled. "Why do you ask that?"

Caroline smirked. "Because some women have fantasies, silly." Her heart began to thump in her chest.

"What is your fantasy?" asked Tantalus as he leaned forward.

She ignored the question. "So do you work in government?" She wanted to deflect the conversation back toward him. She took a cigarette from a pack in her purse. She offered him a one, but he declined.

There was something remarkable about the woman sitting across from him. She possessed a confident quality that was provocative, elemental, and maybe even kindred to his spirit. He glimpsed in the mysterious vortex of her eyes a shadow of sexual intrigue. Perhaps it was the erotic effect of the alcohol or just the recklessness of the moment, but he felt comfortable with her, relaxed. He felt no need to be circumspect with this woman. He felt a kind of immunity from whatever judgment she could render, so he spoke with candor.

"Yes, I work in Congress, and before that I worked in Albany."

"Albany?" she inquired with a puff of smoke.

"A shithole of a town."

"Were you engaged or married?"

He scowled. "Not even close, darling."

Caroline's face showed a spark of feigned interest. Tantalus noticed the glimmer.

"Where are you from originally?"

"Northshore Park, Long Island."

"I've heard of it. It's an affluent community." She looked down at his hands as he poured beer into his glass. His hands were large, a massive, powerful weapon that could be balled into a sizeable fist. She looked carefully at his face. It was a deceptive face, darkly handsome with thick black hair, combed slickly back, and the dominance of two blue eyes, strangely possessing a glimmer of brutal intensity. She had seen faces like his before; it was a handsome face of a scoundrel, of a man who could not be trusted.

After an hour and forty-five minutes of flirtatious conversation and several shots of tequila, the bar began to swirl slightly, so she switched seats to sit beside him and then whispered in his ear, "Pick any hole. I'm yours."

Tantalus was stunned for a moment. His mouth opened slightly and then congealed into a knowing, lustful smile. The uninhibited vulgarity of her offer seemed incongruous with the maturity of her manner. She was difficult to assess. However, he was not one to hesitate in these situations.

"I'm too drunk to drive. I'll go with you," she said brazenly as she stood up.

Hurriedly he led her through the crowd and out the door. She smelled of cigarettes and sweet perfume, and he voraciously tasted her when they were in his car. As he turned the ignition, he wondered if it had been too easy. What did he care? The risks were hers and not his. Tantalus drove and imagined what he would do to the woman next to him named Caroline.

Caroline sat beside him in the black sports car as its engine purred loudly and then climbed up a steep hill into the woods. They drove down streets that gradually narrowed, then came more trees, more darkness, and the space between homes grew wider. Soon the homes were no longer visible behind gates, trees, and barrier walls built of stacked rocks that concealed palatial homes. They were in McLean. She knew which home was his. She had been there three hours earlier when he drove out from his house. She was down the street, in her car, watching, waiting, stalking the stalker until he emerged in his sports car.

He turned left through his open gate and drove up an incline to the driveway in front of his house. There was an expansive lawn and a stately stone exterior. She estimated the home to be at least $3.4 million, maybe as much as $ 4 million. He pulled the car into his three-car garage, parked it next to his two other cars, and escorted her to his den for a drink. Spacious rooms with double doors opened to more spacious rooms, many entirely unfurnished. There were two-story vaulted ceilings, grandiose columns, and a dual ascending staircase that curved upward three floors. There were five bedrooms and six marbled bathrooms. A mahogany library, tellingly devoid of books. Tantalus in his boastful tour flipped on a light and illuminated his outdoor Olympic-size heated swimming pool. The house was a vacuous monument to ego, with a paucity of personal possessions. Nevertheless, it reminded her of the house on Long Island. A home from which she was now banished.

"Nice house."

"I just moved in several months ago. The prior owner was a drug dealer. I heard the FBI seized one million in cash stuffed in duffel bags from all the closets."

"Did you find any hidden loot?" she asked coyly as she ran a finger along the frame of a painting. "That would have been a nice housewarming present. How did you afford all this?"

"Politics can pay off sometimes," responded Tantalus cryptically.

"Like poker or like slots?" she asked flirtatiously. "Do you bluff or fill the slot?"

Tantalus stood still.

"And you keep in shape," responded Caroline as she turned toward him with a smile of seduction. She closed on him and laid a hand on his pants, squeezing his erection.

"You're not very shy, are you," Tantalus said coolly. He was not used to being sexual prey; he was naturally the predator. He led her upstairs by her hand.

As she walked up the stairs, she began to regret the ruse and she thought then of running from the house. She had never met her limit. She was in his bedroom. Stereo electronics and a large-screen television encompassed a wall. Custom lighting illuminated mounted sports memorabilia that appeared to have high value. An overflowing bag of golf clubs leaned against the wall.

"You're a golfer?" she asked.

"Among other sports. Not that good at golf, but you could say I know how to swing a golf club," he said with an unsavory smile.

Before her was a large bed with four pillars, and she instinctively felt what was coming. He picked up a remote control and a gas fireplace at the far end of the room came to flaming life.

"I need to use the bathroom." She began to head for his en suite bathroom.

"Not that one," warned Tantalus in a voice both gruff and unexpectedly alarmed. "Use the one down the hall."

She entered the bathroom down the hall. In the bright and brassy light, she reapplied her pink lipstick in the mirror. Her hand trembled slightly. She removed a container with cocaine from her purse. She delicately sprinkled a little of the snow-white powder on the gleaming marble of the bathroom counter and snorted it. The drug melted rapidly in her delicate nose, releasing euphoria through her body. With dreamy, impassioned eyes, she studied her reflection in the mirror above the sink. The pupils of her eyes opened wide with excitement. She had come to seduce the truth from him, to pry it loose with the wild friction of her passion, as she had done so many times, with so many men. Nevertheless, there was something deeply disturbing about Seth Tantalus. She could see an unstable and eerie element coming closer to the surface the more intimate they became. There was an evident element of danger about him.

She composed herself. There had been situations more precarious than this one, and she had always extricated herself without permanent harm. It was like one of those thrilling carnival rides that tested one's mettle. No harm done. She wanted to keep on the heart-thumping ride. Ride it to the very end.

When she returned, Tantalus was standing by the bed. He had checked her purse for identification and had only found a New York driver's license. He checked her cell phone, but it was locked. He led her by the hand to the edge of the bed and brought her close with his arms. He had already decided to shred any pretense of civil behavior.

With one hand caught in the golden tangle of her hair, he forced her face upward to accept his probing tongue.

She could handle this, she thought. That idea stayed in her mind until, without warning, he ripped her top off, with buttons flying, and then his hand painfully twisted her thick mane of blonde hair. She was forced to her knees.

"You're not in control now, are you?" he asked savagely.

"I want to go. I've made a mistake," she said meekly.

She had experienced worse treatment before, but there was a razor edge of terror to this that transcended any experience. He raised his hand to her face.

"Don't hit my face." She didn't care what he did, as long as she survived with her beauty intact. He ran his meaty thumb obscenely across her mouth, smudging her lipstick and then ripped off her bra.

"Where did you get these scars?" Tantalus asked, noticing the first imperfection in his prey.

"An auto accident several years ago." She looked down at the floor, afraid to make contact with his eyes.

She began to mentally block out the rest, but she did not resist. She yielded passively to his misogynistic will and every warped desire. The tightening of rope around her arms and ankles, the agonizing assault of his repeated thrusts into her from every orifice. There was nothing pleasurable; she was fighting only to maintain herself. She was not even conscious of the fact that she had begun to cry. She could not remember why she had come to this place; could not remember her purpose. At some point his avid sexual energy had spent itself, and she was conscious of lying face down on his bed, tied spread-eagle. Mercifully, he was cutting the ropes loose.

"You hate women, don't you," she asked in a voice choked with emotion.

"I used a condom, didn't I," snarled Tantalus.

"That would seem to be out of your character," she stated as she dressed.

"I don't like to take chances," responded Tantalus.

"Who were you trying to protect with the condom, me or you?" She understood that rape with a condom was difficult to prove.

He came to stand directly in front of her, and then the firm palm of a hand came crashing across her face. He had expected this act to intimidate her, but she obviously was used to this kind of punishment, for she glared defiantly at him.

"Get your stuff and get out."

"You don't really like women, do you?" she persisted in her inquiry.

Tantalus had turned with his back toward her, and she could then see a tattooed eye on his back watching her. He watched her facial reaction in a mirror. She then noticed beneath the eerie inked eye tattoo a strange purple discoloration, perhaps a birthmark, or maybe not.

She steeled herself to ask the essential question. "In Albany, did you know Cathy Wilet?" At this point, she was not sure if she wanted to know the answer from him to that particular question.

Tantalus turned and scowled.

"Who the fuck is she? Anyway, does it matter? Do you think just because I slept with you I owe you a full accounting of my life? We're two adults. We got what we wanted. Now it's time for you to leave. And no, I didn't know any Leslie Warren."

Caroline was startled. "I said Cathy Wilet. Did you say Leslie Warren?"

"No. Who are they? Just get the hell out, now! I'm done." Tantalus said, exasperated. He was drunk and tired and getting annoyed with her.

"I heard you say Leslie Warren," she repeated with shortness of breath. In a pause, they glared at each other. She needed to get out of the house quickly and so she switched emotional gears.

Her dress had shredded. "I need a shirt," she asked plaintively as she held out the ripped garment. He tossed her one of his white cotton shirts. She wore the shirt over the ripped upper part of her outfit.

Without further words, he led her outside the front door. She looked pathetic and disheveled.

"Good night, honey," he said mockingly as he slammed shut the door and loudly locked it.

Caroline Tierney kicked the door in anger and then stood trembling in the night. The only sound came from the dark woods around the house: a crescendo of high-pitch cicadas, filling the night's silent void with their inhuman shriek. She tried to light a cigarette, but her hand was shaking. She thought of calling the police and reporting a rape, but he was likely guilty of other lethal crimes and she wanted nothing more than to be rid of him and quickly away. A yellow cab appeared much quicker that she had anticipated. Perhaps this was a regular custom for the cab company, she thought, picking up at his front door the roughly discarded women of Seth Tantalus.

CHAPTER 35

At his house, Seth Tantalus lay in bed while thunder trembled and an unrelenting flow of water cascaded over his expansive roof and across his landscape. It had rained violently on and off for days now. Rainwater that at first purged his feelings and lulled him to sleep now was eroding his sense of security. The natural ground was turning to pools of liquefied mud. And Tantalus wondered whether he had dug deeply enough. Even a Fairfax detective had alluded to it on the news.

Several nights ago, he had watched the evening news and a segment on the Leslie Warren case appeared. Standing in front of police headquarters, when asked about the status of the Leslie Warren case, a Fairfax detective said, "We'll see what the rains bring up." He heard the detective with an explicitly emphasized drawl, implicitly acknowledging the notion of her buried body and a murder.

"We'll see what the rain brings up," said Tantalus to himself; it had a southern poetic ring. Another clap of thunder shuttered the house. He sat up in bed, startled. A bright burst of light momentarily filled the room. The storm was passing in the night. He wanted to suppress his morbid fears, but there was the growing inexorable impulse to return to the site where he had buried Leslie Warren. He should have dug deeper, he thought. He needed to dig deeper.

Caroline arrived back at her hotel, and the copious downpours and turbulence of the storm had followed her. She lay awake in her bed with a single night lamp on, listening to the fusillade of rain against the window. Her hands were still shaking, and she could not calm down. She had thought she could control Tantalus, catch him off guard. And she did in a way. She heard him say the name Warren when she asked about Wilet. He was a menacing brute, an utter brute who could be capable of murder. Murder and rape.

The hotel room spun violently. She ran for the bathroom, positioning herself in front of the toilet. She retched and then vomited into the swirling water a shot of whisky she had taken to calm her shattered nerves.

She had never met Seth Tantalus before tonight, but she wondered if they somehow could have crossed each other's path in Albany. They may have been intimately connected in the most promiscuous of ways. She had so many casual sexual encounters, it was possible. She reflected on her own role in persuading Speaker Mariano to change the transcript time of adjournment. She wondered if she had inadvertently concealed Tantalus's role or even Congressman Green's role. Unwittingly, she was intertwined with these murders from the very beginning.

As soon as she began to undress, she broke down, sobbing in the process. Her body hurt in the most intimate and cruel way. Tantalus had hurt her. The hurt was deep, deeper than the physical pain he inflicted, deeper than she could admit to herself. A dam had broken. The fragile bulwark of her psyche had shattered against the hard malice of Seth Tantalus. And her tears now flowed like the torrent of rain outside.

CHAPTER 36

It was their first night in the woods, alone they thought. They had suffered through chill and mud, but Kerri Taylor and Beth Linsey were now comfortably ensconced in a single sleeping bag. The gloomy threat of rain had marred their hike here, but the evening had brightened before sunset. Now a vast constellation of stars hung like a vivid speckled canvas over their heads. They had picked a secluded section of the park for their expedition. They did not want their intimacy to be interrupted or scrutinized by the curious straggler or nature explorer. Under the tent for the first time in their mutual twenty-one years, they had made lesbian love to one another. It was a moment that they both anticipated and mutually expected. They had just exchanged a deep-tongued kiss when Kerri heard something moving in the woods.

"Did you hear that?" Kerri asked as they ceased their carnal amusement and focused on the reverberating natural hum of the woods around them. Kerri slipped her jeans back on with sudden alarm.

Beth shook her head no. "I can't believe you're so skittish. You know, sometimes your imagination plays tricks on you out here."

They looked at each other with attuned night eyes and sharpened senses. "I'm going to add some sticks to the fire," said Kerri.

"I thought it was out," Beth remarked.

Kerri slid out of the nylon sleeping bag and with a stick stirred the embers of a flame that had nearly expired. The light stirred feebly to a golden glow. Beth now had also slid out of the sleeping bag and put her pants back on. She then withdrew gel stick for her lips from a bag. She was crouching down and applying it when she too heard a boisterous rustling of leaves and branches. Now they both paused in their movements and looked at each other with mutual concern.

"I heard it," said Kerri softly.

A loud snap of branches came from the darkness. "A bear," whispered Beth.

They huddled next to each other and conferred quietly.

"It sounded big," said Kerri.

"Get your flashlight," directed Beth as she searched her belongings for hers.

There were more smashing sounds of branches breaking in the night. They were a hundred yards from a lake, and the sound seemed to emanate from steep terrain that led down toward the water. Beth wanted to ascertain the source of the sound, but Kerri's heart was beating in her throat. The dark air became deep with tension.

"Don't go," pleaded Kerri. "It's dangerous."

"It's just an animal," replied Beth assuredly.

"It's not a small animal," rasped Kerri.

Kerri switched on her flashlight and tested her beam in a direction away from the sound.

"Kerri, keep the flashlight off until I say so," said Beth, assuming charge in the matter.

With caution, Beth then moved away from the campsite toward the edge of the woods farther down by the water. Kerri stayed behind, ready to aim the flashlight, and watched as Beth tentatively advanced toward the edge of undergrowth. A beacon of light slashed the trees directly above Beth, and they both now knew that the threat was human. Seeing the flashlight beam, Beth ran back quickly. She ignored Kerri and began to frantically grope through their camping equipment. Kerri had no idea what Beth was doing.

"Shhh. Quiet," said Beth as she retrieved a .357 handgun from a backpack.

———

The prior night's rough sexual encounter and a rough, sleepless night had convinced him to return to the site the following day. But now, Tantalus's jeans were caked in mud, and he was cursing his condition. With one hand he swept his flashlight along the area looking for a landmark, while carrying a shovel in the other. "Shit," he said out loud to himself. The spot had seemed isolated and barren when he had buried Warren. Now he was vexed at finding so much human debris. He paused in his movements and contemplated his plan. He had already stomped all over where he had thought he had buried Warren, but erosion from the rain had altered the landscape so that he was now uncertain where he had entombed her.

Studying the ground, he saw scattered beer bottles and what looked like a pile of discarded cans and containers. He also now realized that the mud had created perfect replicas of his boot prints. He was vexed at finding so much human debris in this section of parkland and concerned over the incriminating trail he was now creating.

Tantalus heard a noise in the distance. He stood still, sinking in viscous mud, trying to discern if the sounds were animal or human. He began to contemplate the malignant and onerous prospect of another murder. He felt his cunning turning to dust. In frustration, he threw his shovel to the ground.

"Never should have come back here," he verbalized to himself in the darkness.

Tantalus moved toward the upward ledge of a rock. He then scanned beyond the tree line and was startled. In the distance, he thought he could see the red embers of a fading campfire and two slim female figures huddled close by it, looking right in his direction. He was sure they could see him. He could not take the chance.

Tantalus turned off his flashlight, put it into his jacket, and pulled a serrated eight-inch hunting knife from his jacket pocket. He was in trouble and angry. He furiously charged down and through the embankment. He loudly broke through the entanglement of branches.

Within seconds, under the dim light of a crescent moon, both Beth and Kerri could see Tantalus emerging, like a huge feral beast, from the undergrowth fifty yards away from them. When Kerri saw a male figure in the distance charging toward them, her pulse surged. She knew his intention was malevolent. Kerri issued a terrified scream. Beth tightened her grip on the gun.

Tantalus now clearly saw the two women and their campsite and realized he had a problem. He could catch one and probably kill her, but the other one would get away. Charging forward while working on this logistical problem of murder, he realized that one woman was now in a posture of a firing position with what looked like a gun pointed directly at him.

Beth steadied herself in a firing position with the handgun aloft, with two outstretched arms, and yelled to Kerri, "Turn the light on him."

Tantalus, ferociously sprinting, had closed the distance between them until a flashlight beam momentarily blinded him. Then the distinct explosion of a gunshot rang out in the darkness, startling him.

"Don't come any closer," yelled a female voice. "I know how to use this gun."

"Shit," Tantalus exclaimed as he crouched down, and then, with the dexterity and agile evasion of the college football player he once was, he broke off his run forward and instead peeled off to the side and then reversed back into the undergrowth. The explosion of the shot was unmistakable, and he knew it was a real bullet and a working gun. In his hasty retreat he almost forgot to the retrieve the shovel, but he found it in the undergrowth. His car was parked less than a mile away and he began the trek back. Thwarted, he abandoned this evening's effort to dig a deeper hole. It would be dawn soon anyway. There was no way, he thought the two girls could identify him. Hopefully, he reasoned, they would not focus on the ground where he had buried the body of Leslie Warren.

Beth's hands were shaking badly, but to her surprise she had been able to control the gun and discharge a round, which tore through the darkness and into the woods.

"I saw him. I saw him clearly. I saw his face," said Beth as she turned toward Kerri. "That guy was a no-good fucking animal."

CHAPTER 37

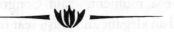

Somatos glanced up at the illuminated oil portrait that hung on the wall outside the floor of the House Chamber. It was six feet high and done in the darkened oil tones of a bygone era. It was a full-length portrait of Daniel Webster, circa 1875. Posterity had transformed this mortal man into an everlasting giant. It was the nature of politics. Somatos's own implacable ambition rose monumentally over his mental landscape. He would add to it, brick by brick, patiently, diligently enlarging its breadth, to build higher and higher. He had seen many young legislators, the rising stars, burn brightly and flare out into obscurity, oblivion. Their names would never be inscribed in the hall of legends; their likeness would never be immortalized in marble; their portraits would never hang in these hallowed halls. They would trade posterity for a few moments, here and there, of cheap, transitory celebrity. Somatos had a very different path in mind.

"Congressman Somatos." The voice was faint yet firm. Congressman Sherwood Scott Jackson was approaching him. In any other setting, the man coming toward him would be regarded as just another old man, shriveled and insignificant. But here the shriveled old man before him, with faint wisps of white hair and a carriage that had curved his small body forward, was endowed by an indefinite but yet perceptible aura of influence.

"Congressman Jackson," responded Somatos, licking his lips. Congressman Jackson of South Carolina was the chair of the Health Policy Subcommittee where Somatos's legislation was pending.

"May I have a moment," said Congressman Jackson as he gestured toward an elegant and plush seat reserved for members of Congress. On tables nearby, the bust likenesses of several long-dead House members watched over them.

"You're creating quite a stir with that draft amendment," said Jackson as he leaned back.

"Well, I am sure you know my district is very different than yours," said Somatos.

"Congressman Somatos. I know your district, and I understand the needs of your constituency," said Jackson slowly. There was a deliberate southern emphasis on every syllable. "You're creating division in the Democrats on the subcommittee. I believe this controversy could be avoided if you were to work out a compromise with Congressman Green. I presume the two of you know each other well from Albany."

Somatos looked into the eyes of the old man across from him. Two shining eyes, sparkling like ancient pools of power, deep and mysterious, focused on Somatos. His countenance was wrinkled and ghostly mottled, but Somatos recognized the unmistakable determination in Jackson's eyes.

"Congressman Jackson, yes, I know Congressman Green. I know him very well, and it is precisely for that very reason why I will not compromise with him. I cannot compromise on this issue," said Somatos firmly.

"Congressman Somatos, you never struck me as an idealist ready to burn his causes for public spectacle. You strike me as a pragmatist."

The old man leaned forward. "I saw you looking at Webster's portrait and at that bust of Henry Clay. These men knew how to negotiate and compromise; you know that. You're not one of these firebrands, are you?" He delivered his words in a snide and derisive way.

"No, I am not a firebrand. I will prevail on this vote."

Jackson laughed, finding amusement in Somatos's optimism. "You don't have your count right. You're two votes off on the amendment as is. We both know that. This is a noble cause, health insurance, but the business groups don't want to assume the costs you're imposing on them."

"I'll compromise once I get it intact out of subcommittee," said Somatos self-assuredly and to the amusement of Jackson.

"Hell, you're not listening to me," said Jackson as his pink cheeks turned red. "You're two votes short."

"Once I get Green I'll have Congressman Laverne."

"You'll never get Green on that bill as is," said Jackson firmly.

"We will see. I do appreciate your counsel on this," said Somatos deferentially.

"It appears my counsel on this has been to no avail."

"That is not true, Congressman Jackson. As I said, I will sit with you and compromise with you once I get it out of the subcommittee intact," said Somatos.

Congressman Jackson stood up slowly and forced a thin smile between his lips. The old man extended his blue-veined hand and shook Somatos's hand. There was odd, palpable strength in this pale tentacle of power. Then he came close to Somatos's face while still firmly grasping his hand.

"You know, Congressman Somatos, politics is like making love on a grand scale. You're trying to do that with this bill. I see that. But sometimes there are risks in being too promiscuous." The old man winked at Somatos with a conspiratorial grin.

In an extraordinary moment, Somatos was at a loss for words.

Congressman Jackson moved slowly down the hall. He was a

sad, fierce old warrior, but Somatos knew that this was an institution where the counsel of old men should never be taken lightly or dismissed out of hand. For a moment, Somatos had the sense that the eyes of every ancient portrait—Hamilton, Clay, Webster—were all fixed on him. He would get Green's vote, and Laverne would follow Green's lead. He would have his two votes, and on a thin majority of one vote, he would pass his amendment.

CHAPTER 38

I t was at 2:00 a.m. when Ryan was awakened by a violent knock on his door. on. Ryan assumed it was Caroline. He opened the door in his underwear to find Anglus and Hestrom standing in the hall in near identical suits, once again intruding on his life.

"Not again. What now? It's over, right?" pleaded Ryan as he turned on a lamp and put on a nearby pair of jeans.

"Sorry to wake you, but we have some information that you may want to know about. You know your linking of Cindy Ambrose in New York as our missing Leslie Warren was critical," said Anglus with sly smile of respect for Ryan.

"We found out that the New York State account associated with the check to Leslie Warren, a.k.a. Cindy Ambrose, was established by the former Speaker of the New York State Assembly. The check was not written by Tantalus. It was issued pursuant to a sealed legal settlement with the New York State Assembly. The account was written from what they call an SDA, a specially designated account of the state of New York. The dollars, in other words, were taxpayer dollars authorized by the Speaker of the state assembly."

Ryan, roused from sleep, could not wholly assimilate this latest news, but Anglus continued speaking. "Do you have any idea why he would do that?"

Ryan looked into Anglus's inscrutable face. Every question from these investigators was posed with an accusatory insinuation.

"No, I do not." Ryan shook his head, trying to comprehend and make sense of this latest information.

"Why did Leslie Warren change her name?" Ryan asked, and before that question was answered, he posed another: "Did she work at the state assembly?"

"We don't have the answer to either question yet," said Anglus, "but the US Attorney's office is issuing subpoenas that the New York State Assembly is fighting. Once a federal judge rules in our favor, we will know the answer."

The questions leaped to Ryan's mind, one after another. He could not think of any legitimate reason why the Speaker would be paying a young woman with state dollars in one lump sum. Ryan, though exonerated now, remained intrigued and transfixed by every turn in the case. "I have no idea why Speaker Mariano would establish such an account. Did you guys have anything else?" A protracted pause hung in the air. "What?" Ryan asked.

"There was an incident in Greenbelt Park several nights ago," began Hestrom. "Two teenage girls were threatened by a young man wielding a knife. The Park Police wired it into the task force because of a possible link to the abduction. A team went out there and interviewed the two women. They indicated that the man appeared to be in the woods past midnight and lurking about when he threatened them."

Ryan wondered where the story was headed.

"We showed the women a photo of you and one of Tantalus."

Ryan braced for bad news; he worried the women had identified him erroneously.

"They identified Seth Tantalus from our photo, so we sent out forensic dogs and our evidence team meticulously inspected the site." Hestrom paused and glanced at Anglus. Ryan wondered if they rehearsed the passing back and forth of conversations in this manner.

"It seems you were right about Tantalus. We've found the body of Leslie Warren, and we executed a search warrant on his house in McLean," stated Anglus without emotion.

"I'm not surprised about Tantalus. You found Leslie Warren's body. That's great," exclaimed Ryan, who smiled with relief at first. Upon seeing the investigators reaction, he then felt immediate guilt at being gleeful upon a gruesome discovery.

"Wait. Wasn't Tantalus working on the Hill today. How could that be?" Ryan asked.

"We didn't get to his house until the evening. Tantalus is missing, but we have forensic evidence to link him with the crime," said Hestrom as he glanced around the room, habitually inspecting for clues.

"Well, he went from Hill staffer to fugitive in a few hours. What a country," Ryan quipped. "I know how he feels, but how could he be missing?"

"He never came home. But we wanted you to know about this latest information."

"Well, that's great," Ryan repeated as he began to walk the men over to the door to remove them from his life once and for all. Anglus and Hestrom began to exit and then turned to Ryan.

"Did you know that Tantalus had a blonde girlfriend? We found blonde hair at the scene. It was in the imprint of Tantalus's boot. It has been sent to Dorus Genetics lab for DNA matching."

The investigators looked at Ryan. Ryan's face was an expressionless blank. He could not grasp their implication.

"Warren was brunette, right?" confirmed Ryan. The investigators drew in their breath and looked at each other. Ryan squinted at the two lawmen and shook his head in incomprehension. "A blonde female—so what?" verbalized Ryan as a thought of Caroline passed through him.

CHAPTER 39

The antique clock melodiously chimed the ten o'clock hour in the fashionable Georgetown Victorian home. Congressman Charles Everett Green was sitting in his den, surrounded by mahogany bookshelves, comfortable in a robe and leather slippers, with the business news on the television. A book about Richard Nixon in his lap held his attention. Unwatched, the blue glow of the television flickered while the congressman, sitting by a lamp, was focused on the plight of the former president.

He turned a page and then felt a curious sensation of a sudden chill. He removed his glasses. There was a palpable sense that a shadow had crept into the room. Diverting his attention from the book, he looked up and saw that the shadow was a flesh-and-blood person. A sharp feeling of panic forced the air from his chest, akin to a heart attack. With a gasp of alarm, the congressman quickly stood up and the book fell from his lap to the floor.

The shadow emerged into ominous focus. His chief of staff, Seth Tantalus, was standing, more precisely lurking, in the doorway.

"Tantalus, how the how hell did you get in here?"

"I let myself in," said Tantalus as he lumbered into the room and sat down on the leather couch across from Green.

"You've got a nice place here," said Tantalus as he surveyed the room, averting direct eye contact.

Congressman Green, standing in his robe, was visibly flustered. "Just what the hell do you think you're doing, Tantalus?"

"I came to talk," said Tantalus calmly. "Where's your wife?"

"My wife is at the Long Island estate. What are you doing here? The police are looking for you; for God's sake, I can't have you here," thundered Green. Incensed at the intrusion but concerned about appearances, he walked over to the window and peeked outside the curtain. The street was dark and quiet.

"Do you have anything to drink? Whisky?" inquired Tantalus with a casual air of indifference to the congressman's obvious distress.

"I'm calling the police. You cannot be here. You're wanted for questioning," Green barked angrily as he began to move toward the phone.

"Go ahead. I'll tell them everything," said Tantalus defiantly.

Green raised the receiver and then gruffly inquired, "Do you have a weapon?"

Tantalus laughed. "Yeah. You could call it a weapon."

Green dismissed the remark, but then, still holding the phone aloft, he paused, as if considering a chess move, deep in thought, and then lowered the receiver.

"You are a profane thug. Are you insane? Mixed up with a murder. My God, we've been in Washington for what, two months?"

Green then, with disgust, looked at his young protégé smugly sitting on the couch. "I knew you were trouble when you told me your political hero was G. Gordon Liddy."

Tantalus laughed and even Green, conceding his concern for the moment, shook his head in general disbelief. Green then strutted over to a small bar. He carefully watched Tantalus from the mirror behind the bar as he extracted ice from a freezer. Tantalus was in a state of agitation, rubbing his hands on his knees. He poured Tantalus a whisky sour and himself a gin and tonic.

"Fifteen minutes, that's all you've got." As he handed the drink to Tantalus, Green noticed that his young aide looked ill, undeniably sick.

"Fifteen minutes for ten years together doesn't seem very fair," observed Tantalus as he examined his drink and then Green, who sat down across from him in a gold-and-red upholstered chair that resembled a throne. Even out of his suit and in a robe, Green maintained a look of nobility. At the hirsute base of his neck, a tuft of gray hair was visible.

"It's political math," said Green, taking a sip of his gin. "Every minute you sit here will cost me a thousand votes. I can't even afford fifteen minutes."

"How many votes will it cost you if they find out about that twenty-two-year-old guy who was running buck naked around your Albany house that night you picked him up?"

Green's face tightened and, almost reflexively, he looked over at the smiling portrait of his wife on the desk beside the fireplace. Yes, he remembered how that young man was trying to blackmail him, but Tantalus, his loyal aide, took care of that matter by smashing the gentleman's nose. Tantalus sucked down a huge portion of his drink. The whisky burned acidly in his throat.

"You've been a loyal staffer," Green said in a gesture of appeasement. "You've conducted yourself with commendable nihilistic zeal on my behalf."

Tantalus erupted in laughter. "Jeez," he said as he shook his head in disbelief. "Commendable nihilistic zeal. You talk like that even in your bathrobe at home. You are one pretentious prick."

"Look, Tantalus, I am going to issue a statement discharging you tomorrow. You need to get a lawyer," counseled Green.

Tantalus laughed again, except this laugh coagulated into a thick, hacking cough that made him painfully grimace. "You're firing me," he cried while gripping his side that twisted now in pain. "Somatos at least kept McNeil on the payroll."

"Have you lost your mind," retorted Green. "In Somatos's district, McNeil's trouble with the police probably gained him ten thousand votes."

Tantalus glowered at Green. "What should I do?"

"Have you spoken with your father? He's a lawyer."

Tantalus cut him off harshly. "I haven't spoken to him in years. He told me after that high school charge I was on my own."

"What high school charge?" Green asked with great confusion. He had ignored so much of Tantalus's nefarious activities over the years that he now wondered how much he had forgotten and how much Tantalus deliberately concealed from him.

"Nothing. Not important."

The book jacket with the Nixon cover lay on the floor, looking up at Green. Green stared at it thoughtfully for a moment. "Look, you need to get a lawyer," he repeated. "Vindication is possible."

"What about Albany?" asked Tantalus, visibly sulking.

Green, still sitting, snapped his head as if shocked by the reference. "What? How does this relate to Albany?"

"It doesn't. I'm just wondering if you and Somatos—" said Tantalus before Green cut him off.

"Look, I don't know what you're involved with here. I don't want to know. Albany is history. My family has aspired to this congressional seat for generations. Generations," he repeated for emphasis. "I've been here seven weeks and already you've created a scandal."

"What if Albany comes up?"

"Look, Somatos will not bring it up. I will not bring it up. And you should not bring it up."

"Somatos will not bring it up?" Tantalus posed the question as he aimlessly wandered around the den. "Just how much does Somatos know?"

Green looked down into the ice in his drink. "He knows what he knows."

"What the hell does that mean?"

"It means that he will not be talking," said Green harshly as he stood up. "Look, whatever trouble you have here, Tantalus, cannot be traced back to Albany. That slipped through the cracks like so many things do. You were worried about the press. Well, the press never picked any of it up. They never see things that we don't want them to see. Their stories always omit facts. They only ever tell half the story. Inaccuracies, distortions . . ."

While Green rambled on, Tantalus ignored him. "I don't know how everything came apart. We were on top and now I'm a fugitive." Tantalus erratically oscillated between humor, pathetic despair, utter incredulity, and barely suppressed rage.

"This is just unbelievable. You've got to clear this up."

"I'm not in a position to do anything," said Green." I can't function as your lawyer. Call Melvin Tallman. Let me get you his card."

Green went to his imperial desk and rummaged through a draw, relieved at finding something he could offer Tantalus to send him on his way. He brought the business card to Tantalus, who sat red-faced on the couch.

Tantalus took the card and looked up at Green. "I need money."

Green looked at him with utter disbelief and then sat back down at his desk. "You should have enough money with all you made on the Dorus stock."

"I'm not liquid. I didn't sell it all."

"What? Are you a greedy idiot?"

"I held some, about a million dollars' worth. I thought it would go higher."

The realization of the dilemma came to Green. "You held some stock. You didn't think Ryan would check your financial disclosures once he saw you at the reception with company lobbyists."

"Water under the bridge. I can't very well go to my bank now, can I?" said Tantalus roughly. He wanted to smash Congressman Green in the face. The old man had a ton of money, new money, Tantalus thought, that was on top of legacy wealth, money that would have not been possible without the risks Tantalus had taken.

"Forget the money."

"Forget the money. I will not forget the money," Tantalus exclaimed. "I still remember when you imparted your wisdom about money to me."

"I don't remember," said Green dismissively.

"You don't remember?" taunted Tantalus. He picked his drink up and carried it over to Green at his desk, who reflexively flinched, thinking that violence was imminent. Tantalus stood towering over Green, drink in hand. He wobbled a little now as he spoke. "Politics can bring prestige, Seth." He lowered his voice and spoke with exaggerated pretentiousness to mock Green's utterances. "But nothing gains the respect of men and women like money. Wealth, not politics, is the foundation of all power. Proximity to power should not be confused with power itself unless it is endowed with wealth." Tantalus concluded this mockery with a laugh to himself. Green watched Tantalus's rendition with a mixture of amazement, horror, and disgust.

"I don't know what in the world you are talking about. Seth, you need to focus on your legal plight."

He then gave Tantalus a long, hard look that evoked some sense of loyalty. He stood up and went across the room. "Wait." At the far end of the room in an elaborate credenza, Green pulled out a small metal box. Fifteen crisp one hundred dollar bills were inside. He brought the money to Tantalus with an open hand, like an offering.

Tantalus put his drink down and counted the crisp money. "That's it."

"That's all the cash I can give you."

Tantalus did not offer a gesture of thanks as he took the money with a swipe of his hand. He then strutted toward the door of the den. Before he left, he turned toward Green. "You know, Congressman, there are crimes—"

Green cut him off in midsentence. "Who do you think you're talking to? There was no crime. There may be incriminating circumstances, but lawyers are paid for these purposes."

Tantalus dismissed this rhetorical rationalization. He was accustomed to Green's logic. He knew Green could never withstand the inevitable onslaught of police and prosecutors. Tantalus looked gravely into the hazy blue-gray eyes of Charles Everett Green.

"I did this for you and the governor."

"Horseshit, Tantalus. You did it for yourself."

Tantalus left the room. Green watched, thankful that his aide did not pass out through the front door but exited instead by the same surreptitious means he had entered. Green laid his drink down and then wondered just how Tantalus had entered. He shook his head, wondering if his career was in jeopardy. He had more twenty-five years' experience in the political arena. He could survive anything, even the fall of his political aide, he thought. He strode over to the telephone and dialed 911. He waited on the telephone while he rehearsed in his mind his lines.

"Yes. This is Congressman Green. My aide Seth Tantalus was just here. He is a fugitive wanted by the police for questioning, and I wanted to report that he broke in here. He just robbed me of two thousand dollars."

CHAPTER 40

An unruly scrum of reporters ambushed Ryan as he walked up the well-worn granite steps leading to the entrance of the Longworth House Office Building. From the tenor of the questions, he deduced that news of Seth Tantalus's flight from justice had become general public knowledge that morning. He had stepped unexpectedly into this predatory press gathering.

"Ryan, are you relieved that the police no longer consider you a suspect in the Warren case?"

Ryan had to laugh. "Yes. I'm pleased I'm no longer a suspect in the case."

"We understand that it was your information that led the police to Seth Tantalus as a possible suspect. How well did you know Tantalus?"

"Not very well. But we had met before. I've told the police everything I know about him and his possible connection to the missing women."

The reporters exploded over the plural "women."

"Did you say 'women'?"

"Is there another woman?"

Ryan paused and then divulged. "I've informed the police regarding Tantalus' possible ties to an Albany abduction."

"What woman?" the press mob shouted in unison.

The mob of reporters and bystanders was such that Ryan ceased all forward momentum. He was stalled, and he reconciled himself to the fact that he would have to endure this ritual indignity that only the press could bestow. Looking boyishly bashful and withdrawn, he was uncomfortable at the scrutiny of the video cameras and photographers. Being exonerated as a suspect was not an achievement that he could take delight in.

"Is your wife relieved?"

Ryan was at a loss for words. He could not answer. He was thankful that a rush of other questions filled the void in his response.

"Do you think that Congressman Green should fire Seth Tantalus?"

Ryan's political tact asserted itself. "Only Congressman Green can make that decision."

Ryan felt a hand on his shoulder; it was Congressman Somatos. He looked fresh and dapper. "I always had full confidence in the character of Ryan McNeil. I think the governor of New York and others who had rushed to judgment owe him a full and complete apology."

Ryan looked down at his shoes. The moment was awkward and unpleasant, and he wanted to talk with Somatos out of the harsh light.

"Do you think the governor owes you an apology?"

As Ryan formulated a response, he could see several capitol policemen rushing over to nudge the press aside.

"I think the governor was premature to call for my termination, and obviously the facts have shown that to be the case. Thank you," stated Ryan as he and Somatos moved forward through a corridor blocked by the police. Inside the halls of the Longworth, Somatos and Ryan moved briskly toward Somatos's office.

"Have you spoken to Annie?"

Ryan looked blankly at Somatos.

"Your wife, Annie, remember her?" said Somatos with an easy smile.

Ryan thought it an odd question. "No. Why?"

"Just wondering. Relax."

Somatos and Ryan entered the office, past relieved and smiling staff, and walked into Somatos's inner office. Ryan shut the door for privacy.

"What do we do now?"

"Do now? You're a hero, Ryan. You helped the police," said Somatos, leaning back in his chair, seemingly elated.

"What about Congressman Green? What about that $770,000?"

Somatos looked at Ryan with incomprehension. "What about Congressman Green. I think he's got a problem, and he will fire Tantalus quickly. It's not good for an elected official to have a fugitive murderer on the payroll. Believe me, I know from near experience. As for the money, let the police figure it out."

"Green changed the transcript time, remember? He must have been covering for Tantalus. Obstruction of justice. Conspiracy. These are crimes."

Somatos's expression changed dramatically. "Are you crazy? You just don't stop. You're self-destructive."

"What?" answered Ryan, startled.

Somatos stood up. "Damn it, Ryan. I asked for the transcript change through Caroline, remember? I will get caught up with Green if you press that button. No way," said Somatos with an emphatic wave of his hand, dismissing the suggestion.

"What are you saying? You want me to lie?" asked Ryan, again feeling betrayed.

"Ryan, no one asked you about the transcript change. No one.

Let's review: Warren's body has been found. Tantalus is linked with the murder. He probably murdered Wilet too. I bet he's got a nice clipping book just like you had in your attic. He's crazy and you're exonerated." Somatos was struggling for breath.

Somatos continued. "Forget about Green. I will handle Green. If you go after Congressman Charles Everett Green of Locust Valley, Long Island, he will bring you down with him, and me too."

Ryan sighed. He appreciated the keen sense in his mentor's instinct. "What about Caroline?"

"Caroline is not your business," said Somatos with snarling intensity.

"The police think Caroline and Tantalus are connected."

"What connection?"

"I don't know. He's probably a sociopath. Maybe he killed Wilet for political reasons or for money or power. He probably thought she was going to give information to the Albany DA against the governor and maybe Green."

"So, Ryan, I don't understand."

"Well, there is one other thing."

Somatos was becoming visibly annoyed. "What now?"

"The police found a blonde woman's hair at the grave where Warren was buried."

Somatos seemed to freeze stiffly. "What are you suggesting?"

Ryan drew in a breath. "Maybe Caroline was involved."

"Why the hell would you think Caroline would be involved?"

"Just a feeling," said Ryan with a melancholy tinge of guilt.

"Well, that doesn't make any sense. What motive?" mumbled Somatos.

"I don't know."

"Well, let the police handle it."

"I have her hair. From a comb she used."

"What?" asked Somatos, confused.

"They could check the hair DNA to see if it matches. She left her hair on my comb," said Ryan almost sheepishly.

"Ryan, what are you thinking? Are you going to drag Caroline through this now?"

"I need to know."

"You need to know what?"

"If she was involved with Seth Tantalus."

"Why?" countered Somatos aggressively. The congressman thought and then spoke. "Politics is a dirty, incestuous business. You knew that. Don't play like some fickle virgin with me. We're from the same block. It's all connected: business and politics and sex. All the reporters can do is get a vicarious thrill."

"You didn't answer the question," pressed Ryan.

Somatos licked his lips and drew in a breath. He reached into his breast pocket for his cigarette holder. "The rumor was that Assemblyman Caluzzi and Tantalus shared the same lover and she was blackmailing Caluzzi. No, it was not Caroline."

"Where did you hear the rumor?"

"Scarletti, the Staten Island Democratic leader, told me." Somatos put a cigarette in his mouth and lit it with his gold lighter. "He said that Caluzzi was being pressed by his mistress and told he had an STD and his wife would not be pleased after all, nor his Staten Island Roman Catholic constituency. Things were closing in on him and he was becoming reckless. I mean it's not every day that an assemblyman tries to rape and murder his intern in his office."

"What are you saying? That murder played better in his district than infidelity?"

"Look, Caluzzi was a mob man, and his district didn't care one way or the other," rebutted Somatos as he blew out a puff of smoke.

"What about Speaker Mariano? Why would he have been paying Leslie Warren or Cindy Ambrose? Just what could 'Leslie' have seen or done to get that money?" asked Ryan, feeling a dread chill up his spine. The implications seemed awful to conceptualize.

"Well, Mariano is dead, Ryan. Dead men don't testify."

"Well, what about the fact he is dead," Ryan stated in such an oblique fashion that Somatos did not catch the implication.

"Heart attack," answered Somatos as he again blew smoke into the air between them.

"So they say," quipped Ryan.

"No, wait a damn minute, Ryan. Mariano was not murdered. Tantalus is the serial murderer here, not Caroline Tierney."

"I just need to know that Caroline was not involved. I think I'm going to give her hair sample to the police so they can check it against the hair they found at Warren's grave. I just need to know the truth."

"I will tell you the truth," said Somatos with a grave expression and with teeth bared fiercely close to Ryan's face. "Beauty is truth and truth beauty; that is all yee know on earth and all yee need to know."

Ryan laughed. "Nick Somatos of the Bronx is quoting Keats to me. That is a deflection."

"OK, then I'll give you another quote: 'There is no truth but power.'"

Ryan repeated the line as a rhetorical question. "There is no truth but power?" He furrowed his brow. "Who said that?"

"I just did," said Somatos, eliciting a laugh from Ryan that ceased abruptly when he realized that Somatos's intense expression did not change.

CHAPTER 41

S eth Tantalus woke in a sweat. His motel alarm had gone off with an insistent buzz. A fever burned in his blood, and he felt sick to his stomach. He was finding it difficult to breathe, so he sat up in bed and began to cough, a deep, rancorous cough that seemed to scrape his ribs. He rose wobbly from the bed and nearly collided with a table on his way to the bathroom. This was his sixth motel room in three weeks, and he was disoriented. How long, he wondered, could he stay on the run?

He had never felt so bad. *So this is it*, he mused in front of the mirror. He studied his reflection. His muscled biceps and torso were still firm, but his face looked haggard. His blue eyes looked glazed and rimmed with red. Then, as he turned to shut the light, in a final moment of reflective vanity, he saw a mark on his back, three inches from his eye-shaped tattoo. He turned sideways and looked at it from an awkward angle. It was a discoloration—purple and blue: a malignant-looking shadow. He twisted sideways and rubbed it with a finger. The skin blanched, but the discoloration remained intact and harsh. A feeling of nausea swept him.

He spent several anxious moments examining it under the dim bathroom light and at different angles, and slowly he began to understand it was, in fact, a manifestation of disease. Death and disease were creeping into his skin and under his eyes. A period of angry denial passed. He shut the light off in the room and lay in bed, watching the ghostly shapes of passing car lights that filtered through the blinds and danced on the mottled ceiling. He wanted his internal ills to be invisible, and the fact that it was so overtly manifesting itself suffused him with anger. He began to burn with the awful and inevitable realization that death's first victim is always vanity. An inexorable feeling of human decay spread through him, like the cracking open of an ancient corpse. The frailty of disease frightened and angered him. *I'm going to look like one of those emaciated queers*, he thought.

My life is over, he thought, *and that bastard Ryan McNeil did it*. He had seen Ryan on the evening news. He had heard Ryan implicate him with both the Wilet and Warren murders. There was no doubt Ryan had put the authorities on his trail. Still, Tantalus could not understand how Ryan knew anything about Wilet.

"That fuckin' McNeil," Tantalus murmured to himself. "That fuckin' bastard McNeil."

CHAPTER 42

R yan wanted nothing more than the whole scandal to be behind
him. He moved into the apartment and settled into a Spartan
existence with one bed and bare necessities. The heat of summer
settled into a routine of bright blue skies and searing sun.

Congressman Green had kept a low profile following Tantalus's
flight from justice. He had quickly fired his chief of staff after his flight
from prosecution, but the speculation was that the charges against
Tantalus could not but reflect on Green. Ryan had heard rumors that
Green would resign, but he placed little credibility in the speculation.
He knew Green to be far too pompous to gracefully accept such a
fate with equanimity. Green in fact denounced his critics as relying
on a "guilt by association," and then he unequivocally stated that he
would not resign.

"I think you should fly to New York tomorrow," said Somatos
as Ryan sat across from him and reviewed a list of items on a yellow
legal pad.

"What's in New York?"

"That speech I was planning to give," said Somatos dryly.

"Do you think I should leave now with the bill pending?"

"I'll be here; I need to be represented at that dinner."

Ryan booked a flight that would leave at 5:30 p.m. and return him at 11:00 p.m. that Thursday. He dreaded the trip.

That Thursday, he left work in a cab that ferried him to Reagan National Airport. There would be no overnight stay, so he was again free of the encumbrance of luggage. He entered the terminal and arrived at his gate fifteen minutes before departure. In the gate area, behind the glass terminal, Ryan watched the plane being readied. A delay was announced: mechanical difficulties. He sat serenely amid rows of suntanned tourists and ebullient children. A saffron ball of sun was suspended just above the horizon.

The flight to New York City would be quick, but the prospect of cold confinement on a jet filled him with sudden, inexplicable apprehension.

"Caution, the moving walkway is ending. Caution, the moving walkway is ending." He began to ponder the metaphorical meaning. The departure board now indicated his flight was delayed for another thirty minutes. Beyond the tarmac, the summer sun descended from view. Ryan sat and watched the crowds. He morbidly mused that there were elements of similarity between funerals and airports. They were both, in some related way, points for departure. Family, friends bid one tearful, emotional farewell. There was the equally fervent hope and infinite faith that one would arrive safely at a better place. Lone business travelers, of course, were the exception. They were grave and serious, endowed with anonymity. Amid the hugs and tears of others, they solemnly walked on airport gangways, consumed with business, headed out into an unknown, uncertain future. Ryan began to envision the plane bursting into a conflagration and consuming his trivial existence within seconds. "The moving walkway is ending." *I can't get on this flight*, he thought.

By the time that the long-delayed boarding had commenced, Ryan had left the airport and was hailing a cab. He had first tried to call Somatos from the airport, but mysteriously there was no answer at the office. Usually a staffer would be on duty until 7:30 or 8:00 p.m.

The Longworth Building was mostly empty, and Ryan entered through the only door that was now open to staff. He presented his congressional identification to the guard. After passing through the obligatory metal detector, he was perfunctorily permitted entry. Hallway lights had been dimmed or shut off, and there were only a few echoing voices and the distant sound of footsteps on highly polished hallway floors. Ryan used his key to open Somatos's outer office door. The outer office was dark.

Somatos's inner office door was shut, but light peeked out from underneath the door. Almost immediately, Ryan could hear what sounded like Caroline's voice. He stilled his movements and then furtively moved close to the shut door, tuning his hearing to the barely audible conversation.

"Congressman Green, I felt compelled to tell my story to Congressman Somatos. I hope you understand," said Caroline timidly.

"Charles," said Somatos, "we've known each other a long time. I find this hard to believe."

"What is this, some kind of blackmail?" said Green angrily.

"I'm offended, Charles, that you could make such an accusation," responded Somatos. "This young lady comes to me with this story and it seems incredible, so I wanted to give you a fair opportunity to respond."

"You're accusing me of participating in murder," snapped Congressman Green.

"I think the charges that this young lady is elucidating would also include obstruction of justice and conspiracy," said Somatos. "Perhaps two murders."

Green responded with his brow raised. "Look, you have no proof. This is galling."

"I do. I went to Speaker Mariano at your request, and he changed the transcript time," insisted Caroline.

"I never requested anything from you, Somatos," said Green. "And young lady, I never saw you before."

"Let's just review, Charles," said Somatos calmly. "This young lady comes to me with this story of how you in Albany requested a transcript change to conceal some activity. Now what she is suggesting I presume is that your aide Seth Tantalus was somehow involved in that Albany abduction of Cathy Wilet and that you were somehow also involved."

"I don't quite recollect that incident, Congressman Somatos. No, I don't believe that to be accurate. I don't ever recall asking you for a transcript change."

"Well, then your memory may be failing you, Charles. At any rate, her story goes on to include a fire that was set conveniently by your aide Seth Tantalus to help the governor. A fire that conveniently also concealed the identity of Cathy Wilet's abductor."

"I can't believe we're having this conversation here," muttered Green.

"Better here, Charles, than in a court of law."

"What do you want, Somatos?" said Green gruffly.

Somatos smiled. He removed a gold pen from his pocket and then reached over to a nearby pad. He wrote on the pad and passed the note to Green. Green read the note that simply stated "HR 3264 Amendment 7."

"I can't believe her story, Charles. I am incredulous, because I believe you to be an honorable man. For example, you know my amendment is coming up in the subcommittee, and I know you are an honorable man, and as an honorable man you would consider how many more children would be covered by health insurance if you voted in favor of that bill."

"So that's what this is about," said Green as he tucked the slip of paper under his jacket.

"Charles, it is just a matter of how I view you. This young lady wants me to believe that you are a cold-blooded conspirator with your aide Seth Tantalus. I don't want to believe that, Charles. But if you force me to believe it, I know that Caroline will attest that it was you that asked her for the transcript change."

Inside the office, Ryan could hear movement. He then moved farther away from the door to avoid detection.

"You'll have my answer on the vote, Somatos. This better be the end of this business. Do you understand? I don't want to see this woman ever again or have you mention her name to me," said Green defiantly.

Somatos's office door swung open; a triangle of light filled the dark outer office. Green emerged. Ryan could see that he appeared to be wearing a tuxedo. Green exited the office with an angry but unflappable and confident strut. Ryan hovered in the shadows, still concealed.

After several moments of quiet: "That was well done, Caroline. I think he is panicked."

"I almost felt sorry for him, showing up in his tuxedo and all."

"Nonsense. The truth of the matter is he is involved with Tantalus. But I don't think he wants it all out there in public. The governor is involved. Tantalus setting a fire for the governor. Can you imagine. Are you sure Tantalus said Leslie Warren when you asked about Cathy Wilet?"

"Yes, I'm sure. How about my money, Nick?"

"Oh yes," said Somatos as he paused in midsentence.

Caroline suppressed a startled scream as she glanced over by the door and could see Ryan hovering in the darkness. "Oh my God, you scared me."

"I never made the flight, Nick. A panic attack, I think. They say that happens when people feel that their lives are about to end," said Ryan seriously.

"We're just doing some last-minute negotiations on that bill, Ryan," said Somatos.

"I can see, Nick. Caroline, you two work well together. Almost as well as Tantalus and Green, but look what happened to them."

"I think I'll leave you two alone," said Somatos. "You must have lots to talk about."

Ryan stood to block Somatos, moving to directly confront him. "It's never ending with you." Ryan struggled to express his condemnation. "Your exploitation of people; it just goes on and on."

Somatos moved close to Ryan's face and spoke softly. "Don't talk to me about the arrogance of power until you've got it in your hands."

Somatos edged his way coolly by Ryan and then he turned to offer his final rejoinder. "And don't call it exploitation, Ryan. You're confusing exploitation with seduction. Seduction means two interested parties. So I don't exploit, Ryan, I seduce."

"The reference is to you and Green or you and Caroline?"

Somatos sneered at Ryan and then left his office and shut the door behind him, leaving Caroline behind.

Caroline glowered at Ryan. "What is it?"

"Tantalus talked to you about Leslie Warren? Then you know Seth killed both of them. You know it, right? Did you tell the police? How involved are you with all of this, Caroline?"

"What do you mean?"

"Were you involved in Cathy Wilet's abduction?"

"I told you. You never mentioned the transcript change to me. I didn't know that there was any relation to Wilet's abduction till I saw you a couple of weeks ago."

"Did you ever sleep with Seth Tantalus?"

Caroline's hand trembled, but she didn't think that Ryan could see it. "No. Of course not."

"You know, Caroline, the police found blonde female hair at

Warren's grave," said Ryan as he moved closer to her, looking directly into her face. "That couldn't be your hair, could it?"

"Of course not," said Caroline stiffly. She began to think how her hair could have gotten to the scene. She remembered Tantalus's rough treatment of her. He had grabbed her by the hair. A strand stuck to his boot, transported to the scene, implicating her—she closed her eyes envisioning it.

"All right, Ryan, I'll tell you the truth. Remember that story I told you about my husband? How he crashed his car through a window while he was doing cocaine? So I left him. Well, Ryan, the truth is that I crashed the car through the window and he left me. That's how I got those scars on my shoulder. Are these the kind of revelations you're looking for?"

"Yes, Caroline. Tell the truth. Why did you leave me back in Albany?"

"I left you, Ryan, because that is the way I am. You can't change it. You can't change me."

Ryan, seeing her disengaged from him, attempted to translate his fierce emotions into soft words, coming close to her face from the side. "Remember what it was like between us? We can have all that we ever wanted: a family, a life, kids, and a house. Why are you pulling back? This investigation will be over. I'll have my life back. Don't you remember what our life was like together?"

He could not help but smile at this conjured image, a long suppressed but ineluctable image of his destiny. There was a time for both of them when such thoughts of their mutual future did not demand the energy of deliberate elucidation. Futility was beating on him, awkward, heavy futility. She was inches from him, but far away in another place. He longed for her, wanted nothing more than for her to fall into his arms.

"We were just kids then, Ryan. Life is in the way now. I look at these young girls today and it's so sad because I'm not them anymore.

Look what time does to us. It destroys everything that was beautiful."
Her eyes welled with tears.

"I have to go," she said on the verge of convulsive emotion. She
sputtered away and left him without looking back. He stood frozen
in the office while she ran down the hallway. He could hear her
heels rapidly clinking away from him. He wanted to run after her.
He was reminded of those moments immortalized in film, those
poignant and pathetic scenes where lovers divide. He despised those
movies. He decided at that moment that he would bring his sample
of Caroline's hair to be tested and determined whether it was the
same hair found at the site where Warren's body had been buried.
The test would remove his doubts and restore his faith in her and, in
a strange way, his own slipping faith in all humanity.

CHAPTER 43

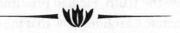

Somatos's office assumed a frantic level of activity in anticipation of the health care vote, and Ryan felt a sense of cautionary hope. The day moved smoothly. A secretary called for Ryan. There was call for him from the Fairfax Police.

"Hello," Ryan answered.

"Hello, Ryan, this is Lars Hestrom. I've got news for you."

Ryan expected that he was calling to convey news of Tantalus's capture.

"Your girlfriend's hair, Caroline Tierney. Dorus Genetics matches it with the hair we found where Leslie Warren was buried. Tierney is now officially a person of interest, and an alert to detain her has been issued. I thought you should hear it first from me."

"Thank you for calling me," said Ryan, stunned.

"You should call us if she tries to contact you," said Hestrom, sounding tough.

"Yes, yes, of course I will," said Ryan automatically.

Ryan had not told Somatos that he submitted her hair to the police, and he debated whether to broach the subject with him.

Political prudence dictated that Somatos be made aware, lest he have communication with her that would compromise him politically or legally, for she was now, like Tantalus, a fugitive. Nevertheless, Ryan could not break the news.

The working hours passed while Ryan waited, looking for an opportunity. He knew Somatos would not be pleased. He had explicitly warned Ryan against submitting Caroline's hair. However, Ryan had to know the truth. He had presumed that the test would conclusively exonerate Caroline. Now that the reverse had happened, Ryan wasn't quite sure what do.

During the day, abruptly, without any prompting, Somatos turned to Ryan and inquired about Caroline.

Ryan answered blankly. He had not heard from her.

"It's sad in a way. You know, she depends upon the kindness of men," observed Somatos.

"I think she depends more upon the weakness of men," responded Ryan. The remark did not need elaboration. Somatos paused, in apparent reflection, and then he did not mention her again to Ryan. The subject of Caroline became for Ryan a flash point that he wanted to avoid. He felt now that no one could be trusted. The politics of murder and missing girls seemed to be an ever-expanding circle, conspiring around him. He had wanted truth, and the truth was so horrible that now he only wanted beauty to come back into his life.

The sheer propulsion of the car as it sped north on the highway gave momentum to Caroline's train of thought. She had lived comfortably in a conjured world of self-denial where snow was sun, deserts were lush, and opportunity beckoned at every turn. Accustomed to the cool luxury of wealth and its appurtenances— the boat, the ostentatious cars, the palatial house and private pool, the vacations of sea and sun—she was now feeling rather lost and disconsolate. Her husband had left her, and he had adroitly deprived her of legal entitlement to his substantial resources. It was a fast and furious life, propelled by the high-octane engine of money, but now, stripped of material enrichment, she felt vulnerable for the first time in a very long time.

She knew in her heart and depth of her soul that she was profoundly lost and alone. The desire to keep moving was now the only thing to preserve her, a desperate need for movement as necessary buoyancy to keep her afloat in a tossing sea of trouble. Whimsically, she flipped from channel to channel on the radio, but the needle of her emotions could not find a grove of melody to soothe her. She drove away from Washington toward New York, and every mile of distance away from Ryan made her uneasy. Drugs and alcohol were a necessary palliative. A yearning for relief, crisp and white, melting upon a mirror. She had been on a cocaine binge the night she drove through the window. Her husband, more concerned about the wreck of his prized luxury car, decided that Caroline was a liability he could no longer afford. His beneficence having been exhausted, she had a faint idealistic notion that either Somatos or Ryan would come to her rescue. Perhaps even Tantalus, she thought before her encounter with him. But the whole matter of murder, and, of course, the politics of it all, now repelled her, sickened her.

Before the Delaware border, she felt consumed with the idea of a swim, to coolly soothe her distress. She had passed so many motels and so many pools that the cooling vision of chlorine and blue depths seemed entirely distracting. Some childhood memory stirred, when her mother was alive and her family was intact and the family pool was a bright blue fixture. The notion of a swim was so compelling that she drove off at the next exit and headed for a motel with a pool.

As she checked in and placed her belongings in the room, she felt that the idea of a swim was both impulsive and absurd. The motel room had the musty odor of summer rugs. However, having gone to this extent, she felt compelled to proceed. Changing into a two-piece bathing suit, she appreciated her form in the mirror. The taut lines of youth were gone, but luckily, she could still appreciate her own appearance. She jauntily headed toward the pool, towels in hand.

Behind a chain-link fence was spread an undisturbed blue rectangle of water, neatly bifurcated by a white string with buoys. Last year, in the lap of luxury, she had swum in her own pool, sometimes at midnight beneath stars and in a haze of alcohol and drugs. This swim would be different. The rays of sun refracted intensely from the watery surface and the small concrete perimeter. She positioned a yellow-ribbed recliner and arranged her belongings. With a sweep of her hand, she tested the water. The chlorinated scent of the pool was redolent in the air, and the water, basking under the brilliant sun, was temperate. She stepped gracefully onto the diving board, tested its elasticity, and dove. The sudden brace of water cooled her agitated body. Invigorated, she swam laps for almost thirty minutes until her arms ached. It was when she emerged, dripping and sleek, that she noticed a family had entered the fence.

Chlorine water ran from her and pooled on the hot concrete while she toweled down. The weight of depression seemed mitigated. Assuming a supine position on the recliner, she basked in the penetrating pleasure of the sun, hoping to restore vitality, while the crystalline voices of two little girls rang gleefully from the family. The thought of children seemed to be appealing at once. The huge hole that had been torn in her life, she considered, maybe could be filled with children. She conjured up a maternal image of herself and dozed in contentment.

By the time Caroline rose, the acute angle of the sun had passed and a tinge of sunburn had appeared on her face. She checked her cell phone, but she did not have any messages. She sauntered to a nearby soda machine. Passing the family, she noticed an intent scrutiny from the mother, who was reading the screen on her cell phone. She deposited several quarters in the soda machine, but the machine failed to dislodge any soda. Frustrated, she fiddled with the buttons until a bare brown chest emerged and pounded the machine hard with a fist. A soda ejected.

"Sometimes it needs to be hit hard," said the man, who had a cigarette dangling from his mouth and a vibrant line of tattoos up his arm.

"I guess you have the magic touch," said Caroline flirtatiously.

"Don't you know it," said the man, basking in the flattery. "Where are you traveling to?" he inquired.

"Nowhere in particular, sweetie."

"No. But you are," said the man with long, dark hair as he laughed, almost snickered. "You're running."

Caroline looked at him blankly. "What?"

"I know who you are," he said as he brought his brown face close to her sun-strained eyes. He smelled faintly of beer.

"Who am I?" Caroline asked with a smile of self-assurance.

"I've seen you before."

"All right, who am I?" reiterated Caroline.

The name he was struggling for came to his mind as he remembered the news article.

"Caroline, right? Caroline something."

She assumed he had read her name at the front desk of the motel.

"Look, I know you're on the run, so I can help you."

"Really?"

"I've got some stuff we can party with."

"Really?"

"You want to party, Caroline? I know that's what you want."

The effrontery of the man was not particularly compelling for her, but the thought of drugs, any drugs, seemed immediately appealing. She wanted to get high. She needed to break free, by any means, natural or artificial, of the deepening depression that was inking her soul an indelible deep blue.

"OK, I'll meet you in room 415 in twenty minutes," said Caroline sharply. "But just one question."

"OK," said the man, feeling smug.

"Why did you approach me?"

The man laughed again. "You don't know. You really don't know what's going on."

Caroline did not like the sound of his remark. Perhaps she was ignorant of some news.

"I'll show you in your room," he said as he strutted away. He flicked his cigarette in some bushes, and Caroline for the first time considered that perhaps only the evil people left in the world smoked these days.

CHAPTER 44

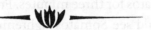

Congressman Sherwood Scott Jackson gaveled the health policy subcommittee to order at 3:00 p.m. The old congressman scowled at the crowd as his gavel ponderously struck four times. The garrulous din from the audience subsided, and people quickly occupied seats. The high-ceilinged committee hearing room consisted of a row of ten congressional members and the chair of the subcommittee seated in the middle on a dais, behind nameplates, under the glare of several strategically placed klieg lights, facing out at on audience of approximately eighty people, mostly lobbyists in expensive suits and policy specialists from relevant federal agencies. Congressman Green, who had been standing behind his seat and chatting amiably with his colleagues, respectfully took his seat. Somatos was several chairs down from Green, looking unusually pensive and preoccupied. As far as Ryan could tell, there had been no communication between the two of them. Ryan took a seat in the back of the room, clutching a legal notepad.

The subcommittee session was considered important but by no means crucial to that day's business of the Congress. Few reporters were in attendance; vested interests were themselves invisible but manifestly represented by the omnipresent well-tailored lobbyists.

The subcommittee had already held several public hearings, and the business to be conducted today was the consideration of twelve amendments to a larger health care financing package that included major revisions to Medicaid. As a clerk announced each amendment, a discussion ensued. Somatos's amendment was called. The chair recognized Somatos for three minutes. From the back of the hearing room, Ryan could see Somatos tightening with nervous pressure. Somatos cleared his throat and spoke in a husky voice, flavored with the distinct dialect of one of New York City's boroughs.

"Mr. Chairman, members of the committee. This amendment would allow the participation of an additional seven million children to be enrolled in government-subsidized health care. The funding comes from a tax surcharge on business. Small businesses under ten million dollars in sales are exempt. So what we are discussing here is a question of priority. Is the profit margin of large corporations a priority or the health of children? I don't know about you, but I rank children above profits any day."

At that remark, Ryan could see the Republicans on the committee rolling their eyes and twisting uncomfortably in their leather seats. Somatos continued his brief statement without rhetorical flourish or any formal eloquence. Time was limited and the vote was imminent.

For thirty minutes, consideration of Somatos's amendment sparked verbal acrimony among the committee members. However, Ryan could see that Congressman Green remained notably taciturn during the exchange. After thirty minutes of pointed questions and inconclusive discussion, the chair called a roll call vote. The vote proceeded alphabetically as expected. In turn, each congressman and woman called "aye" or "nay." When Green's name was called, he called out to defer, rocking back and forth in his chair in a contemplative posture. While the roll call preceded, both Congressman Green and Congressman Laverne had been passed over and were again to be called by the clerk. The amendment was two votes short. Ryan's eyes volleyed between Somatos and Green. Somatos had his sight fixed on Green, like an assassin.

The clerk again requested the vote of Congressman Green. Ryan could see Green visibly vacillate and then after a hesitation call "aye." The vote of Congressman Laverne followed: "Aye." The amendment passed by a single vote. A low but perceptible hum emanated from the audience. Lobbyists briskly left the room to operate their cell phones, visibly chagrined by a vote count that had been proven wrong. Somatos's amendment had passed; Ryan presumed that Green had yielded to Somatos's pressure. Somatos did not show any emotion. It was neither the time nor place for a showing of pride.

"Congratulations, Congressman," Ryan offered to Somatos in his office thirty minutes after the vote while the staff huddled around him. Somatos beamed proudly at his legislation's passage, like a new father.

"It would seem that Congressman Green is an honorable man," said Somatos with a sardonic wink directly at Ryan.

"You don't think that Green will take permanent offense at the way you extracted his support?" asked Ryan.

"Extorted his support?"

Ryan grimaced. "I said extracted."

"There is no defense for a man who, in excess of his wealth, has kicked the great alter of justice out of sight. Green knows that it's all part of the game."

Unlike Somatos, who seemed energized, Ryan's political energy had been enervated. The vote was a victory for Somatos, but there was no pleasure for Ryan. His strength had been sapped.

"Another exercise in power politics to what end?" asked Ryan of his mentor, expansively.

"You're too seasoned to be cynical at this stage, Ryan. What do they say back home? Don't hate the player; hate the game."

Abruptly, Somatos went into his office. In a sudden shift of emotion, he went to his window and looked out. Ryan followed him in and then wondered what had engendered such sudden solemnity. After a pensive moment, Somatos turned back toward Ryan. A sentimental mist seemed to cloud the usually bright wolf eyes. He seemed about to speak, but then he turned his back again to Ryan to look out the window at nothing in particular.

CHAPTER 45

The motel room window was illuminated repetitively with the sweep of car headlights from the highway. The smell of cigarettes and stale alcohol permeated the room. Stretched lethargically on the bed, Caroline was naked and her clothes strewn disheveled and tossed in a rumpled mass that cascaded from her suitcase. Caroline stared at the news and her photo on her cell phone. She considered it first with a kind of narcissistic flattery. The surreptitious photo had been taken recently when she was having brunch with Ryan, and Caroline realized that Ryan had been cropped from it. After she vainly considered the photo, the ramification of the news article affected her. She was wanted for questioning as an accomplice to Seth Tantalus in the murder of Leslie Warren. How absurd, thought Caroline. She considered how her hair might have been transported to the crime scene. She speculated that in her struggle with Tantalus at his house he had savagely pulled her by the hair. Some strands, she thought, had come loose and affixed to his clothing or even a shoe or boot. Unfortunately, this evidence carried to the crime scene. Thus, she had become implicated in the most inadvertent and tragic way.

She felt powerless to exonerate herself. She simply did not have the energy.

Her life was reduced to a jagged shamble of rough-edged duplicity and deceit. She had run out of money, her wealth melted like a luxurious mound of snow in summer, without the faintest trace. Most importantly, her wounded ego was stung by Ryan's betrayal of her. He must have given the police a hair sample for identification. The prospect of a grand jury, a trial, publicity—it was all loathsome. She was not involved directly with the murder of Leslie Warren, but perhaps, she thought, in some way, she was guilty of some crime.

At the far end of a tunnel, there was a lurid light in her eyes or perhaps in her mind. Futilely, she wanted to close her eyes against this intrusion but discovered to her silent horror she could not. There was the detached and morbid sensation of not having control of one's body. In a strange and surreal way, she was still able to think in the way that people think in dreams, vividly and in flashes. Like a horrifying dream that defies awakening, she could not break free of its hold. It was a coma perhaps, a death-defying half sleep, a cruel and motionless dreamlike state. She was coherent enough to be cognizant of the fact that she had been on a drug-and-whisky-laden binge. She had acted impulsively with reckless abandon fueled by sentimentality, anger, euphoria, and regret. There was the sensation of a tear running down her cheek. She wished there was a way to call for help. There was not.

For hours, she hovered in this abstract and half-conscious state until her slowly beating heart succumbed. The once beautiful and expressive blue eyes transfixed their gaze, and her body was utterly and completely still. Her brain, deprived of oxygen, slowly ceased to function, and the once beautiful body that had ruled over so many men began the inevitable accelerated decline that death brings.

It was several hours before a maid discovered the body of Caroline Tierney. According to the police report, the maid had entered the room at about nine o clock that night. The startled maid, a recent immigrant from Honduras, found the naked, lifeless body. The police report omitted the unknown fact that the maid also found a duffel bag with fifteen thousand dollars in cash, which she hurriedly concealed in her car before alerting the hotel manager. "She had a beautiful body," said the maid admiringly.

For the police investigators at the scene, there was initial confusion regarding the death. Several hours elapsed before a confirmed identification could be made and a state coroner could with certainty identify the deceased as Caroline Tierney and the cause of death as a lethal combination of cocaine, Valium, and whisky.

CHAPTER 46

Dusk settled finely over the city of monuments, museums, and modern order. The Capitol dome was a luminescent vision, a lofty cake white in the deep blue twilight, rivaled only by a silver globe of moon hung low in the sky. Ryan emerged from the legislative building and gazed up at the white rotunda peak, capping the glory of government. The dome before him was an omnipotent magnet of aspiration that bended, refined, and even distorted the will of men and women who sought the prestige of its power. The heat of day cooled, and the emerging night was soothed by a breeze from the river. He hailed a cab and directed it toward Georgetown. Ryan envisioned a quiet, finely prepared meal in a Georgetown restaurant, alone.

Ryan's cab accelerated past the elongated grassy stretch of the mall, past the illuminated spire of the Washington Monument, along the tree-lined streets, thronged with traffic, and then up the boulevards that blared with a cacophony of horns and sirens indigenous to any metropolis. At Georgetown, the cab became lodged in traffic and Ryan exited.

The exquisite aroma of exotic cuisine from a hundred restaurants flavored the air. On the streets, a pulsing throb of pedestrians moved in lively groups. Ryan could overhear multiple animated conversations from the prancing women on their cell phones and swaggering men in suits who passed him on the street. Around him now were street beggars and young university revelers, the poor, the wealthy, and the well-to-do. Bureaucrats and diplomats and power brokers mingled and weighed their dinner options. The night was alive with frivolity and laughter, and the world of Washington seemed like an open banquet to be feasted on by those who had ascended to its pleasant perch.

"What's up, man."

"What?"

"Your ego need a shine?"

It took a moment for Ryan to focus on the fact that the young man wanted to shine his shoes. Ryan laughed. He had spent several hours drinking and now at 11:00 p.m., someone wanted to shine his shoes on a street corner in Georgetown. "Sure, why not," offered Ryan, feeling magnanimous. He sat down on the improvised shoeshine chair while the young man, with great alacrity and zest, polished a raised shoe with a dirty buffer. The street crowds, worn from the evening of eating, drinking, and revelry, edged past him with indifference and, strangely to Ryan, almost an ostensible disdain.

"You look down," said the African-American teenager.

Ryan noticed that the young man's pants and shirt were tattered in places. He placed his age at about sixteen.

"Just a bad luck streak," said Ryan casually.

"No way. You're the man, you got it all," said the young man as he focused on the shoe.

"What do you mean?"

"You know. You got a wife, a house, right?" said the teenager, looking up with an optimistic smile.

"Why no. My wife is filing for divorce and will likely get the house. So I don't," said Ryan.

"Well, you got money, right?"

"No, not exactly. I'm in debt now," replied Ryan.

The young man looked up, concerned that he wouldn't be paid for his service.

"Well, you got kids, a car, right?"

"No. I had a car, but it was wrecked. My stepdaughter is no longer with me. No," said Ryan, whose mood under this line of inquiry was becoming melancholy.

The young shoe shiner buffed mightily and prepared for the next shoe. The prospect of a generous tip was fading, but he sustained an unmitigated enthusiasm for his job.

"Well, mister, you don't have no wife, no kids, no car, no house, no money." The young man paused thoughtfully. "You got a girlfriend?"

"Well, no, not really," said Ryan as he pondered a faded, almost painful image of Caroline.

"Shit," replied the young man. He directed Ryan to raise his other foot. "Well, let me see," he said. He was continuing to shine vigorously but was becoming distracted. "You have a good job, right?"

"Yes, I did," said Ryan.

The young man paused his polishing and looked up at Ryan. "You did?"

"Well," said Ryan, "I still have it, but I think I'm going to be fired."

"Oh," said the young man as he resumed his work. "So you ain't got no wife, no kids, no house, no car, no money, no sex, and you think you might lose your job."

It was a succinct recitation of his current circumstance, more than Ryan himself could have elucidated. "Yes, that about sums it up."

"Well, man, you are a pathetic white man," said the young man as he finished the last buffing, "but you still got more than me and most people."

"Yes, I see your point," said Ryan, feeling as depressed as ever.

The boy saw Ryan's dejected state and wanted to offer him some encouraging recommendation. "Look, man, why don't you head to N and Fifteenth." He handed Ryan a wrinkled business promotion card.

Ryan read the card. It said, "Free admittance to the Babylon Club." Ryan laughed aloud.

"Man, go. It will do you good," counseled the young man.

"All right. I just might do that," said Ryan. He stood up and gave the young man a twenty dollar bill. A loud boom of music came down the street, emanating from a black Jeep, slowly cruising, packed with a full crew of African-American kids, in revelry.

The night was young, and Ryan felt emboldened. It had been years since he entered a strip club, not because of some sense of propriety but rather because he simply regarded the whole affair as somewhat juvenile, almost depressing. But this kind of activity seemed to suit his somber mood, so he walked through the thronged streets toward the club.

Outside the Babylon Club, an enormous bouncer in a T-shirt and black jacket and with an intimidating gaze inspected each patron before permitting entrance. Ryan handed him the free admittance card. He looked Ryan up and down, nodded his assent, and then spoke into a hand-held walkie-talkie: "One coming in."

The club was much darker than the street, with purple and black walls, and dark furnishings. A miasma of cigarette smoke intensified the ambience. The only light came from a mirrored stage where a tall, tan goddess, entirely undressed and bathed in spotlight, was making love to a brass railing. Another bouncer directed Ryan to a seat toward the back, a seat that established some physical decency between the woman's sex organs and one's face.

Ryan ordered a beer and watched the show with an amused detachment. Rock music blared from unseen speakers, throbbing with relentless percussion. Next to Ryan sat a young professional with a wad of cash set on his table like Monopoly money. He seemed either quite drunk or thoroughly engrossed in the affair on stage. The tall, tan goddess descended the stage to a round of applause, a garter on one leg holding a thick green bouquet of cash. Within seconds, as the blonde displayed her gratitude to the audience, she was substituted by an Asian woman emerging from the darkness, dressed in a negligee and who appeared to have a very large chest, disproportionate to her petite figure.

"I like this one," said the young man seated next to Ryan. Ryan nodded as he drank mightily, gulping down the beer, intent on dulling the senses.

"This one has a set on her that could float a ship," the yuppie observed. Ryan again nodded polite agreement. He ordered a second beer. The waitress's chest, two large artificial globes of flesh, floated into Ryan's face.

The young man next to Ryan stood up, approached the stage, and, with some dexterity, placed a twenty dollar bill into the garter of the gyrating Asian. Ryan looked at him somewhat baffled at his generosity.

"I made five thousand dollars today in the stock market. Day trading. Last week I made ten thousand. Spent at least three thousand in here. One of the girls gave me one hell of a hummer in my Mercedes."

Ryan intensified his conquest of beer. After the fourth beer, the changing scene of women seemed to establish a kind of mindless trance. There had been at least six dancers now. Ryan was amused at their little conventions of periodically wiping down the mirrors with glass cleaner and polishing the brass rails. An immaculate stage seemed integral to the integrity of their performances. They moved among the audience and whispered appreciation, but their voices betrayed them as harsh, coarse. The sight of these nimble, high-heeled women did little to lift his spirits. However, on stage their smooth, creamy bodies, framed in darkness, softly highlighted by the iridescence of neon lights, became Playboy models of perfection that held his attention. Long legs stretched wondrously, erect breasts thrust provocatively forward, and Ryan felt himself worshipping at a kind of shrine, paying homage to the sublime beauty of a woman's body.

Ryan lost count of the beers he had consumed, and the dancer now, a brunette, was undulating her bare sex organ so efficiently that Ryan felt an erection stirring. From the audience, a big athletic type came before the stage. He stood before the dancer and, proximate to her sex, was hungrily breathing in her feminine scent. "I like it shaved, honey. The other girls have too much hair down there," he said loudly as he slipped money into her garter.

Ryan snapped alertly from his alcohol-hazed mind. The lights from the stage momentarily illuminated the young man as he slipped the money into the silk garter. Ryan thought in that crass, illuminated moment he had seen Seth Tantalus.

The man had returned to his seat, enshrouded in darkness and a vapor cloud of cigarette smoke. Ryan scanned the club. Tantalus was closer to the front door. *A hell of a situation*, thought Ryan to himself. He was trapped with his nemesis, a murderer, in a strip club of all places. He had walked into the killer's lair. Ryan turned in his seat and peered through the darkness toward the man. There was a resemblance to Seth Tantalus: thick, dark hair swept back, huge jaw, the stance that seemed arrogantly aggressive.

Ryan rose from his chair and made his way through the closely positioned tables to the rear of the club. In the back, between the restrooms, Ryan removed his cell phone. Keeping an eye on activity by the stage, he dialed the 911 operator. The music from the club would make the conversation difficult.

"What is your emergency?" inquired the harried police dispatcher, in routine fashion.

"I just want to alert you that a fugitive in the Leslie Warren abduction is here in the Babylon Club at Fifteenth and N Street."

"What?" the dispatcher asked, seemingly confused or unable to clearly hear Ryan.

"The Leslie Warren abduction suspect is at the Babylon Club," repeated Ryan, more forcefully and drawing attention from a nearby waitress dressed in a bikini.

"All right," said the dispatcher slowly, "a fugitive for the Leslie Warren abduction is at the Babylon Club in DC."

"Yes."

"Who are you?" the dispatcher demanded.

"Never mind." Ryan hung up the phone and at that moment recognized that he, himself, was at one point a suspect in the abduction. The way his luck had been running, he mused, the police would come and arrest him.

He looked up and could see directly in front of him a wobbly Seth Tantalus searching out the darkness for a lavatory to relieve himself. Ryan was standing right by the men's room door. Tantalus focused on Ryan. A look of disbelief quickly changed to one of belligerent rage.

"Son of a bitch," Tantalus exclaimed.

Ryan paused, battle ready, but before Tantalus could lunge he was locked by two bull-necked bouncers, who had anticipated trouble from the inebriated patron. The bouncers had their hands full. Tantalus was violently enraged. Only by the fact that the bouncers matched Tantalus in size were they able to successfully constrain him and force him back toward the front door.

"I'm going to kill you and your whole family, you little prick."

The action in the club ceased. Dancers moved into corners, guarded by more bouncers. In a violent spectacle, Tantalus was pulled forcefully through the club. Tables were turned and beers spilt. The music stopped playing.

By the time Tantalus was pushed out onto the street, he could hear the distant wail of sirens. Confronted by three sizable bouncers, and the police on the way, he sprinted angrily down the street into the hot night.

Inside the club, within minutes, normalcy resumed. Tables were set upright, music played again, and the dancers slowly resumed their gyrations. A number of patrons, recognizing that Ryan was the focus of the enraged man's ire, watched him with protracted stares. Ryan regarded their suspicions with a composed propriety, waiting several minutes unobtrusively in a corner of the club, and then he left before the police arrived. He exited the club and was out on the street. Cautiously, he looked around. Confronted with the raw, angry menace of Seth Tantalus, Ryan now felt the threat. As long as Tantalus was a fugitive, Ryan knew his life could not return to some semblance of normalcy.

CHAPTER 47

R yan entered his apartment and collapsed in bed. He was too tired to shower or even fully undress. The alcohol had injected an overwhelming lassitude into his body: it demanded sleep, dreams, peace. Weighty thoughts dissolved into ethereal slumber. His body turned and slid into sleep.

He can see the upstairs corridor of his house. It is dark and quiet. Check on Jessica. Make sure she is safe. He moves down the hall carefully, quietly. Jessica is in bed, sleeping peacefully. He is reassured. Then he hears moaning. A coarse groan. Ryan moves back down the hall to Annie's bedroom. The corridor is long and dark. The walls shift, and he must balance himself as he moves forward. He recognizes Annie's moans. They are deep, impassioned. He opens his bedroom door. Annie's back is arched and her dark mane of hair is wild. Her breasts are thrust forward, sensually. She is sitting arched in bed; more accurately she is straddling something. No, someone. Ryan enters the room. Annie continues her movements, gyrating her hips in rhythmic fashion. Ryan remembers the way she used to ride him to climax. He is almost beside her. She does not turn. More groans. Now she turns and smiles at Ryan. It is a beguiling smile. There is a sense of evil. See what you're missing, it says. Ryan's pulse is quickening. Jealousy. Raw jealously burns into him. Who is the man? They have stopped their mutual movements. He too is smiling at Ryan. It is a wide, bare smile with teeth that seem to glimmer malevolently in the darkness. It is a wide wolfish smile. Somatos. A phone is ringing: an insistent electronic squeal.

Ryan awoke. His cell phone was ringing incessantly. Ryan could not answer the phone. He was dehydrated, and his head pulsed painfully. Complacently, he allowed the phone to ring so that the voice mail would intercept the call. Still inebriated, he walked unsteadily to the kitchen and drank two full glasses of water through parched lips. He sat down on the bed and removed the remainder of his clothes. Horrible dream, he thought. Horrid. He looked at the phone. He did not recognize the number and entered his voice mail code. Immediately, he recognized the voice as Somatos. Uncharacteristically, the voice was subdued, almost confused. It was moments before Ryan focused on what Somatos was saying.

"Ryan. Ryan. I've just received a call from the Maryland State Police. I've been notified that they have found Caroline Tierney dead of a drug overdose. They believe it is suicide. There was no note found, but they did find a business card from me with some writing on it, and they felt that I needed to be notified." Somatos paused on the recording. "I've also found out since we last spoke that she was wanted by the police as an accomplice of Seth Tantalus. Submitting that hair sample was a mistake, Ryan. Well, it makes no difference now; she is dead. Call me."

Ryan considered whether the phone call was still part of a dream. But even in his semi-inebriated state, he recognized the reality of the call and the fact that Caroline was dead. Ryan reclined back down on the bed.

A haunting murmur of mortality whispered in his ear, an incessant chattering that made sleep impossible. The barely furnished room was a depressing cell of solitude. Dawn would render comforting dimension and life infused color to the nebulous night. But for now the minutes past midnight clicked in his mind, agonizingly, tortuously, ominously. Her death seemed inconceivable, portentous, horrifying, and wrenchingly sad. Ryan McNeil's grieving for Caroline Tierney came in the form of a thousand needles of pain. There was an unbearable discomfort. He could not sleep now. He could not be still. He could not quell the turbulent riot of emotions that rampaged within him. Maybe it wasn't suicide, he contemplated. *Maybe Tantalus got to her. No. No, that makes no sense.* But Tantalus was crazy, Ryan considered. Maybe Tantalus thought killing Caroline would inflict revenge on Ryan.

Caroline was dead, and Ryan choked on emotion. Deciphering her motives had always been impossible. She was now another permanent enigma, like Wilet, like Warren, like Annie. Except, of course, Caroline was dead and Annie was still alive. *Is she still alive?*

Ryan sat up in bed. Tantalus had trailed Ryan from Albany to Washington D.C.. With the sordid encounter in the strip club and now Caroline's death, maybe Tantalus was targeting all the people in Ryan's life. Ryan picked up his cell phone. He wanted to call Annie, but each time he entered the numbers he stopped before entering the last digit. He would appear foolish calling his ex-wife to bemoan the fact that his lover had killed herself. He could not call. *Maybe they are in danger*, thought Ryan. Jessica and Annie could be a target of Tantalus. *Revenge.* The revenge of a killer with nothing to lose, improbable, illogical, but there was a symmetry to it that appeared to fit the entire pattern, thought Ryan.

The clock showed the time to be 3:40 a.m. Ryan could get to Annie's house in thirty minutes. He began to dress, at first slowly and then with frantic effort. *Just to be sure she is safe,* he thought. Ryan dashed from the apartment building into the street. It was a serene summer night. On the deserted street, Ryan hailed a cab and recited his old address. *Just be sure that they are safe*, thought Ryan. He sat anxiously in the back seat while a Jamaican cab driver talked to his buddies on the cab radio.

The cab discharged him on the suburban street across from his old house. There were no lights on inside the house, and the street was tranquil. Ryan let the cab leave. There were no suspicious cars and no traffic. The nocturnal hoot of an owl punctuated the minutes. He stood stranded on the street. The night was warm, muggy, and Ryan felt a damp frustration, standing like a spy in the open. Around him was the gossamer stillness of a summer night. He had left nearly five weeks before, but that short period now seemed substantial, almost daunting. He felt constrained from crossing the street. He could see no activity by the windows, but to walk up to the front door of his house now seemed to require a determined act of temerity. Perhaps this feeling was a product of an overexcited imagination, he considered.

Ryan checked his watch. The timepiece had frozen still at 3:35. The second hand was not moving. The battery must have died, he thought. He withdrew his cell phone and dialed Annie's house phone. He paced while the phone rang for several minutes, then went to voice mail. He started to utter a word and then disconnected. Maybe they were sleeping. Maybe the phone was off.

He drew in a deep, conscious breath. The sweet suburban air, even under starlight, was aromatic from the cultivation of lawns and flowering bushes. He felt a kind of calmness pass through him. His calmness dissipated quickly while he looked carefully again at the front door. He could see a shadow that did not seem quite right. Was the front door ajar? It did not seem possible. He stared at the door, fixing his powers of perception. The door looked open. *This is silly,* he thought. *Why not walk up and check.*

He walked across what had been his lawn to the front door. In the inanimate night, his movements, he thought, must have appeared suspicious and conspicuous. There was no subtle way to approach the issue; he needed to check to see if the door was properly shut. He gave a gentle push and the door swung open into darkness. Ryan's body surged with adrenaline.

Ryan peered into the indefinite darkness. He could barely discern the outline of his living room. He stood for a few moments, paused on this precipice, while his sight adjusted to the darkness. Finally, he entered. The arrangement of furniture seemed familiar. Nothing seemed amiss. An unreality clung to the moment. He was standing in his former life. Why? He was not sure whether to turn on a light, call out, or step back outside. He was still, surveying the room. He moved forward into the living room. There were no sounds. He wondered if his deep breathing was audible. Wait, a mechanical sound. *What was that sound?*

The front door shut slowly, seemingly automatically. Ryan turned and could see Seth Tantalus standing by the door with a gun pointed directly at him. Even in shadows and darkness, the gun had a distinct metallic glint that immediately conveyed lethal reality. Tantalus was in front of him and the gun was firmly in his hand. Conjecture and rational thought were subsumed. Ryan's mind was now on a plane of primitive reality.

"I thought you had moved back in," said Tantalus nonchalantly.

"No, I hadn't."

"I knew you would be here, though. You've got a strange desire to protect woman, don't you, Ryan?" said Tantalus with raw antagonism.

"What have you done with Annie and Jessica?" demanded Ryan.

"Nothing. They're tied up," said Tantalus calmly.

"If there is any harm to them..."

"I said their tied up."

Ryan was relieved that Tantalus was conversing. He had feared summary execution by an impetuous sociopath. If harm had come to Jessica or Annie, Ryan pledged to himself fierce, violent retribution. He would not hold back his hatred; he would yield to base human reflex. He would kill Tantalus if he could.

Tantalus continued: "It was you I wanted. I can't believe how you could screw things up, Ryan. Un-fucking believable."

"What do mean, Seth?"

"How did you trace Wilet and Warren back to me? I still don't understand how that happened."

"I knew it could not be a coincidence that you had tried to drop those clothes at my house and then threw it at my car. I knew it had to be tied to Wilet."

"What are you talking about?" demanded Tantalus. His voice became suddenly savage and loud. Surely, thought Ryan, Annie could hear it if she was still alive.

"You were trying to frame me for both murders," asserted Ryan.

"How did they tie you back to Wilet, though?" asked Tantalus. Clearly this conundrum disturbed him.

"I kept clippings of her disappearance," said Ryan.

"Clippings? Why did you do that?"

"Well, I saw the car you took her in, and I . . ."

"What the hell are you talking about," interjected Tantalus, his face contorted with confusion.

"The limo, the car."

"You saw her when she was abducted. Shit, unbelievable." Tantalus waved his gun, almost distracted by this news.

"You didn't know?" said Ryan, waiting for a moment to lunge, hoping that Tantalus would be distracted.

"Oh, I killed Wilet, but I wasn't driving that car, you dumb son of a bitch," said Tantalus.

For a moment Ryan could not concentrate on the gun. "What?"

"You're so naïve, Ryan. So damn naive. No, I wasn't driving the car. You learned nothing from Somatos, didn't you."

The remark struck Ryan as a non sequitur. What thing of relevance was he to have learned from Somatos?

"I'll tell you, Ryan," said Tantalus as he again steadied his malevolent aim in what Ryan perceived to be the direction of his head. "I was dating Wilet; she was a good lay. I was screwing a lot of women, though. I just did not give a shit. I had already planned the fire in Tower Two to destroy some documents on the ombudsman appointments. A favor for the fuckin' governor, who knew those documents would sink him. But the governor is too smart to pay out directly. So he does us a favor by vetoing Somatos's genetic testing legislation. Through the veto, Green and I made a ton of money by investing in the one company that would profit when our legislation was signed years later. I had already told Wilet about the stock and the fire I was going to set—some bragging, you know how it is. I must have slept with a hundred women in Albany. But this Wilet bitch was bent out of shape. She said she was going to tell the Albany DA that I was planning on destroying the Ombudsman evidence for the governor. She had all the documents and didn't give a damn about politics. She just wanted to screw me over."

Tantalus's voice was angry now and emphatic. Ryan could sense a rising crescendo that would lead to violence.

"I tried talking to her, but she wouldn't listen. So I lost my temper and one thing led to another. You know, I expected the police to catch up with me, but they never did. I guess I got all the evidence in the fire. I had no idea you kept a jerk-off collection of Wilet memorabilia." Tantalus could feel the fever in his blood, boiling over, throbbing in his head and wrenching him internally.

"And Warren?" asked Ryan, seeking postponement of the inevitable.

"That bitch just happened to recognize me from Caluzzi's office."

"Caluzzi? The assemblyman that tried to rape his intern?" Now it was Ryan who was distracted and challenged by a new conundrum. "What are you talking about, Tantalus? What the hell did Leslie Warren or Cindy Ambrose have to do with Caluzzi?"

Tantalus unleashed a loud, perverse laugh.

"I thought you had it all figured out, Ryan. Leslie Warren was Caluzzi's intern. Remember the intern that killed him the night he tried to rape her? Cindy Ambrose changed her name to Leslie Warren, but it was her."

Ryan shook his head in disbelief. He remembered the news report of the young intern, with concealed identity, who had murdered Caluzzi, defending herself against a sexual assault by the assemblyman.

"You don't have anything figured out, do you, Ryan? I was in Annabees and this Cindy Ambrose chick comes up to me and says, 'Don't I know you from Albany? Didn't I see you with Assemblyman Caluzzi?' I lie. I say, 'No, not me.' I don't know who she is. So I ask her if she was a friend of Cathy Wilet. She says, 'The missing girl, the murdered girl?' I explained that I was her boyfriend and maybe she knew me through Cathy. And then I realize how stupid I was. I made the connection in her mind."

Ryan could not fathom the logic. "So what? I don't get it. Why murder her? Was she blackmailing you? Did you pay her the $770,000?"

"I wouldn't give that bitch a dime. I don't know anything about that money. She saw me with Caluzzi. I realize she may have heard me talking to Caluzzi about driving the car. She had no basis for connecting that conversation with Wilet until I told her I was Wilet's boyfriend. She had no idea who I was until then. She had only been working in the assembly for six weeks. I was just another young legislative director down in the assembly, talking to Caluzzi about driving a car. She was gone after she killed him in self-defense. I never saw her again. She never saw me again. Leslie Warren Ambrose, whatever her name, justifiably kills Caluzzi, the one crazy guy that could be a problem for me—which was a lucky break for me—but then I had to kill her. Not so lucky for her."

"Caluzzi drove the car that night? He abducted Wilet? Why Caluzzi?"

"Ryan, you are an idiot. Caluzzi was all mobbed up, remember? His brother was in a crime family. His brother was a contract killer. Somatos told me that Caluzzi would likely drive the car. Somatos told me to ask Caluzzi and I did. To tell you the truth, I have no idea who drove the car that night. I never saw the guy that dropped her off. Could have been Caluzzi; could have been Somatos."

"Wait a second. What are you saying about Somatos? He wasn't driving any damn car," Ryan raged. "You're the one with the gun and you're the murderer."

"How can you be so sure? I wasn't the one driving the limo that took her. It was the driver who saw you and wanted to make sure that you couldn't finger anyone," snarled Tantalus.

Aimlessly, the gun wavered. This was the opportunity. No time to think further. Ryan sucked his breath in and pounced with full force of rage and resolution. Lunging forward, he grabbed Tantalus's firing arm with both hands, twisting the muzzle to the side, trying to break Tantalus's hold on the weapon. Fortuitously for Ryan, Tantalus was slow to react. His upper body tightened stiffly, and to Ryan he was as immobile as an enormous statue. In the darkness there were grunts, animal like and ferocious. Tantalus's superior physical leverage allowed him to steady himself firmly while forcing Ryan back. Tantalus knew it was a matter of seconds before he would break free of Ryan's frantic hold and then be able to throw Ryan to the floor and fire the weapon point blank.

Without warning, there was an explosion. Ryan closed his eyes and then opened them. There was a slimy, viscous mass on his face. Tantalus was on the ground. Ryan was stunned and stepped back. A few seconds elapsed before he realized that he was speckled in blood and brain matter. Amazingly, he realized that his brain was miraculously intact and Seth Tantalus's head had fatally exploded. Ryan turned and there was Annie McNeil holding a gun straight out with both hands. Intensely, she was frozen in a rigid firing position.

Ryan drenched in Tantalus's blood, wiped his face with his hand. He looked at Annie with a sense of palpable relief.

"Where did you get the gun?"

"My ex," said Annie sharply. She was standing stiffly with the gun still poised.

"I didn't know you could shoot," Ryan said thankfully, as the tightness in his chest loosened. "Is Jessica ok?"

"Jessica is fine upstairs. She was able to free herself and untie me. And yes, I can shoot very well, Ryan," she said with evident hostility.

Now Ryan realized that Annie was maintaining her firing position. "What's wrong?"

"I know about Caroline Tierney."

Ryan looked at her with utter incomprehension. "You know what?"

"How could you, Ryan? You bastard."

Ryan was bewildered. "What are you talking about, Annie? You heard Tantalus. He's the one that came here to hurt you; to hurt Jessica. He's a murderer," exclaimed Ryan.

"He came here because of you, Ryan," screamed Annie viciously. "You brought this horror into this house." Her words were shrill and sharp as a dagger. "You're as evil as him."

Ryan could not comprehend the condemnation. "How am I evil, Annie? What the hell are you talking about?"

"I'm talking about Caroline Tierney, the blonde. I saw you with her, you know. I went to the hotel and the two of you just walked right past me. You didn't even notice, Ryan." Annie paused and drew in a deep breath for her righteous condemnation of Ryan. "You're a degenerate. A serial womanizer."

Ryan would have laughed the matter off, if not for the fact that Annie was still pointing a weapon in an ominous firing position at him.

"She was a slut. A slut," she repeated shrilly. "You slept with her before our marriage and during our marriage, and you didn't care if you made me sick, did you?"

"No, I was not sleeping with Caroline," said Ryan emphatically, with the realization that his wife was deadly serious.

"Don't lie, Ryan. Somatos told me everything."

Ryan was bewildered. "Somatos?"

"He told me that you were sleeping with her and with that other slut too. You didn't care if I lived or died. You didn't care if Jessica had a mother or not, did you? Every sexual act with you was dangerous and diseased," Annie screamed in righteous condemnation.

The accusation was so wild and irrational to Ryan that he smiled nervously.

"Are you crazy? I was fighting to protect both you and Jessica. That's why I'm here."

"We don't need your protection, Ryan. I'm the one with the gun, and I am capable of protecting myself and Jessica. Somatos told me that Caroline is dead and that you would probably come to me for comfort."

"Somatos?" The sense of betrayal beat on Ryan with fierce wings of fury. "Somatos is deceiving you, Annie."

"Is she dead? Tell me. Tell me the truth."

"Yes. She is dead, but Somatos is manipulating you for his own benefit."

"He has no reason to, Ryan," said Annie plainly. "I'm sorry, but you deserve it."

"Deserve what?" Ryan countered.

The answer never issued back. Instead, with the same calmness and deliberate calculation with which she had triggered the weapon moments before, Annie McNeil aimed and pulled the trigger again, this time discharging a bullet directly at the head of Ryan McNeil. Before the explosion of the bullet, the expression on his face was one of pure incredulity: more utter amazement than fright. Ryan heard the sound of the gun, but the elapsed time was too minimal for him to comprehend that his wife had shot him. After the explosion there was no expression, for his face was gone. Ryan catastrophically fell to the ground, his brains shattered into a fragmentary, hideous mass. Both Ryan McNeil and Seth Tantalus were now commingled on the carpeted floor in a horrid pool of blood and brains and livid corpse.

Her first instinct was to run upstairs and check on Jessica. She had told her to hide in her bedroom closet. Upstairs, she opened the door to the closet and found her. The little girl was meekly curled into a sobbing ball on the floor, knees drawn tightly up to her chin. Her eyes were shut tightly, twisting her face. She was immured in her own little world. Annie embraced and comforted her. Close to her face, wet with tears, she instructed her to stay upstairs, for there had been a horrible, horrible accident downstairs and the police had to come. Fresh tears spouted like a fountain from the little girl. Annie tenderly picked her up and carried her to her bedroom, where she laid her on the bed and secured her under the protection of covers. Coming close to her ear, she murmured maternal reassurance. The little girl, still in a quivering state of fear, nodded childish concurrence.

Annie went back downstairs and then stood reflectively still for a moment, surveying the carnal wreckage in the living room. A huge hemorrhage stain had spread out across the white carpet. Immediately, she recognized that most of the furniture was now irreparably ruined.

Outside, a rose-colored dawn bloomed beyond the window, like a fast-growing flower. Annie sat bolt upright in a white upholstered chair flecked with blood and hideous bits of brain matter. The scene before her became transfigured. Clarifying light entered through the windows, rendering the gore of blood and lifeless flesh around her more vivid. Gradually, this gruesome scene became substantial, less dreamlike, less surreal. Nevertheless, over this morbid horror hovered a kind of strange serenity. The pause offered a respite in which she was able, in her mind, to effectively sweep clear the remaining detritus of her marriage, the corporeal remnant of which was sprawled on the floor before her. For her, the new dawn had swept in like a cleansing wave, smoothing her conscience, eradicating those little mental bubbles of guilt. In her mind she calmly composed her exculpatory tale.

After this mental preparation, she went to the telephone

and dialed 911. The fact that her hands were not trembling at all surprised her but in a strange way also pleased her. As she waited for the operator, she realized as well that she was utterly composed, self-assured. In fact, there was almost a sense of relief. She had conclusively resolved the issue.

Soon birds blithely chirped outside, a precursor of a typical summer day, and then their mellifluous song was displaced by the siren wail of the police, harsh and emphatic, a violent rending of the morning peace. She was ready for their peremptory intrusion and for their accusatory questions. For on this new day she had nothing to fear. Absolutely nothing at all. She was as certain as one could be of that fact.

CHAPTER 48

66 So let me understand what you're saying, Ms. McNeil," said
Lars Hestrom as he questioned Annie McNeil in the same
room of the Fairfax Police Department headquarters where Ryan
was questioned seven weeks before. She was sitting across from
Hestrom while Mike Anglus stood farther back against the wall,
arms folded in a stance of reserved judgment.

Annie was wearing a white cotton summer dress, slim at the
waist, and her large bosom tugged at the top, where a pink pearl
necklace dangled. Her meticulously coiffed dark hair cascaded to her
shoulders. Both Anglus and Hestrom had not fully appreciated the
voluptuous figure of the woman before. Now they seemed entranced
by her composure and her story of feminine self-defense against two
men. Hestrom, looking down at his notes from the initial police
interview at the scene, recited the information.

"Ms. McNeil, you said that you heard an intruder break in so you
went to get your gun. You came downstairs. You saw the intruder
and fired into the dark. The first bullet struck Ryan McNeil. You then
realized that you had accidentally shot your husband, from whom

you had been separated, and who had entered the home without your knowledge."

Annie, with a morose, pained expression, nodded in agreement.

Hestrom, scrutinizing her as carefully as he had Ryan, saw only innocence.

"Then you saw the intruder Seth Tantalus had a weapon pointed at you, but in that ensuing moment you were able to fire a second round, killing him."

"Yes. Yes. That is exactly how it happened," said Annie. Her emerald-green eyes were free from expression, her chin set like stone, a perfect portrait of resolution, spousal loss, and melancholy regret.

"So it was only after you shot your husband did you realize your error?"

"Estranged husband, yes," she corrected him. "It was a night of tragedy and horror." She had rehearsed the line in her mind.

She paused and looked at the inscrutable expressions of Anglus and Hestrom. "It was a mess. There was blood everywhere. I will have to get rid of the rugs and the couch. That blood was evil, pure evil you know, from that criminal Tantalus."

Hestrom winced and then glanced to Anglus, who stepped forward.

"You know, Tantalus is much larger, taller than your husband. You confused the two of them in the dark?"

Annie in response did not blink before she answered.

"A man is a man. In darkness, they can appear the same to a woman. You know, sometimes your perception is not right, especially in the dark. I had to act quickly. I did not recognize Ryan in the shadows. Naturally, I never would have shot him if I had. You make wrong split-second decisions. You as police officers can understand how that is."

Both men nodded grimly and sympathetically. "We understand that it was a horrible experience. Ms. McNeil, we will get back in touch, but your story seems to correspond with the physical evidence we found at the scene. You are free to go."

Annie smiled and then stood up. The stressed creases of her face seemed to relax. Her chest jutted forward, and both men mutually admired her. The talk of spilled blood and mistaken violence seemed to flow incongruously from the rouged lips of the woman in the white cotton summer dress. Nevertheless, she exuded pure innocence in the matter.

"How are things at home, Ms. McNeil? Your daughter?"

"Oh, she's OK. I explained everything to her, and Congressman Somatos has been coming by to help out. He is a wonderful man, you know." She beamed a flawless white smile at them.

"Well, if we can help in any way," offered Anglus. He thought that maybe he would stop by her house and check on her. They opened the door for her, and a uniformed officer escorted her out.

"What do you think?" inquired Anglus of Hestrom.

"I think I'm glad this case is over," sighed Hestrom as they both sat down. To the seasoned investigators, the innocence of Annie McNeil was beyond reproach, beyond any need for further inquiry or speculation. The poor woman had tragically shot her husband by accident.

"I think she's holding a lot in," said Hestrom.

"Not really," said Anglus with a lascivious smile. "I think I saw most of it hanging out."

Annie emerged from the Fairfax Police Department and began to walk across the sun-splashed plaza. At the far edge she could see the dark limousine. She approached tentatively, until the back-seat tinted window lowered and Somatos beckoned her in. Normally, his manners would have dictated that he hold open the door, but he did not want to be seen or especially captured in this awkward moment on camera. One could never be sure where the press was hidden these days. Annie slid in beside him with a smile while she smoothed the lap of her cotton dress. Somatos directed the driver to the Apollo Restaurant in Georgetown.

"How are you, Annie?" asked Somatos as he took hold of her hand. "Are you holding up all right? I hope the police didn't trouble you. This was your second interview with them?"

"It was fine, Congressman," said Annie, and then she corrected herself. "Nick."

"Well, if you need anything at all, please feel free to call upon me," said Somatos magnanimously with a broad, open smile. Annie studied the deep tan hue of his face, with teeth perfectly white: the inscrutable but photogenic countenance of a true politician. The ride progressed, and Annie became silent, almost sullen. A question begged to be asked.

"What is it, Annie? What's wrong?"

"Nick, I have to ask you. That night I heard Seth Tantalus say that he wasn't driving the car that took Wilet in Albany, and I also heard him say that he didn't pay Warren $770,000."

"No. We mustn't talk about this," said Somatos, agitated.

"I just need to know, Nick," inquired Annie gently.

Somatos turned away from her, sighed, and weighed his options, looking out the window of the limousine as it moved along the highway. He then turned back and looked directly at her. "Annie, I looked into that payment of $770,000 to Warren. It came from a former New York State Speaker who is now dead. He was paying Cindy Ambrose, who changed her name to Leslie Warren because she had sued the state."

Annie was intrigued. "Leslie Warren sued the state?"

"Yes. Leslie Warren had been brutally assaulted by an assemblyman. She had a case pending that accused the Assembly Intern Committee of not adequately protecting her from Assemblyman Caluzzi. The Speaker at that time was named as a culpable party in the lawsuit. So he established a state escrow account in the budget and had the matter settled out of court. He had a state judge seal the record. I am sure after the publicity she wanted to start a new life so she changed her name and secured a new identity with the assistance of the Speaker and our magnificent New York court system that fought the federal prosecutors very hard to preserve her true identity."

Annie mulled the logic of the information, but her inquisitiveness was not fully satisfied.

"What about the driver of the car that took Cathy Wilet? If it wasn't Seth Tantalus, who was it?"

"This is best put behind us, Annie," said Somatos firmly.

"Just tell me: Were you involved?" asked Annie softly.

"I've been judged of moral character, Annie. I am a United States congressman. No, I am not a murderer," asserted Somatos. "I no more murdered Cathy Wilet than you murdered your husband."

Annie flinched visibly. Somatos, seeing the reaction, consolingly extended his hand and placed her hand inside his. "I know how hard this must be on you," he comforted. "Ryan was a good man."

The limousine turned onto Memorial Bridge. The Potomac glittered majestically in the late-afternoon sun beside the pearl-white Lincoln Memorial. Somatos lowered his tinted window and, on the pedestrian sidewalk of the bridge, caught a quick glimpse of a young girl, running in shorts, long tan legs and flowing blonde hair, and a long-suppressed vision hurtled forward in his mind and almost escaped his lips.

He turned to Annie. Somatos paused, pensively, and then he offered sage counsel with her sea green eyes emotively locked on him. "Annie, just remember in life everyone is guilty of something. Only babies and young children are wholly innocent."

Annie could only smile at his politician's logic; she found it endearing. Mostly, though, she was hungry now, and only contemplating what food to order at the Apollo Restaurant.

CHAPTER 49

Three Months Later

Somatos emerged from portico shadows that formed under the massive pillared facade of the Capitol.

"Congressman Somatos, are you pleased about the closure of the inquiry into the deaths of Leslie Warren, Seth Tantalus and Ryan McNeil? Are you satisfied now that the cases are formally closed?" The reporter asked his questions as Somatos trotted blithely down the steps of the Capitol. A throng of reporters coalesced around him, eager for some profound words to play on the news that evening or transcribe for tomorrow's newspapers. Somatos looked down at his feet; there was no fitting platitude to utter. For a few seconds he contemplated the proper demeanor to convey. He then looked up in composure and began to speak fluently. Three news cameras captured his image in their lens and recorded it while other reporters jotted efficiently on notepads.

"Ryan McNeil's death was untimely and horrible. He was a

young man who dedicated his life to public service first with the New York State Assembly and later with the United States Congress. He was brave and he was instrumental in uncovering the identity of the murderer of Leslie Warren in Virginia and Cathy Wilet in New York. Without his help, it is unlikely these horrific crimes would have been solved. This country is better for having had Ryan McNeil serve it. I am a better man for having known him. Annie McNeil dearly loved her husband. Her daughter, Jessica, dearly loved him as a stepfather. As you know, I requested the Speaker of the House to approve the life insurance policy so that Annie McNeil will receive the full three million dollar triple-indemnity policy. I think it was the right and proper act."

"Congressman, are you pleased that your health policy amendment was signed into law by the president yesterday?"

"Yes. That would not have been possible without the work of Ryan McNeil," said Somatos gravely. "Thank you very much."

A pageant of splendid victory played in Somatos's mind. He could hear the imagined herald of trumpets, a high formal note, and the unseen clamor of crowds bellowing his acclaim. Senator Nickolas Somatos—anything was possible now, within his reach. He had dispensed to the poor, pathetic masses what they needed. They would have a quality of health care commensurate with the medical treatment afforded the wealthy that lived beyond the pavement and concrete and brick of his district, out in the green places where cocktails were served by pools and open lawns, those lemonade porch, barbecue deck places indifferent to the yearnings, hopes, and needs of his urban constituents. It was a noble and righteous cause, secured by ignoble and devious means, but that was the price, thought Somatos, a cheap price to pay.

Somatos thought back to the day he had attended the funeral of Ryan Patrick McNeil—a gray day of intermittent rain. It was a small ceremony, steeped in the sanctimonious ritual of the church. A few family and friends of the decedent, the depleted remnants of a once great clan. Behind the hearse, a handful of black limousines, somber and sleek, rode out to the cemetery, their headlights burning through the mist that seemed to shroud the day. At the cemetery, a few reporters and photographers stood a respectful distance, huddled under the great green awning of a nearby oak tree. In his mind, he thought, *Fair youth, beneath the trees, thou canst not leave.*

He had stood solemnly beside the dignified widow, steadying her on the uneven ground of the graveside. He could see her periodically blinking dashes of drizzle from her emerald-green eyes. Suddenly the sky rumbled with the percussion of thunder, and the rain then came in a deluge. He was ready with a black umbrella, extending it over the dark shroud on her head while the rain on the umbrella reverberated a sorrowful, sustained drumbeat. Standing there with Annie McNeil while Ryan's casket was lowered into a pit of mud, the sound of the rainfall on the umbrella seemed to Somatos an eternal, haunting echo of bereavement.

Ryan McNeil died a victim of his own idealism, rationalized Somatos. In his mind, Ryan was a mistaken casualty in unfathomable darkness. It was a darkness cast by the confused shadows of human souls, lost in a cave of captivity, unable to decipher the meaning of what they see while seeking what they do not know, while the gods hovered purposefully above.

Somatos moved farther down the granite steps of the Capitol. It was September, but the sun was bright and powerful, almost blinding to the eye. Somatos basked in the benevolent warmth and removed a pair of sunglasses from his pocket. He adjusted the shades on his face and smiled contentedly to himself. He felt supremely confident; the future lay before him like a prize to be graciously accepted. He had not only survived, he had flourished where all others had failed. A magnificent, transcendent light of greatness was within his grasp. He felt as if he could soon firmly seize it, not on this day, but perhaps the next day, not only for this time, but for all time.

EPILOGUE

Congressman's Wedding Attended by the Governor

A Special to the *New York Herald*—The wedding of Congressman Nickolas Somatos of New York City to Annie McNeil of Fairfax, Virginia, was attended by prominent officials from across the state, including the honorable governor of New York. Political pundits noted that Somatos's new family could only help in the race to be the governor's successor. The governor, who last month abruptly announced his retirement, has publicly declared his support for Somatos to succeed him. Congressman Charles Green also attended despite the fact that earlier in the week the Nassau County Democratic machine had forced him to withdraw from the Democratic ballot for reelection in November. Somatos's new family, including eight-year-old stepdaughter Jessica, handled the crowd like seasoned veterans. In fact, Ms. McNeil knows something of politics. Ms. McNeil was married to the former legislative director for the congressman but nevertheless seemed enthralled by the gathering of notables. Her former husband, Ryan McNeil, is deceased, having died in an accident. Seven months ago, Ms. McNeil gained some notoriety in a case that involved Seth Tantalus, a former aide to Congressman Green, who was suspected of several abductions and murders in both Virginia and New York. Mr. Tantalus was killed by Ms. McNeil after he broke into her home and threatened her. There was no mention of the incident at today's ceremony.

The End

ABOUT THE AUTHOR

Barry R. Ziman started his career as a Director of Legislation in New York State in the 1980s. In the 90s, he became a lobbyist first in New York City and later in Washington, DC. He is a graduate of the Bronx High School of Science and the State University of New York College at Oneonta.